"Never been married. Never plan to be."

Erica took a step toward Garrett. "But if you think anything is going to happen between us, guess again. You are so not my type it isn't even funny."

They might as well have been alone in the apartment for the charge in the air. Flirting with her was dangerous. Still, Garrett couldn't rein himself in. "So what is your type?"

"Not a cop, that's for sure," she said.

"What do you have against cops?"

"You wouldn't get it."

"Try me."

"Don't think so." Erica's dark brown eyes were laced with something he couldn't put a finger on. Something that looked an awful lot like fear.

Someone had badly hurt her and the little boy. All Garrett wanted was to get his hands on the guy who had.

Dear Reader,

I can't tell you how proud I am to be a writer of Harlequin romance books. For me to find myself included in the company's 60th anniversary celebration is nothing less than a triple scoop of double fudge ice cream topping my writing cake.

See, me and Harlequin Books—we go back a long way. Harlequin stories became a part of my life as a young teenager, and I'm quite sure I will never have read my fill of romances. There's nothing that can make me smile, cry or turn pages faster than the expectation of that long-awaited first kiss and those wonderful happily-ever-after endings. As long as these eyes can see there'll be a romance book on my bedside table. And it'll likely be a Harlequin book.

More than anything, though, I want to thank you, our readers, for keeping Harlequin Books alive and vital and publishing some of the bestselling books on the market today. Without you, I couldn't have so much fun writing. Thanks for picking up this book!

I hope you enjoyed Noah and Sophie's story in *First Come Twins,* the first in my AN ISLAND TO REMEMBER series. With any luck, reading about Garrett and Erica will feel a little like coming home to a place you love and people you've missed.

Watch for *Then Comes Baby,* another Mirabelle Island story, coming in December 2009. And welcome back to Mirabelle!

Helen Brenna

Next Comes Love
Helen Brenna

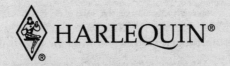

TORONTO • NEW YORK • LONDON
AMSTERDAM • PARIS • SYDNEY • HAMBURG
STOCKHOLM • ATHENS • TOKYO • MILAN • MADRID
PRAGUE • WARSAW • BUDAPEST • AUCKLAND

Recycling programs
for this product may
not exist in your area.

ISBN-13: 978-0-373-71594-7

NEXT COMES LOVE

Copyright © 2009 by Helen Brenna.

ABOUT THE AUTHOR

Helen Brenna grew up in a small town in central Minnesota, the seventh of eight children. Although she never dreamed of writing books, she's always been a voracious reader of romances. So after taking a break from her accounting career, she tried her hand at writing the romances she loves to read. Since her first book was published in 2007, she's won Romance Writers of America's prestigious RITA® Award, a *Romantic Times BOOKreviews* Reviewer's Choice Award and Virginia Romance Writers' Holt Medallion.

Helen still lives in Minnesota with her husband, two children and far too many pets. She'd love hearing from you. E-mail her at helenbrenna@comcast.net or send mail to P.O. Box 24107, Minneapolis, MN 55424. Visit her Web site at www.helenbrenna.com or chat with Helen and other authors at RidingWithTheTopDown.blogspot.com.

Books by Helen Brenna

HARLEQUIN SUPERROMANCE
1403—TREASURE
1425—DAD FOR LIFE
1519—FINDING MR. RIGHT
1582—FIRST COME TWINS*

HARLEQUIN NASCAR
PEAK PERFORMANCE
FROM THE OUTSIDE

*An Island to Remember

For Jerry Twomey

Thanks, Dad, for helping me believe
I could do just about anything!

Acknowledgments

Many thanks to friends who help make my days
a little brighter.
Carolyn Fletcher, Pam Hoyt, Linda Maxwell,
LaDonna Fallen, Sybil Crevier, Ann Kyrilis,
Carol Tlachac, Denise Tatryn, Jan Abbott,
Roxanne Dayton, Maureen Wenner and
Kerry Adelmann. Thanks, guys, for always being there.

As always, my editor Johanna Raisanen's pearls of
wisdom, and in this book's case several carats',
worth of diamonds, helped make this book the best
it could be. Thanks, Johanna, for all you do.

And to my agent, Tina Wexler, for your encouragement
and calm in the face of my creative outbursts—
okay, meltdowns—thanks, and I luv ya.

CHAPTER ONE

NO MALLS. NO CLUBS. No nightlife.

This place is gonna suck.

Erica Corelli kept her thoughts resolutely to herself while the ferry cruised by Mirabelle Island's shoreline, passing gingerbread houses, sailboats and yachts, manicured gardens and white picket fences. A couple of Southsiders from Chicago fit into this idyllic setting about as well as gum wads on the streets of the Magic Kingdom.

The late-April afternoon sun moved lower on the horizon. Erica pushed away from the boat's metal railing and hid her misgivings with a smile. "It's pretty, isn't it, Jason?" She ruffled the six-year-old's short hair. She'd hated having to cut and dye brown his naturally blond curls, but there'd been no way around it.

"Like a fairyland," Jason whispered, his eyes wide. It was one of the few times he'd put down his handheld video game long enough to take in the view. "Are you sure they'll let us live here?"

No, Erica wasn't sure. "We're as good as anybody here, kiddo, and don't you let anyone tell you any different."

She glanced at the employment ad she'd found in the local newspaper back on Wisconsin's mainland for a place called Duffy's Pub. She would've preferred to cook, but she could bartend with the best of them, and waitress if there were no other options. If she could find a job, any job, and a place to live, they'd be all right. For a while, anyway.

Jason stuffed the video game into the front pocket of his sweatshirt and shuffled closer to her side. "Are you going to make me go to school?" he asked.

There had to be kids living on the island, right? So there had to be at least one school. "Don't you want to go?"

His brow furrowed as he shook his head in short motions back and forth. It didn't seem right for a kid to be this somber and introspective.

"We'll see." Erica flipped through a glossy tourist brochure looking for details. Over ten square miles, it said. She had no idea what a square mile looked like, but it sounded small.

She'd been to Mirabelle only once when she'd been about ten and back then everything had seemed big. She'd loved that noisy cars and city buses weren't allowed on the island. Everyone walked or took carriages, or rode bikes and horses. She remembered thinking that this island had to be the most perfect place on earth. The kind of place where happily-ever-afters hung on trees like bright red apples waiting to be picked. The kind of place where, any minute, a knight might ride out of the forest, scoop up a princess and carry her off to his castle.

Right. These days, she'd settle for Mirabelle still being the kind of place a child could feel safe, if only for a few weeks.

A chilly spring wind blew across the deep waters of Lake Superior and hit the back of her neck. She flipped the sweatshirt hood over Jason's head and zipped her own leather jacket up tight.

As if sensing Erica's doubts, Jason said, "Is this my fault? Did I do something wrong?"

"Don't you ever think that, okay?" She knelt in front of him, eye to eye. "Okay?"

Jason nodded.

"It's gonna be all right. Better than all right, even. We'll have fun here. Before you know it you'll be back home. Safe and sound."

With a short toot of its horn, the ferry announced its arrival at the Mirabelle Island marina. A slight tremor ran through the deck as the huge boat settled against the pier. With a short burst of activity, ramps were lowered and the other passengers, a sum total of five other people, trotted off the boat.

"This is it." Erica helped Jason hoist up his own backpack, then she grabbed their suitcases. "You ready?"

He nodded.

"Here we go."

They stepped off the ferry and headed toward what looked like the center of town. Although it was early spring and the overflowing baskets of flowers hanging from the black iron lampposts were noticeably absent, the island was much as Erica remembered. Stately trees, oaks, maples, on the verge of leafing out, and several types of evergreens, lined the cobblestone road. Cobblestone. For real.

A candy shop, painted fire-engine red with white shutters, like something out of a painting, sat at the nearest corner. A blue-and-white restaurant, the Bayside Café, claimed to grill up the best half-pound cheeseburger in the entire state of Wisconsin, while the ice cream shop next door offered a selection of gourmet coffees. An art gallery, bank, post office and flower shop all sported identical green-and-white-striped awnings. To top it all off, a chapel, an immaculate white building with narrow, stained glass windows, sat up on the hill, overseeing it all. They probably had perfect white weddings in that church.

She glanced longingly back at the ferry already pulling away from the pier. So much for that. Erica took a deep breath and glanced down at Jason. Smiling awkwardly, she handed him the Green Bay Packers cap she'd bought at a gas station. "Do you mind wearing this?"

He looked from the hat to her and back again and without a word jammed it on his head.

She rested her hands on his bony shoulders, doing her best to comfort him. "Would it be okay if we came up with a nickname for you?"

He looked at her quizzically and then, understanding, he whispered, soft and small, "Sure."

"Do you have any ideas?" She grinned, trying to lighten things up. "Ralph? Pedro? Maynard?"

As if he hadn't even heard her measly attempts at humor he frowned in concentration. So serious. "How 'bout Zach?" he said.

"Zach. Sounds good." Erica's heart swelled with admiration. "This is going to be hard, kiddo, I know." She hesitated, taking Jason's small hands into her own. "From now on you have to call me Mom."

GARRETT TAYLOR SAT AT THE counter next to several other residents in the Bayside Café and washed down with a gulp of water the last of his early dinner, a dry, relatively tasteless tuna salad sandwich. What he wouldn't have done at that moment for a genuine, spicy, saucy Chicago-style pizza. Might have to learn how to cook one himself, he thought ruefully as he watched the comings and goings in the harbor.

This time of year, there were only a couple ferry runs a day. By all accounts, come June and the start of the summer tourist season there'd be a ferry scheduled practically every hour, each one overflowing with wedding guests and travelers all looking for quaint and quiet. Garrett let the rest of the island residents handle quaint. For the last eight or so months, as Mirabelle's new chief of police, he'd taken care of the quiet.

The late afternoon ferry docked and a few Mirabelle residents who worked or had been running errands on the mainland hopped onto the pier and headed home or to their respective businesses. The last to step onto dry land was a young boy with his mother. She dragged a couple suitcases behind her, making it look as if they intended to stay a short while. He'd never seen her before or the kid.

Not that Garrett minded strangers. Tourism was the island's bread and butter, but Mirabelle's strangers were usually vacationers or college students looking for summer jobs, a lot of them from Chicago or the Twin Cities. This one, with her dark, chin-length blunt haircut, leather jacket and high-heeled boots was neither. She stuck out like a Harley parked in a row of Cadillacs.

"Well, lookie what the cat dragged in." Herman Stotz, Mirabelle's assistant police chief, whistled softly and nodded toward the street.

During the off season, Garrett and Herman both worked part-time, generally splitting daily shifts, so they'd gotten into the habit of meeting for lunch or dinner several times a week to discuss police business. "Know her?" Garrett asked.

"No, sirree. Her, I'd remember."

Garrett flipped a ten onto the counter and pulled on his uniform jacket. Herman followed suit.

"Have a good evening, Dolores," Garrett called to the café owner.

"Thanks, Garrett. Herman. See ya later."

As Garrett turned, Hannah Johnson, Sarah Marshik and Missy Charms, the three women sitting at the table directly behind Garrett and Herman, glanced up. Hannah, a blue-eyed, blond-haired daisy of a woman, taught at the island's only school. Sarah owned the flower shop and doubled as the island wedding planner. And Missy, a horoscope-reading new-ager, owned the gift shop next door to Sarah.

Someone or another was usually trying to hook him up with one of the island's three most eligible women, but Hannah was the only likely match for Garrett. Missy was too far out there and Sarah was far too classy for the likes of Garrett, not to mention she was a widow with a young son. Although moving to Mirabelle was a first step in changing his life, getting married and having kids were whole different issues he wasn't ready to tackle. Besides, his Mirabelle plan called for settling in slowly. No quick decisions. No acting on impulse.

"Bye, Garrett," Sarah said, smiling widely.

"Hey, Garrett," Missy said, grinning, "Why don't you stop by the gift shop later and I'll give you a tarot reading."

"I'll be sure to do that, Missy." Chuckling, he nodded at Hannah. "See you later, Hannah."

"Bye, Garrett." She gave him a small wave. "Herman."

"Ladies." Herman nodded at their table.

Garrett stopped by the café's glass front door and watched the woman who had come off the ferry cross the street before hitting their block. On closer examination, he wouldn't have called her pretty. Sexy was more like it. Those boots alone with spiked heels and buttons up the back set her in a whole different category of woman. The only boots he'd ever seen on Mirabelle were of the rubber sole and thick lining variety. Add skinny jeans and cleavage—no, he was not going to look again—to the package, and this was a wild one. Those lips. So full they hardly even dipped in the middle. Brown eyes. Wide-set and intense. *Man alive.*

Garrett got ready to head outside. If he timed it for right…about…now… He pushed open the door, impeding sidewalk progress. "Whoops. Excuse me."

The woman stopped. After one wary glance at his face, her focus dropped to the badge on his police-issue jacket. Caramel highlights ran through her dark curls like milk chocolate ribbons in a dark chocolate cake. After a so-quick-it-was-barely-there flash of uncertainty, she looked as if she might bite his head clear off given the right motivation.

Mmm, mmm, mmm. From cub to tigress in seconds flat.

Something primal fired to life at his core, and he immediately tamped it back down. *Not your type, G.T.* "Need some help with that suitcase?" he asked, holding her gaze.

"Do I *look* like I need help?" She didn't even smile. A raised eyebrow was the only expression of emotion on her face.

"You look completely self-sufficient. But we could all use a hand every now and then."

"I'd be glad to help you with one of those suitcases, ma'am," Herman said, sucking up. "Or the boy's backpack."

"We'll be fine." She glanced at Herman.

Garrett slipped on his mirrored sunglasses and glanced down at the boy. He couldn't see much of his face what with the baseball cap pulled low on his brow, but at this angle a bruise on his neck was visible under the shadow of his hooded sweatshirt. "What's your name, buddy?"

"Um... Zach," he said, glancing up at his mom with a worried expression.

"As in Zachary?" That bruise was a thumbprint if Garrett had ever seen one. The only question was whose thumb.

"Just Zach." The mom started to turn.

Before she took a single step, he held out his hand. "I'm Garrett Taylor. This is Herman Stotz. And you are?"

"Unless I've broken any of your laws—" she ignored his outstretched hand and continued down the sidewalk, holding her son's hand "—none of your business."

Garrett resisted the urge to pull her back and explain in no uncertain terms that everything that happened on Mirabelle was his business. Everything and everyone. But this was Mirabelle, he reminded himself, not Chicago, and that hotheaded, shoot-from-the-hip-regardless-of-the-consequences Garrett Taylor was best kept under wraps. For everyone's sake.

"Whooeee," Herman whistled quietly. "That one's going to cause you some trouble."

Garrett watched them walk away. "Only if I rise to the bait." That, he resolved, was *not* going to happen, even after he found who had caused that boy's bruise. And he would soon find out, no doubt about that.

CHAPTER TWO

STUPID, STUPID, STUPID. Erica chastised herself as she headed toward Duffy's Pub. *None of your business.* What the hell had she been thinking making a comment like that? Then again, how could any red-blooded woman even hope to think after looking into that man's piercing pale gray eyes?

To make matters worse he was a cop and not one of those doughnut-eating, potbellied middle-aged beat walkers, either. This guy had the lean face of an athlete and, from what she could tell, the muscles that went with that territory, making him all the more disturbing in her book.

Where she'd grown up, cops walked a fine line between two worlds. Most of them had grown up on tough streets, some even had juvie records, and a lot of them tripped big time on the power behind that badge. There was nothing worse than a man with a mean streak claiming to be on the right side of the law, and she'd known a few of those men in her lifetime. Men like Billy Samson.

Okay. So she'd stepped out onto this island on the wrong foot. What was done was done. If she didn't lighten up and smile every once in a while, or at least quit acting as if every person she met was planning on stealing her purse—a purse that held every penny she owned—she would continue to stick out like a sore thumb.

This was small-town Wisconsin. People here waved when they passed you on the street and held doors open for pregnant women and old ladies. As hard as it might be, she was going to have to try and fit in.

"Are we in trouble?" Jason asked, glancing back at the cops.

"Absolutely not. We didn't do anything wrong." She squeezed his hand. "But to be safe keep your hat on inside."

Erica opened the heavy wooden door to Duffy's Pub and stepped into a dark and dank-feeling foyer, making her feel as if she were heading into a cave. That'd be the first thing she'd change if given the option. A restaurant gave only one first impression and in a place like Mirabelle that served a lot of Chicagoans on vacation, the last first impression a business owner wanted to give was dingy.

They went inside and found a couple people catching happy hour at an antique oval bar. The old jukebox in the corner was lit up but silent, and only one of several TVs mounted overhead was on and, thankfully, tuned to a national sports channel. Not that anyone was paying attention to it anyway. The main dining area with an impressive view of Lake Superior had only two tables occupied. Although the place had promise, it was clear from the looks of the wood paneling and faded curtains there hadn't been an update in décor for at least a decade.

A lanky older guy, probably in his early sixties with a scraggly gray beard and startling blue eyes was cleaning glasses behind the bar. He glanced up as they approached. "What can I get for you two?"

"Nothing for me." Erica lifted Jason onto a bar stool and sat next to him.

"How 'bout you, buckeroo?" the man asked.

Jason glanced up at Erica. One look into that sweet face and Erica's heart leaped into her throat. Not used to being responsible for a child, she had no clue as to his tastes. "Do you like root beer?" As soon as the question was out of her mouth she wanted to bite it back. She was supposed to know these things. From now on, she was going to have to be more careful.

Jason nodded and the old guy poured some soda into a mug and set it on the bar. Jason took a sip and then pulled the video game out of his pocket and started up again on whatever it was he'd been playing all day, his gaze focused and his thumbs working overtime.

"Is Lynn around?" Erica set the classified ad on the counter. "I'd like to talk to her."

"Ayep, hold on." He poked his head through a door behind the bar and called, "Lynnie! Someone's here about a job."

Erica quickly flipped open a menu and perused the pub's offerings, hoping to get an idea of what she was getting herself into. Diner fare. Could be worse. She glanced up when a woman with long, wavy grayish white hair and round, ruddy cheeks pushed through the swinging doors from what appeared to be the kitchen.

After wiping off her palms on an apron tied around her waist, the woman held out a hand. "I'm Lynn Duffy. What can I do for you?"

"Erica." She firmly shook the woman's hand. What was the last name on that fake ID she'd bought? *Oh, yeah.* "Jackson. Erica Jackson. You're looking for restaurant help?"

"Bartender, waitress, cook. You name it, I pretty much need it. In a few weeks there'll be a whole crew of college kids coming to work through the summer, but there are always a few who don't show up. One of my bartenders just backed out. You worked in restaurants before?"

Erica nodded. "For the last ten years."

"Whereabouts?"

"Couple different places. In…northeast Minneapolis." She'd been there several times visiting an old high school friend, so if necessary she could name a few well-known establishments.

"What can you do?"

"Bartend, waitress, cook," Erica answered. "You name it, I can pretty much do it."

"All right." Lynn smiled. "I can use someone like you. We got about a month before the summer tourist season gets in full swing, so let's start you out behind the bar, and we'll go from there."

"Just like that?" No references, no applications, no personality tests? Erica eyed the other woman skeptically. There had to be a catch. Nothing was that easy.

"Well, now that you mention it," Lynn said. "There is one condition. Can you stay through the summer?"

Four months on this tiny island? Not likely. Erica hoped to be back to her old job and her own apartment in a couple weeks, give or take, but she needed the money now. "Sure," she said, making a promise to give the woman everything she had for as long as she had to, but not one minute longer. "Through the summer was our plan."

"Well, then you're hired," Lynn said. "This is my husband, Arlo." She patted the old guy's shoulder. "Generally, he runs the carriage and horseback riding business, and I take care of the pub. Can you start tomorrow night?"

"I was hoping for mostly daytime hours." She flicked her head toward Jason. "So I can work while he's in school."

At the mention of school, Jason looked up from his game and frowned. How did he do that, stay totally focused on that handheld device and yet hear everything going on around him?

"Well now, there we got our first snag." Lynn set a hand on her hip. "We don't open until eleven in the morning and we close late on weeknights, even later on weekends. I need waitresses during the day and a bartender at night."

Erica had been in the restaurant business for as long as she could remember, so she'd become quite a night owl, heading out with coworkers and friends after hours. All that was going to have to change. She had a kid to worry about now. Obviously, she hadn't thought this job all the way through, but she wasn't qualified to do anything else.

"School's out in another month. Then what are you going to do?" Lynn asked.

With any luck she wouldn't be here long enough to have to worry about summer, but she had to uphold the pretense of caring. "Is there a day care on the island?"

"Not that I'm aware of." Lynn glanced down at Jason. "Snag number two."

Jason suddenly put his game away, grabbed Erica's hand and shifted on his bar stool, moving close to her side. "It's my problem," Erica said, sticking out her chin. "I'll figure it out."

"You got about a month to do that," Lynn warned. "When the tourist season starts the beginning of June things are going to get crazy around here."

"Can you recommend a house or apartment to rent that's close to the restaurant? I need to find a place to live. Furnished, if possible."

Lynn laughed. "Dearie, on this island everything is close." She threw a questioning glance at her husband. "What do you think?"

He shrugged.

"What about the storm damage?"

He shrugged again.

"The college kids?"

Erica glanced between the two of them, clueless as to what was going on. Without saying much of anything they each seemed to know exactly what the other was thinking.

"Oh, all right." Lynn turned back to Erica. "First come first serve, I suppose."

"What is?" Erica asked.

"The two apartments we rent out above the restaurant here." She pointed upward. "They suffered some water damage last week from some straight-line winds that came in off the lake, but the roof has been fixed, so that's the main thing. If you don't mind the inconvenience of some minor construction…"

"How long before the repairs are finished?"

After a quick glance at Arlo, Lynn turned back to Erica. "A couple days. Week tops."

Erica imagined Jason sleeping above a bar. "Is it noisy?"

"Never had any complaints." Lynn shook her head. "The ceiling's been pretty well soundproofed. Rent's four hundred a month. You won't find anything less expensive on the island. Mind you, they're nothing special, but they are furnished."

"I'll take one."

"You might want to look first."

They were cheap. "As long as the rooms are clean and the roof doesn't leak anymore, that's all that matters." Erica unzipped her purse and counted through her quickly dwindling supply of cash. She'd cleared out her savings account before leaving Chicago, but most of it had been chewed up with having to buy that rust bucket of a car she'd had to leave on the mainland. Add in some clothes, suitcases and a couple games for Jason's handheld gamer, and she was about wiped out. If she paid a full month's rent, she wouldn't have much left for groceries.

She hated to ask this—she and pride having had an intimate and committed relationship—but she couldn't use her charge cards and, with Jason in tow, Erica didn't have much of a choice. "Can I pay you the other half of the rent with my first check?" She held out two hundred dollars.

Lynn didn't say anything, only held Erica's gaze for a very long and uncomfortable moment.

"I'm good for the rest," Erica said. With any luck she wouldn't need to be.

Arlo cleared his throat.

"Oh, all right," Lynn said. "I'll tell you what. Since the storm damage is in the process of getting fixed, you can have the first two weeks free."

"You don't need to do that."

"You haven't seen the damage." Lynn cocked her head at Erica. "So when can you start?"

Something told her Jason would need some time to adjust. "I need a day to get settled."

"How 'bout Wednesday then? That'll give you a couple days under your belt before the weekend. Unless you'd rather experience baptism by Friday night."

"Wednesday's fine."

"Stop down here before eleven. We'll get some paperwork done and I'll show you around." Lynn took a key ring off a hook near the kitchen door and pointed at their two suitcases. "That all you got?"

Erica nodded. She had this much only because she'd thought to stop at one of those megastores along the highway for some essentials, figuring it would look odd for a supposed mother and son to be traveling without so much as a toothbrush.

"Arlo, why don't you help Erica get those bags upstairs?"

"Ayep. Figured as much." Arlo grabbed the larger bag.

Erica had no sooner helped Jason down from the bar stool than the restaurant door opened, letting in a blast of cool air and silhouetting the shape of a man. The cop. She may have only met him once, but that muscular frame was unmistakable.

He walked inside, nodded at the group of customers at the bar and then turned to greet the Duffys. "How you doing, Lynn? Arlo?"

"Well, this day has certainly gotten brighter, Garrett," Lynn said. "We hired ourselves a new bartender. Erica Jackson, this is Garrett Taylor, our police chief here on Mirabelle."

So she'd brushed off the chief. *Figures.*

"We've already met." He nodded. "Erica. Zach."

Jason looked down at the ground, and Erica gave his hand a quick reassuring squeeze. "Chief Taylor," she said, forcing a smile.

"Come on, let's go," Arlo said. "I don't have all day."

Erica took Jason's hand and followed Arlo, sidestepping the cop. That man was dangerous on so many levels, it wasn't even funny, and he was definitely not the type of person she'd expected to find here on quiet little Mirabelle.

"See you around," the cop called after her.

Not if she could help it.

THE KITCHEN DOOR SWUNG closed behind Erica Jackson and her son, and Garrett, though trying his damnedest, couldn't keep his big mouth shut. "So what's their story?"

"How should I know?" Lynn went behind the bar and washed glasses.

"You didn't ask?"

"As long as she does her job it's none of my business. As long as she doesn't cause any trouble on the island it's none of yours."

Yeah, yeah, yeah. "How long she planning on staying?"

"At least through the summer."

"So she's renting one of your apartments?"

"You betcha." She squeezed out a soapy rag and wiped down the bar.

"Where'd they come from?"

Lynn glared at him. "Said she'd worked in northeast Minneapolis."

That he could—maybe—believe. From what he'd heard from other cops that part of the Twin Cities was a tough neighborhood, but he would've put money on her being from Chicago. Little Italy maybe with that dark hair and skin and those brown eyes.

Lynn paused in the middle of a long swipe down the shiny bar and set her hands on her hips. "I swear, Garrett, you are the most paranoid person I've ever met."

"That's what happens when you work fifteen years with the Chicago PD."

"Well, you're not in Chicago any more," Lynn said. "How much harm can a pretty mom and her boy possibly cause on our island?"

Plenty. That woman was trouble, or trouble was following her. Maybe both.

"Garrett Taylor."

When Lynn spoke his name like that, she reminded him of his mother, a stern, but loving woman. How she'd raised four boys, much of the time without a husband, and without any of those boys following their father's footsteps by ending up in jail, for very long anyway, was beyond him.

"Jim Bennett was police chief on this island for twenty some years, so there's no doubt he's a hard act to follow. You've been here less than a year and it's been an adjustment for a few people. Most of us happen to like you, so I'm going to tell you something for your own good."

Ah, hell.

"I need a bartender, and I don't want you hassling this young woman like you did that man Ron Setterberg hired over the winter to help remodel his rental shop."

"That guy had a felony record for dealing."

"And he'd done his time. He wasn't the first person who'd come to Mirabelle to start over."

As far as Garrett was concerned repeat offenders could start over on someone else's island.

"Why did you come to Mirabelle?" she asked, putting one hand on her hip.

"You know why." At least she knew what he'd told everyone, that he'd grown sick of the violence, that he'd simply lost the stomach for the heightening brutality of the crimes. The truth was that he'd hated who he was becoming. And he'd had a hard time looking at the man he saw in the mirror. A man who had begun to resemble his father more and more every day.

Before Garrett had come to Mirabelle he'd been treading a fine line for years, but after what had happened that hot night last summer he had to get out or risk becoming one of the very criminals he hunted. These last several months, which had included a thankfully long, quiet and cold winter, had all but erased that hardened, edgy cop, the cop who'd more than once taken matters in his own hands. The last thing he wanted to do was dredge that man back up for no good reason.

"You don't need to go looking for trouble," Lynn said. "On an island this size you can see it coming from miles away."

He nodded. "You want to know what happened to that guy Ron hired last year?"

She didn't say anything, only held his gaze.

"He left here and got a job over on the mainland. Two weeks later he was arrested for possession." Garrett stood and headed for the door. "So you want me to back off, Lynn. That's fine. For now."

CHAPTER THREE

ERICA FOLLOWED ARLO out the back door of the restaurant, into a narrow alley and up the metal stairs on the side of the building. He took his time, his feet clanging loudly on every step as if his hip were bothering him.

"You don't need to go all the way up," Erica offered. "I'm sure we can find the apartment on our own."

"Well, I might be getting old," he said. "The day I stop moving is the day I die."

Whatever.

He unlocked the door to the first of two apartments above the pub. "This one's got the nicer view out the bedroom windows."

She poked her head inside. So much for fairy tales. From the outside, the building had looked well-kept enough with the redbrick having recently been power washed and a fresh coat of white paint on the shutters and trim, but apparently all a person had to do was lift Mirabelle's picture perfect rug to find the proverbial dust.

But then the Duffys usually rented to college students on summer break. Knowing there might be any number of parties, no landlord in his or her right mind would spend much on décor. Then there was the storm damage. Part of the ceiling and drywall on the inside wall bordering what, most likely, was the other apartment was badly water-stained.

A ladder and various other construction supplies and tools were piled up in the living room.

"Was that caused by the storm?"

"Ayep. The roof was repaired last week. The interior will be next." He dropped their luggage off inside the door. "Well, there ya go. I know it isn't much to look at, but things have been a bit tight around here moneywise."

Holding Jason's hand, Erica stepped into the apartment. The place smelled old with hints of linoleum and cement in the stale, slightly musty air. There was one large front room, combining kitchen, dining and living space. It was sparsely furnished with only a battered oak kitchen table, an old couch, a TV, two chairs that had seen better days and a coffee table that had been strategically placed to hide part of a stain in the worn brown carpet.

Positives. There had to be a few.

She reminded herself that it came cheap, and it seemed safe. As far as she could tell there was only one way up to the apartments, and the metal steps leading to the second floor were noisy. Very likely she'd hear someone coming long before he reached her front door. At least the place, other than the storm damage, looked clean.

"Thanks, Arlo." Erica glanced at Jason. "This'll be great, right?"

He didn't respond, but simply stuck to her side as he glanced doubtfully around.

"Guess I need to turn on a few things." With fatherlike concern—at least how Erica imagined a father might act since she'd never known hers—Arlo walked around the apartment, plugging in lamps, turning on the refrigerator and lighting the pilot on the water heater. He pointed at a telephone on the kitchen counter. "That line won't work 'til you get it reconnected." He sniffed the air. "Crack a couple of windows and that oughtta take care of the staleness. Lynnie usually leaves clean linens in the hall closet."

She followed him around, listening as he explained how everything worked. If she'd been alone and responsible only for herself, she wouldn't have even bothered making one of those beds before curling up and sleeping. The last few days of zigzagging through Minnesota and Wisconsin had been nothing short of a nightmare. She'd snatched little more than catnaps in the car since yesterday afternoon.

Outside the bathroom, she found the closet and another door. She jiggled the knob and found it locked. "Where does this lead?"

"To the restaurant kitchen downstairs."

"Is it always locked?"

"There's a dead bolt on the other side."

Which meant if she unbolted the other side of this door, Jason could get downstairs if he needed her. It also meant if an undesirable got in downstairs, he could, theoretically, get into this apartment. "I need a chain put on this side," she said, realizing too late how demanding she sounded. "I mean, if you don't mind."

Arlo nodded. "I don't see why not. I'll have it taken care of this weekend." He handed her the keys. "Guess we'll be seeing you tomorrow."

"Arlo?"

"Ayep."

"Is there a grocery store on the island?"

"Newman's on Main." He pointed to his left. "Couple blocks west of the pub."

"Where's the school?"

"Up past the church. On the east side." He pointed in the other direction toward the ferry pier. "I hear some of the young couples say it's a small, but good school." He smiled at her and patted Jason's head. "If your work schedule puts you in a pinch with the boy, let me know. He can always come up to the stables and help me out with the horses."

Jason's head shot up and interest flickered in his eyes, but he didn't say anything.

Why would this man offer to help? He didn't know her, didn't owe her a thing. She struggled with something appropriate to say, then finally settled on a quiet, "Thank you."

As soon as Arlo disappeared down the steps, she bolted the front door, latched the chain and checked the locks on the windows. For the first time in days, she felt as if she could breathe. The smile she felt forming on her face wasn't the least bit forced for Jason's sake. "Let's go check out the kitchen."

Cooking had always been an outlet for pent-up energy for Erica, so not having a kitchen to mess around in had about killed her. She opened a few cupboards to find mismatched plates, cups and silverware. The state of the pots and pans, flea-market finds at best, almost brought a tear to her eye when she thought of the set of professional cookware she'd left back at her own apartment. And the knives? They probably hadn't seen a decent edge for years.

"Nothing fancy, but we'll live," she murmured.

Next, she and Jason walked down the hall and found two bedrooms, each with a bare double bed, bedside table and dresser. The bathroom was barely large enough for the two of them to stand side by side. Hard water stains ringed the sink, and the toilet looked like a throwback from the '50s.

This was nothing like the house with a backyard and swing set that Jason had left behind along with all of his friends, but they were both going to have to make the best of this new home for a short while.

Home. This little boy wasn't the only one who'd left his life behind. She'd woken up one morning same as always, and a single phone call had changed everything. In a matter of a few hours, she'd had to leave her apartment, her friends, her job, her life. For this. And for how long? A week, a month, longer?

Where the hell are you, Marie? Call me. Dammit.

"Well?" She took Jason's hands and swung her arms. "What do you think?"

"How long do we have to stay here?"

"As long as it takes, kiddo."

AFTER A QUICK TRIP to the island's sadly lacking grocery store for a few items—Erica hadn't the energy for more—she whipped up a stir-fry back at their new apartment and she and Jason ate while watching some silly sitcom. Less than a half an hour after the warm food hit his stomach, Jason fell sound asleep on the couch.

She found a couple of old-fashioned chenille bedspreads along with sheets and towels wrapped in plastic in the hall closet, quietly made both beds, and then carried Jason down to one of the rooms. Like an overdone noodle, he hung limp in her arms and didn't even crack open an eye as she laid him down and took off his shoes.

Pulling the covers over him, she waited a moment to make sure he'd stay asleep and then snuck out of the room, leaving the door open only a few inches. She went back to the TV, turned down the volume and flipped to a national headline news station. Half an hour later, she turned the TV off. Nothing. No mention of Jason or Marie.

Antsy now, Erica paced in the living room. If she'd been back home, she'd still be at work. After work, she'd have grabbed a beer or something to eat with coworkers, maybe even hit a club or two. Some loud music and dancing sounded good right about now to let off some steam, but this wasn't Chicago.

Maybe Marie had left a message. Erica went to the kitchen counter, drew her cell phone from her purse and turned it on. Nothing new. Maybe her half sister had finally wisened up and left that sonofabitch of a husband and was in hiding. Cop or no cop, Erica'd had a bad feeling about Billy Samson from the moment he'd convinced Marie to marry him right out of high school. For years, Erica had tried talking her sister into leaving him, but Marie had always been quick to defend her husband. Maybe something had finally happened. A last straw. Some sanity. Erica had been fine without a man all these years. Marie would've done fine, too.

Maybe there was something she'd missed in her sister's voice mail. She pulled up her saved messages and listened.

"I know I haven't kept in touch the way I should have, Erica. I'm so, so sorry." Marie's voice came over the cell phone, sounding emotional and rushed. "I need your help and there's no one else I can go to. Please. Pick up Jason from school. Meet me at Charlie's at two o'clock. I'll be able to get away easier once I know Jason is safe."

There was a long pause and then, "If I don't show," she whispered, her voice now panicked, "leave. Get out of town. Go someplace safe. Don't trust anyone. Don't—don't—use your cell phone. I'll call and leave a message when I can. Whatever you do, take care of Jason." She paused again. "Safe and sound, Rick. Keep him safe and sound."

The line went abruptly dead, as if Marie was in a hurry. There was nothing else. No clues for Erica. No secret code, no hidden meaning.

Safe and sound. Those were the words Erica had always whispered to Marie when they'd been kids and scared and hugging each other. During storms or after nightmares. When their mother hadn't come home at night, or when she'd come home with another man.

The fact that Marie had used a childhood nickname for the first time in many, many years had tugged at Erica in a way she hadn't expected. She'd dropped everything and done exactly as Marie had asked, and when her sister hadn't shown up at the restaurant they used to meet at for lunch now and again—luncheons that had gotten less and less frequent after Marie had gotten married—she'd ordered Jason a burger, fries and a chocolate shake and waited.

When four o'clock came and went, Erica, again, did exactly what her sister had asked. She had taken Jason and left. They'd driven north out of Chicago and hadn't looked back. Running away had gone against her every instinct, but there'd been no other option.

Whatever you do, take care of Jason.

Dammit! The last place she wanted to be was here baby-sitting. She didn't know how to take care of any child, let alone a boy frightened of his own shadow. She should be in Chicago, finding and helping Marie.

Oh, God, Marie. Where are you? I told you this was going to happen. I told you and you wouldn't listen to me. You defended that asshole. Why?

Since she'd left that Chicago restaurant, Erica had held it firmly together. She'd refused to let Jason see the fear in her heart. Now, she shook with all the impotence and anger and let the tears fall. Hugging herself, she fell back against the wall and cried.

After a long while, she wiped her cheeks dry and straightened her shoulders. *Okay, you had your little falling apart. Now do something. Do it.*

She flicked open her cell phone and ran through the list of saved numbers. She was about to connect to her sister's cell when Marie's warning flashed through her mind. *Don't use your cell phone.* Until she knew more about what was going on she had to trust her sister's instincts.

Erica snapped the phone closed, quietly snuck down the stairs and ran through the alley to the pay phone she'd noticed earlier on the street.

The night was dark, quiet. In Chicago, with the constant

glow of the city the stars always seemed to look faded, as if a hazy wash had been painted over the sky. Up here, the sky was a sea of black velvet pinpricked with brilliance.

She reached the cobblestone street, and hesitated as the light from Duffy's, as well as a couple other restaurants, spilled onto the sidewalk. Several lampposts illuminated the street.

She shoved some money into the pay phone, dialed into her cell phone account and waited. Four messages sat in her in-box. The first one was from her boss, wondering why she hadn't shown up for work and the second two were from co-workers asking, surprisingly, if she needed help. She hadn't thought they'd had that kind of relationship. They hung out sometimes after work, but she'd never thought of them as friends. Her instincts had her wanting to call at least one of them back, but she couldn't.

The last message was a hang-up for which the number had been blocked. Could that have been Marie? No, she would've left a message.

Erica shoved more money into the phone, blocked the number and dialed Marie's cell phone. It rang several times before a click sounded as if the call had been answered, but instead of a customary acknowledgment there was silence on the other end of the line. Complete and eerie silence.

Don't trust anyone. Erica held her breath. It took everything in her not to whisper her sister's name.

"Erica?" Finally, a man spoke over the line. "Is that you?" It was Billy. His voice, too slow and too deep, as if he were trying to convince himself he had things under control had always driven her crazy. "Where the hell are you?" he asked. "Where's Marie?"

Where's Marie? What the—?

Her heart hammering in her chest, Erica disconnected the call and glanced nervously around. She was alone. She looked up a number on her cell and dialed on the pay phone.

After several rings, the call was connected. "Yo." A man's gravelly voice sounded over the line.

"Teddy? It's Erica Corelli." She paused, hoping like hell he'd remember her. He'd been the only one of her mother's boyfriends she could remember with any affection. "Yeah, I know it's been a long time. I need your help."

THERE WAS NO WAY Billy was going to be able to trace that call, but he would've bet anything it had been Marie's sister quietly listening on the other end.

Dammit! He snapped his wife's cell phone closed and glanced out his car window up to the top corner of the apartment building, looking for movement. From this vantage point, parked in shadows on the dark street, he could see it all, the illuminated parking lot and front and rear entrances. Near as he could tell, Erica hadn't been home since she'd signed out Jason from school.

Even her car, a relatively new, black, two-door sports coupe hadn't been moved from its parking spot directly under the lamppost. The restaurant folks had said she hadn't shown up for work, either. This was so unlike her, they'd said, all worried and concerned.

He'd give them worried, all right, once he got his hands on Erica. Why the hell had Marie listed her sister as the emergency contact at school anyway? Just thinking about it got him worked up. No one took what belonged to him. No one. The kid was already halfway to a momma's boy, having spent way too much time with Marie. The last thing Jason needed was more one on one with another weak-kneed Corelli.

Then again, that Erica had always been stronger and smarter than her little sister. Seemed like whenever Marie spent time with Erica, she'd come home with all kinds of ideas, getting on his case about this and that.

His blood boiled thinking about it. Damn her, but she

knew how to push his buttons. Day and night. Until he knocked her back into shape. Marie should've been glad he'd limited her visits with her sister. Unfortunately, that meant he now knew very little about Erica. She could cook, and that was about all he knew from the few holiday meals they'd shared, but Billy had no clue where the damned woman would go to hide or who she'd turn to for help.

A pair of headlights came around the corner, and the car pulled into the parking lot. A guy got out and headed toward the apartment's security door. This was it. Time for Billy to take some precautions.

He double-timed it toward the building entrance and caught the front door before it swung closed. Avoiding the elevator, Billy climbed the stairs to the third floor. He used the key he'd found in Marie's things and let himself into Erica's apartment. Then he went from one dark room to the next, searching for anything that might clue him in to where she'd gone.

The place looked clean with no sign of last-minute packing. That meant Erica had done something very few people could manage. With nothing more than the clothes on her back, she'd left and didn't bother with a backward glance. Smart and strong. She might prove tough to find.

After carefully going through a small file cabinet, he located a bank statement and wrote down the account number. Same with the credit card and cell phone. He doubted she'd be stupid enough to use any of it, but he had to cover his bases.

Then he stood in the middle of each room and looked around. There had to be something here that would lead him to her. After carefully digging through closets, the medicine cabinet, in the back of kitchen cupboards, under the bed and finally her bedside table, he found nothing except for the spare key to her car.

He sat on the edge of the bed and picked up the framed photo on the bedside table. Marie, Erica and Annette, their mother. It'd been taken only a few years before Annette had died. As far as he knew, Marie and Erica had no surviving relatives, and their fathers were long gone.

Since Erica hadn't been planning this, her reaction would've been instinctive. She'd most likely gone someplace she felt comfortable. Someplace she felt safe. Someplace he wouldn't know about.

He stared at the picture, trying to remember where it had been taken. Some restaurant for Annette's birthday or something. He studied Marie's smile. *Dammit, woman. You couldn't let it go, could you?* He stared up at the ceiling and felt actual tears drain down his throat. Then he clenched his jaw and his fists. *I'm not going to blubber over you. You don't deserve it.*

Setting the photo back down, he picked up the only other one he'd seen in the apartment. Once again, it was Marie, Erica and Annette. They were sitting in a horse-drawn carriage. It was a crappy Polaroid, but Billy had seen this before. Marie had something similar she'd kept on her dresser. She'd always said that this vacation, when she'd been about eight, had been the best time of her life.

That's one of the things that had driven him crazy about Marie. All she'd wanted was fairy tales and romance. Who had time for that shit? He snorted into the quiet, stale air and almost threw the photo across the room. He felt like trashing the entire damned place, but he couldn't. When questions started being asked—and they would be soon enough—every finger had to point to Erica.

He walked to the closet, grabbed a couple suitcases, set them on the bed and threw in one thing after another. Makeup, lotions, brushes, clothes. Next, he'd have to make sure her car wouldn't be found. When Erica never came home—and he was going to make sure she never did—it would look as if she'd planned all along to disappear without a trace.

CHAPTER FOUR

THE LATHE MACHINE whirred as Garrett turned the last hickory post for the nightstand he was making for one of the guest rooms in the cabin he'd bought on Mirabelle. A basic, rustic-looking frame, this simple table with one drawer certainly wasn't one of the more challenging pieces of furniture he'd ever built, and he was looking forward to moving on.

He'd hoped to start making something special, unique and classic for the furniture in his own bedroom, the last room in the entire house to be outfitted, but a specific design had eluded him all these months.

No matter, though. He loved working with wood, soft, hard, cross-grained or burled. The exact medium didn't matter. In his woodshop, he was always in control. He never lost his temper, he never got angry, he never lashed out. The Zenlike concentration it required to make something from nothing with his hands never failed to soothe his soul. Until this morning.

He couldn't concentrate, couldn't keep his mind on the machine and had almost sliced the skin off several knuckles. The reason was undeniable. *Erica Jackson.* Her dark eyes, guarded and heavy with worry, haunted him. She was hiding something, and until he knew what, he wasn't going to be able to get her out of his mind.

His hold slipped and the post slid away, causing his arm to fall forward. *Dammit anyway.* He'd better quit while he was still in one piece. He switched off the machine and pushed his safety glasses onto the top of his head. So much for finishing off the table. He walked over to the laptop that he often kept in the small office off his woodworking shop and logged on to various databases to see what he could find on Erica Jackson.

In Chicago, his resources had been virtually unlimited, but here he was on his own. He typed her name into his computer, figuring he'd check out Minnesota first since she'd claimed to have lived in northeast Minneapolis.

His hand hovered over the return button as a silent debate echoed through his mind on the ethics of background checks given little or no cause. He'd told Lynn he'd back off, but what would be the harm in doing a background check? If the woman was clean, no harm done. If she wasn't, he might be doing Lynn and Arlo a favor.

Bang. Without another thought on the matter, he hit Enter and waited for the search information to pop onto the screen. One match. A woman in her forties. Too old. Maybe his Erica was from Chicago as he'd first suspected. He checked the Illinois and Wisconsin databases, as well as all the surrounding states. Still no matches in the correct age range. He tried various spellings. Nothing.

Zach Jackson? He typed in the name. Several listings appeared, but none of the ages matched.

Erica, if that was even her name, was lying. Why?

He'd thought he'd shaken off Chicago, where armed robberies and murders were commonplace, but apparently Mirabelle alone wasn't enough. A mysterious character stepping off the ferry was all it took to pop him right back into ready mode.

On impulse, he picked up the phone and dialed his old partner. John Wilmes answered on the first ring. "Hey, John. It's Garrett."

"Garrett who?"

"Smart-ass."

"Ah, Garrett Smart Ass. I remember him. Tall, dark and stupid. Not that I'm still harboring ill will about him deserting me or anything."

"How you been, buddy?" Balancing the phone between his ear and shoulder, Garrett proceeded to clean wood dust out from under his nails with a metal file and then slathered on heavy lotion. Working with wood sucked every last bit of moisture from his hands.

"Same old, same old. Everything messier and nastier than the day before. And that new partner they saddled me with? I hate training in these green boys. We need you, you know? No one else around has your intuition."

Intuition was a nice, sugarcoated way of describing Garrett's ability to think like the lowest scum of the earth. John's comment, the one that'd had Garrett interviewing for this job a year ago, ran through Garrett's mind as if it was yesterday. *Damn, G.T., you think just like them. Good thing you're on our side.*

Except that Garrett had stepped one and a half feet over the line onto the lawless side on too many occasions. The last time, he'd set out to kill a man and had about finished the job.

"When you coming back?" John asked.

Garrett wasn't leaving Mirabelle. This place spoke to his soul in a peaceful, quiet way. Working as a part-time cop and a part-time wood/construction worker was exactly what he needed to keep the demons away. And the setup here—ten acres with a split log cabin and a detached garage—well, he couldn't have asked for more.

Although the original house had been built in the '20s, subsequent owners had added on several rooms and a loft and then gutted and remodeled the entire interior. The utility building was perfect for a woodworking shop. It was well insulated, had its own furnace and was big enough for not only all of his machinery, including, amongst other things, saws, sanders, routers, but also the stock of wood that he'd been buying for years in the hopes of some day designing and building his own furniture.

"I'm serious," John said. "We need you here."

"Yeah, like a hole in the head." Garrett had never been a by-the-numbers police officer and his chief had made it clear he wasn't all that broken up about Garrett leaving the CPD. "I come back," Garrett said, "and in a couple months time, they'll be putting me behind bars."

"You're not the first cop to go vigilante, and you won't be the last."

"I won't cross that line. Not again." Breaking the rules was one thing. He'd run into a lot of situations that didn't fit the standard operating procedures, but it had scared the shit out of him, discovering exactly what he was capable of, getting a good look at the ugliness inside of him. Here on Mirabelle, he could forget what he'd almost become. He could force himself into a pure and virtuous mold, and no one was the wiser. "That's the nice thing about Mirabelle. The worst I have to deal with up here is shoplifting or a bar brawl here or there."

"Four more years, three months and fifteen days until Sally and me are joining you up there in God's country. You better start scoping out the houses for us."

"This island isn't big enough for the two of us."

"Well, between now and then, you're going to have to make room. Now, whaddya want?"

"Checking up on a couple new residents. Erica and Zach Jackson."

"Runaways?"

"No. Mother and son. Mom's probably in her…" Garrett paused, picturing Erica in his mind. It was easy to do. She'd pretty much consumed his every thought since she'd stepped off the ferry. "Mid to late twenties. Early thirties at most."

"What else do you know?"

"Nothing." That's exactly what Garrett had on Erica. He drummed his fingers on the battered desktop. He couldn't peg her and call it a day, that's what bothered him more than anything. *Dammit to hell.* Mirabelle was making him soft. He hadn't even noticed whether or not she'd been wearing a wedding ring. She had a kid, so there had to be a dad. Where was he? Divorced? Uninvolved? Dead?

"Let me check into it and get back to you," John said. "It's going to take a while, though. We're swamped down here."

"Get to it when you can. Appreciate it." Then there was the boy's bruise. "Tread lightly, John, okay? I don't want you bringing attention to them if it turns out they're running *from* someone."

"IT'S NOT THE END OF THE world." Erica stood next to Jason in front of the elementary school their first morning on the island. "We're just here to check it out today, okay?"

After sleeping in quite late, they'd stopped at Miller's, the combination ice cream parlor and coffee shop for a muffin and juice for Jason and a double latte for Erica and had then set off for the school. They'd found the one-story tan brick building that looked as if it'd been built in the sixties, up the hill beyond the chapel, exactly where Arlo had said it would be. Now Jason only stood there, frowning, something Erica had seen far too much of these past few days.

"What do you want me to do," she said, "homeschool you?"

His glance was hopeful.

"Don't even think about it, kiddo. You'd be going to school if you were back home, right?"

He nodded.

"So this is what your mom would want," she whispered, pulling his baseball cap lower on his brow. "Right?"

He nodded again and dropped his gaze to the sidewalk.

"Then let's go." She held the door open and they found the office on the right.

The secretary, a grandmotherly sort, glanced up and said, "Can I help you?"

Erica froze without a clue what to say.

"You two must be new to the island."

"Um…yeah. Zach and I…just moved to Mirabelle. How do I go about…?"

"Enrolling him in school?"

"Exactly."

The woman explained the process while piling up paperwork. "Just fill all this out and bring it back as soon as you can."

Erica took a quick glance at the information required on the forms. She was going to have to lie through her teeth and hope these folks wouldn't complete too deep a records check before school wrapped up for the year.

"We don't live or die by policy here on Mirabelle, though," the secretary went on to explain. "We'll get your son into his classroom as soon as you're both ready."

The principal came out and introduced herself, and Erica and Jason were given a tour of the building, which included meeting the woman who would be Jason's teacher, Hannah Johnson.

"Good to meet you." The teacher smiled and shook Erica's hand. The woman was blonde, blue-eyed and could have been the poster model for cute as a button. As opposite from Erica as sunshine from rain.

Jason hung a sullen step or two behind Erica.

Hannah knelt down. "Hi, Zach. I'm looking forward to having you in our class."

He never said a word, not even when his soon-to-be teacher gave him an information sheet to fill out so she could get to know him better. As they finished and headed back toward the entrance, classes were being let out for lunch and a rush of students flooded the halls.

A small boy, who looked to be no more than Jason's age and who wasn't paying the slightest bit of attention, ran headlong into Jason, knocking him down.

"Hey!" Erica grabbed the kid's arm and held him back. "Watch where you're going."

"Oh, my gosh!" A perky-looking young mother came running toward them through the front entrance. "Is your son all right?"

Jason looked shaken, but no worse for wear. Erica helped him up. "You okay, kiddo?"

He nodded, refusing to look at the other boy.

"Brian, tell him you're sorry," the woman said.

"Sorry."

"I'm Sarah Marshik." She held out a manicured hand. "This is my son, Brian. I have lunch with him once a week."

How very motherly of her. "Erica." What was their last name again? "Jackson. This is…" She couldn't seem to say the words *my son*. "Zach."

"You got to the island yesterday, didn't you?"

Erica nodded, feeling rather dowdy next to Sarah. Wearing a gorgeous wool coat over a silk shirt and dress pants, the woman looked as if she should be trolling the designer shops on Michigan Avenue in downtown Chicago.

"I was grabbing something to eat at the Bayside Café when you got off the ferry," Sarah explained. "Have you found a place to live?"

"Yeah," she answered reluctantly. The last thing Erica wanted was to make friends on this island, but the more she fit in the better she and Jason would disappear into the fabric of this foreign land. "One of the apartments above the pub."

"I'm down the street from you. On Main. Brian and I live above my flower shop."

They stood in silence for a few moments, before Sarah said, "Well, if Zach's looking for someone to play with, or for that matter—" she grinned and dug around in her purse "—you need some flowers or even a wedding planner." She handed Erica a business card. "Give me a call. That's my home number, too. If there's anything I can do to help, let me know."

"Will do."

Sarah and her son were heading down the school corridor toward the lunchroom when Erica realized there was something this woman might be able to do for her. "Hey, Sarah?"

The woman turned.

"Can you suggest a babysitter? I'm going to be working for the Duffys and may need someone to watch over Zach here and there."

"Oh, that's a tough one," Sarah said, frowning. "There are several teenagers on the island, but a couple troublemakers in the bunch." She wrote names on her card and handed it back to Erica. "Try these two, but I'd love to do some kind of playdate trade-off with you. My shop is open every day of the week and it's always hard keeping Brian busy."

"Okay." *What would Marie say?* "Once I get my work schedule, I'll give you a call."

"Great!"

As Sarah turned around, Erica glanced down at Jason. He was leaning against her, resting his head against her thigh and looking not a little conflicted as he watched Brian heading into the lunchroom, holding his mother's hand.

"I want to stay with you," he said.

A sense of complete inadequacy rushed through her. What could she say? What could she do to help ease his fears? "I know, kiddo." It was sorely inadequate, but all she had. "Come on. Let's explore the island a little and then get some groceries before we head…home."

Such as it was.

CHAPTER FIVE

HAVING FINISHED A short shift at the station, Garrett changed out of his uniform and into work clothes and climbed the steps to the second floor of the Duffys' building. He knocked on the door to Erica Jackson's apartment. No answer. After knocking again and still not getting any response, he let himself in with the key Lynn had given him when she'd hired him to repair the storm damage.

"Hello?" he called after cracking open the door. No response. They had to be gone. He stepped into the apartment, leaving the door open behind him and looking around. Unable to snuff his cop's curiosity, he checked out the bedrooms. One suitcase sat open on the floor in each room. Two suitcases for an entire summer. Could be they traveled light or couldn't afford much, could be she was lying about staying, or it could be they'd left wherever they'd come from in a hurry. The answer to that question would shed a distinctly different light on Mirabelle's newest residents.

The bigger suitcase was probably Erica's, and he probably had time to shuffle through the contents. He ran a hand over his face, debating. *Oh, hell. Knock it off, G.T.* Having John check for criminal records was one thing, but Lynn was right. Unless this woman and her son did something to warrant closer examination, he had no right violating their personal space.

He walked back out to the living room and went to work.

He was on the ladder, tearing down the damaged sections of Sheetrock on the ceiling and wall when footsteps sounded on the metal steps in the alleyway.

On hearing her hesitate at the open door, he spun around and called out, "It's just me." She'd hung back and he couldn't see her. "Garrett Taylor. Doing some repair work."

Keeping Zach firmly behind her, she moved into the doorway, her arms loaded down with grocery bags. As soon as she saw him, she said, "It's okay, Zach. Come on in."

As she stalked into the kitchen the boy followed, carrying his backpack and a baseball bat. Looking fairly miffed, she set the bags on the counter. "What the hell are you doing in my apartment?"

Everyone's carefree attitude on this island had been hard for him to adjust to, as well, so he did his best not to study her every move, not to read into everything she said. "Sorry if I scared you. The Duffys hired me to repair the damage from last week's storm."

"I thought you were the police chief."

"That's only a part-time job on Mirabelle. I do construction work on the side."

Her expression said she was trying to make sense of something.

"The Duffys told me to let myself in. That okay with you?"

"You mean, you have a key?"

He almost laughed at the look of disbelief on her face. "It seemed the easiest thing to do. No one was living here when I started the repairs. If you want—"

"Yes, I do want," she said, unloading the groceries. "Give it back to them, please."

"I'll leave the key with you." Even if she was now living on Mirabelle, where some residents still didn't lock their houses before going to sleep at night, he couldn't blame her for being careful.

"I want you—" She stopped, seeming to check the attitude. "I'd like you out of here by six."

"Can do."

The boy watched him for a moment, a look of serious concentration on his face. "Zach," she said, "Come sit up here and let's do that information sheet they gave you at school while I make us some dinner."

The boy hopped up onto the stool at the counter, and Garrett went back to ripping out the damaged parts of the ceiling and wall. Behind him, he heard her banging around in the cabinets. She was still royally pissed. Much to his surprise, he found himself enjoying making her mad. It sure seemed easy enough to manage.

Before too long, she was chopping something. In the small apartment, the smell wafted up to him within seconds. Onions. There was the sound of a pan being set on the stovetop and then sizzling. More chopping. Tomatoes. Simmering in the pan. Then something frying. Italian sausage.

The smells brought him back to his mother's kitchen. He hadn't had many home-cooked meals since she'd passed away a few years back. Oh, he'd been to his married brother's house for holidays and such, and his sister-in-law was a wonderful cook, but nothing ever tasted the same as Mom's. He'd even tried re-creating a few of her recipes himself. He might be able to work magic with wood, but he was crap in a kitchen.

Now garlic and fresh basil. His stomach grumbled. He hadn't eaten anything since meeting Herman at the sandwich shop at Rock Point Lodge earlier in the day and it was now close to five.

Covers slid on top of pots, and then he heard her talking quietly to Zach. "What do you want me to put down for this question?" she asked.

He glanced behind him to find her leaning over Zach and

writing on a piece of paper on the counter. "That's a good answer," she said, rubbing his shoulders.

It was an intimate exchange and caught Garrett completely off guard. He went back to work, wondering how people managed being parents, let alone good ones. What if he turned out like his own father?

"I have to use the bathroom," she said. "I don't want you getting into Chief Taylor's way, Zach, so stay right here, okay?" Her footsteps sounded down the hall and then all was quiet.

Garrett had told Lynn he'd back off, but he'd never promised not to fish around, and kids were notorious for giving things away. He glanced behind him to find Zach standing right next to the ladder. What luck? "Hey, there," he said softly.

"Hi." Intently, he studied Garrett's progress, the video game in his hand forgotten.

"You like watching this stuff, huh?"

Zach nodded.

"Do you ever get to help your dad around the house with repairs?"

"No." He shook his head. "My dad's a cop, too, but he doesn't fix things."

A cop? No shit. That Garrett hadn't expected. "You want to be a cop when you grow up?"

Zach stared silently at him for a moment, and then resolutely shook his head. "No."

Interesting. Every young son of a cop Garrett knew wanted to follow in his dad's footsteps. They were usually so proud of their fathers. Now if he could only ask who'd given the kid the bruises, he'd have a few key pieces of the puzzle put together, but digging into that would only scare off the boy.

The bathroom door opened and Erica came down the hall. "Zach! I asked you to stay back."

"He's okay where he is," Garrett said. "I won't drop anything on him."

While glaring up at Garrett, she steered Zach gently back toward the island counter in the kitchen. If he had to put money on it, she wasn't the one behind that boy's bruise.

"Come on, kiddo," she said. "Dinner's ready anyway, so let's eat." He heard her scooping food onto plates. After several minutes, she asked, "Are you hungry, Chief Taylor?"

She was trying to be polite, but the reluctance in her voice was damned near comical. For such a tough cookie, the woman was an open book. "Call me Garrett. And no, I'm all right. I need to finish tearing this out before I can stop."

While they sat at the table and ate, Garrett finished pulling away all the damaged parts of the ceiling and drywall. Then he set about cleaning up the mess he'd made, dumping chunks of Sheetrock in a wheelbarrow, rolling it over to the metal landing outside and tipping everything into a Dumpster in the alley below.

"Can I watch TV now?" the boy asked after he'd finished eating and was setting his plate on the counter next to the sink.

Erica paused in cleaning up the kitchen and glanced over at Garrett. "Will he get in your way?"

"No, not at all." He smiled at Zach. "This'll be my last load anyway."

Zach turned on the TV and sat on the couch. He looked like a kid with a lot on his mind, someone who could use some friendly contact. Moving had to be tough.

"So what's your favorite show?" Garrett asked while he was cleaning up the last of the mess.

"I dunno."

"Did you and your mom check out the school today?"

Zach glanced at him. "Yeah."

"What did you think?"

He frowned. "It's okay."

"You look like you'll be in…second grade?"

As Erica wiped down the stove and counter she glanced toward them, clearly monitoring their conversation.

"First."

"Oh, so you'll have Miss Johnson." Garrett nodded solemnly.

"What?" Zach asked, sitting forward. "What's she like?"

He glanced toward the kitchen. The expression on Erica's face said the tigress was ready to pounce at any second if he said anything remotely inappropriate. "I know a boy named Brian in her class," Garrett explained.

"I met him today."

"You did? Well, he claims she's the best. Nicest teacher in the school. Heck, she's the nicest teacher I've ever met. Gives her kids lollipops on Fridays."

"No way."

"Yep. And she's pretty, isn't she?"

"Sorta."

A half smile formed on Erica's face as she finished the dishes in the sink.

"Give it a chance," Garrett said, putting the last of the debris in the wheelbarrow. "You might like it here."

Erica had her head down and was washing dishes as he took the last wheelbarrow load outside. By the time he was finished he was covered in Sheetrock dust. He stored the wheelbarrow out of the way at the end of the balcony, then took off his shirt and shook it off over the railing. He ran his hands through his hair and brushed off as much of the drywall dust and chunks as possible.

When he turned around, Erica was watching him through the doorway. Most women would've discreetly looked away, but Erica was most assuredly unlike any woman he'd ever known. She met his gaze without even a hint of a smile, and Garrett thanked his lucky stars that Zach was in the apartment, or there was no telling what might've happened next.

He yanked himself back. *No fast women. Period.* Once he finally made the decision to settle down, he was going for a sweet, uncomplicated homebody, someone who could bring out the best in him, if there was such a thing. Just because Erica Jackson looked like she could cook did not make her Susie Homemaker.

He tugged his shirt on and went back into the apartment to the glorious smells of fresh basil, garlic, Italian sausage, tomatoes, onions, peppers. "Mind if I wash my hands?"

"Go ahead." She reached into a bag on the counter and set a pump container next to the sink. "Here's some soap."

As he was standing at the sink, scrubbing away, Garrett glanced at the big pot of rich, thick sauce on the stove and his stomach gurgled loudly. "Sorry." He wiped his hands off on a towel lying on the counter.

"Oh, all right, fine." She grabbed a plate out of the cupboard. "Take some. In fact, take a lot."

"Hey, don't worry about it. My stomach can wait until I get home."

"I have trouble with small portions." She held out the clean plate. "And, uh, Zach didn't eat much."

He looked at the pot again. "Actually, I am a little hungry. You sure?"

"Do you want some or not?"

He took the plate and dished himself up some pasta, ladled on some meaty sauce and dug in, standing right there in the kitchen. Savory flavors exploded in his mouth. Fresh, spiced perfectly, not too sweet. Hands down, this was the best sauce he'd ever tasted and that included his mother's. "Where'd you learn to cook like this?"

"I don't know. I just do," she said gruffly, and went back to washing dishes. "My mom was gone a lot while we were growing up, so I cooked for my sister and myself. I guess I got bored with the same old stuff and experimented."

"Do me a favor and talk Lynn into putting this on the menu."

"You're from Chicago, aren't you?" she asked, out of the blue.

"Mmm-hmm," he said, still chewing. "How'd you know?"

"You got the sound."

"Funny, so do you." He studied her reaction. Nothing. But then he hadn't really expected one.

"So why'd you come to Mirabelle?" she asked.

How did he go about telling someone that he'd gotten too good at solving crimes because he'd started to think too much like the murders, rapists and robbers. "Get away from the rat race."

She didn't believe him. It was written all over those pretty brown eyes.

"Why did *you* come here?" he asked.

"Once when I was a little girl I came here with my mom and my sister." She stopped drying the pan in her hands and focused on Zach sitting in the living room watching TV. "It was the best three days of my life."

Whoa.

The admission had no sooner left her mouth than she glanced up at him, appearing no less surprised to have spoken those words than he'd been to hear them. He cleared his throat. "Do you know if there's a broom and dustpan in here somewhere?" he asked, hoping to cover the sudden awkwardness that had sprung between them.

"I saw one in the closet."

After washing his dish in the sink and setting it in the rack to dry, he followed her down the narrow hall and stood behind her. This close, he realized that without the boots she'd been wearing the other day she was more petite than he'd thought. The top of her head barely came to his shoulders. She was so tiny he could probably fling her up on his shoulders and carry her around for a few hours before he'd notice she was there.

She spun around with the broom and held it toward him. "Here."

"Thanks." He grabbed the handle, but didn't move. No wedding ring. Suddenly, the he-man in him didn't want to move. Susie Homemaker or not, she was damned sexy. "So where's Zach's dad?"

"Chicago."

That he could believe. "Married? Divorced?"

"Neither. Never been married. Never plan to be." She took a step toward him, the challenge clear in the way she held out her chin. "But if you think anything is going to happen between us, guess again. You are so not my type it isn't even funny."

Dang. The sound of the TV reminded him the boy was behind them, but they may as well have been alone in the apartment for the charge in the air. If Zach hadn't been in the living room, he might've picked her up and carried her back onto one of those beds.

"So what is your type?" Flirting with her was dangerous. He knew it, and still he couldn't rein himself in.

"Not a cop, that's for sure."

"What do you got against cops?"

"You wouldn't understand."

"Try me."

She glared at him. "Don't think so." She went to step around him, but he didn't move.

Touch me. Put your hand on my arm, better yet my chest, and move me. Touch me once and I'll bet you don't let go. Like a curse, she'd settled over him. All he wanted in that moment was her under him, her arms around him.

"Typical cop," she whispered. "Thinking you're all that."

"Zach's dad is a cop, isn't he?" Garrett whispered. The smell of her, basil and a haunting citrus smell that seemed to come off her hair, made his mouth water.

She narrowed those big brown eyes at him, her wheels turning. Would she lie, or tell the truth? "Yeah, Zach's dad is a cop. And he's an asshole. First class."

The truth again. She was full of surprises, but then something in the way she'd owned up seemed too confident, too up-front that told him her cut went deeper. "That's not the whole story, though, is it?"

She only stared at him.

"Zach's dad isn't the whole problem. What happened, Erica?"

"I don't know what you're talking about." She studied him, took in his arms, his chest, but the appreciation in her eyes was laced with something he couldn't put a finger on, something that looked an awful lot like fear.

She was afraid of him? Him?

Garrett became acutely aware of the difference in their respective sizes, the way he had her backed into a hallway. He never, ever would've hurt her, but the fact that he could bench-press about twice her weight suddenly seemed like a terrible defect.

"I'm sorry." He stepped back. "For…all the dust."

"You gotta do what you gotta do." She broke eye contact and carefully skirted by him, making sure they didn't come into contact.

Someone had badly hurt her and the boy, and all Garrett wanted to do was get his hands on the asshole.

CHAPTER SIX

THE BIG, BURLY MAN, a man with muscles on top of muscles, doing construction work while the little woman cooked dinner in the kitchen. Was there anything more sickeningly domestic in the world? Just the thought of it made Erica want to toss her pasta right back up.

Then again, the look on Garrett's face when he'd tasted her sauce may have been worth it. He'd actually closed his eyes for a second and, he probably didn't even realize it, but a small sound of pleasure had escaped his throat. If she was honest with herself, just watching him work dressed in faded jeans and a gray T-shirt may have been enough to make cooking for him worthwhile. When he took off said shirt, exposing a back rippling with strength, she would've gladly whipped up some tiramisu for him if she'd had the ingredients.

"Thanks for dinner," he said, coming back out into the kitchen.

It was those eyes. "You're welcome." They were the palest gray she'd ever seen. The look of those hands, so big and strong, almost made her swoon.

"I'll finish sweeping up the mess I made on the floor over there and then get out of your hair."

Not to mention his voice, soft and deliberate. He didn't need to speak loudly to get attention. She'd bet all he had to do was walk into a room to get every head to turn.

"That's okay, I can sweep." She needed him gone. The

worst thing that could happen right now was a collision under the sheets with, of all the possible men out there, a police chief. "I'll take care of it in the morning."

"It won't take me more than a few minutes."

"Zach and I are ready to wind down. It's been a long day."

"All right." He pulled a key ring out of his pocket and held it out, his biceps bulging. "Here's your key."

Erica should've been afraid of a man the size of Garrett Taylor. She wasn't, not in the slightest. In fact, her skin burned with a strange awareness. One touch from him and she felt as if she might actually explode. She held her hand out and waited.

He glanced at her open palm and then into her eyes and dropped the key, clearly misreading her actions. "Thanks." No way was she setting him straight.

"I'll be back tomorrow to finish the repairs."

She'd try her best to be gone. "Thanks for the warning."

"See you later, Zach!" he called.

"Bye," Jason said without turning from the TV.

It had already grown dark outside by the time Garrett left the apartment. She listened to the sound of his feet pounding down the steps, then locked and chained the front door and rechecked every window. Then she sat down on the old couch next to Jason to watch TV.

"He's nice," Jason said after a few quiet moments.

"You think?"

"Yeah."

The man certainly seemed comfortable carrying on a conversation with Jason.

"Do you think he'll tell my dad where we are?"

Erica looked down at her nephew, her heart breaking for him. She'd never once explained that they were running from Billy, but he understood all the same. "I don't know."

"My dad always says," Jason whispered, still looking at the TV, "that cops stick together."

That's what worried her, almost as much as her obvious attraction to Garrett Taylor.

He was a man, she reminded herself, and she'd never had much respect for the opposite sex. How could she when her entire childhood had included a revolving door of the unreliable, untrustworthy louts?

She'd never known her father. He'd left before she'd been born. There'd been Marie's dad, from all accounts a bigger asshole than Erica's. Then a whole stream of other jerks had followed, including a couple of creepy cops, one extremely abusive, until Teddy, the only nice guy in the bunch.

Teddy had been a record, hanging around for almost an entire school year, and just when Erica was settling in to the idea that she might actually be able to count on the guy, she'd woken up one morning to find him gone. When Erica had asked what had happened, her mother had shrugged and moved on. To another bottle. Another man. Another job. Another apartment, dragging her and Marie behind in the muck.

Not surprising, Erica's own life had turned into a succession of broken relationships, but she'd be damned if she was going to give any man the upper hand. "I don't know about you, kiddo, but I'm exhausted," Erica said. "Let's get ready for bed."

After shutting off the TV, they trudged down the hall together. She finished putting his clothes in the dresser about the time he was done brushing his teeth. He wandered out of the bathroom, and she turned to find him in the middle of a big yawn. "You must be tired," she said. "It's been a long day."

He only nodded and shuffled into the room. "Do I have pajamas?" he mumbled.

"That's your dresser over there. I put all your clothes inside." What little they had anyway. She was going to have to rectify that as soon as she got her first paycheck.

He opened the top drawer, took out his pajamas and

pulled his T-shirt up and over his head. When he turned around, Erica sucked in a breath. "Oh, my God, Jason!" A large, ugly bruise covered his left upper arm and shoulder. "What happened to you?"

He glanced down at his arm as if he'd forgotten and quickly pulled his pajama top over his head, covering himself. "I don't know." His eyes shifted away from hers. "I must've fallen or something."

No one got a bruise like that without remembering how it happened. Billy. Erica would've bet anything that this had been the final straw for Marie. "Did something happen at home?" she said, testing. "Or school?"

He shrugged. "I got in some kid's way during recess and he pushed me down. I guess I hit my shoulder."

She might not know him as well she'd like, but it was clear from the way he wouldn't hold her gaze that he wasn't telling her the truth. Still, she didn't feel comfortable pushing him, at least not yet.

Frustration burned a wide and deep hole inside her, bringing back all kinds of bad memories, memories of being small and helpless. She'd sworn long, long ago she would never turn away from a conflict, never run away. *Never again.* What had she been forced to do? Run.

But this was about Jason, not her, and she vowed to do everything in her power to protect him.

"Does it hurt?" she asked.

"Not anymore." He climbed onto the bed and sat on top of the bedspread. "Am I going to school tomorrow?"

Smart kid, changing the subject and using empathy to get his way. "There's only about a month of school left before summer break, and I think it'll be a good way to meet other kids your age."

"I don't want to meet anyone." He crossed his scrawny arms over his chest. "I want to stay with you."

"I'm going to have to work, kiddo. We'll have to keep you busy doing something."

"I can keep myself busy."

His shoulders sagged and a tear or two pooled in his eyes, and Erica immediately regretted her tough-luck attitude. She was completely out of her league. What would Marie say? The few times she'd seen her sister with Jason, Marie had always seemed like a natural and competent mother. Where had that come from? Certainly not their mother.

"I'll tell you what," Erica said, compromising. "You can take tomorrow off. Get the lay of the land, so to speak. Then on Thursday and Friday, you go to school. Check it out. See what you think. Anyone can do two days, right?"

"I guess so. If you want me to go to school, I'll go. Mommy said I was supposed to do whatever you told me to do."

"Marie said that? When?"

"Last week. She told me that if you ever came to get me, I was supposed to go with you and do whatever you said."

Marie had known something was going to happen.

A flood of tears flowed into Erica's eyes. Quickly, she looked away. Guilt and shame washed over her for not having been able to help her sister before now, for not snatching her away from Billy, but Marie had always been so quick to defend her husband and make light of his controlling behavior. In fact, the more Erica had pushed the more Marie had distanced herself.

It's going to be okay. Marie's smart. She's hiding until whatever happened blows over.

Erica surreptitiously swiped at her cheeks and turned back to Jason. "I think you're going to like the school here. Your teacher seemed really nice, but if all the rest are witches with bad breath, crooked noses and moles on their chins, you can hang with me."

That caused a small smile.

She fluffed his pillow. "Go on. Climb in."

He shoved his feet under the covers and pulled them up to his chin.

"G'night, kiddo." She brushed his bangs aside, kissed his forehead and then flicked off the light.

"Erica?"

"Yeah?" Tonight, she didn't have the heart to remind him to call her mom even in private.

"Where's my mommy?"

She'd known that question was coming. In fact, she was surprised it'd taken him this long. "I'm not sure, Jason." She remembered Marie saying that sounded better than "I don't know."

Sitting down on the edge of the bed, she picked up his hand. At the first sounds of him sniffling, her back stiffened. He was crying. Now what was she supposed to do? She was his aunt, not his mother. When she heard him dry his eyes with the sleeve of his pajamas and try to suck it up, something inside her melted. Opened. Unlocked.

"She'll call us when she can, Jason. I know she will. She loves you very much and she'd do anything for you." Erica pulled her nephew into her arms and hugged him tightly. Suddenly she wanted him as close to her as he wanted to be close. "You know your mom never would've left you unless she couldn't help it."

Jason nodded and tears dribbled down his cheek, one right after another. "I miss her."

"Me, too." Erica hugged him close and rocked him gently. Though she couldn't recall ever having rocked anyone in her life, let alone having been rocked, the motion felt natural, comforting even to her. After he'd calmed down, she let him go. "I have something for you."

"What?"

"Hold on." She ran out into the kitchen, rummaged

through her purse and came back with a wallet-sized photo. "Here."

When Jason looked at it, he smiled.

"I took that picture of you and your mom at Thanksgiving last year. I'll get a frame for it tomorrow, okay?"

"Okay."

She took it out of his hand, set it on the bedside table and flicked off the lamp.

"Will you stay here with me?" he asked.

She hesitated. "Sure. Right next to you."

She lay down on the other side of the bed and held his hand in hers. It wasn't long before Jason gave up the fight and fell completely limp with sleep. His breathing turned quiet and even.

After a few moments, she disentangled her fingers from his and went out to the kitchen. Flicking off lights, she paced. This waiting was killing her. Without a second thought, she raced out of the apartment, down to the pay phone and dialed the number to her mother's old boyfriend. "Teddy?" she said. "Have you found her?"

"MY DAUGHTER ALWAYS COMES to stay for a week over the Fourth of July," Shirley Gilbert said from the steps of her garishly pink Victorian bed-and-breakfast a block off Main Street. "She's a teacher, you know. Divorced. No kids."

Hint. Hint. "Well, I'll keep an eye out for her when the Fourth rolls around," Garrett said, more than ready to get on his way.

He walked down the sidewalk, pulling a cart loaded down with a busted-up antique desk. One of Mrs. Gilbert's guests had tripped and fallen into the desk, breaking a leg and causing a malfunction in the rolltop cover. She'd asked him to fix it and the job required some tools from his workshop, so after working on the Duffys' apartment, he'd stopped to pick up the pieces. "I'll get this back to you as soon as I can."

"All right then," she called after him. "Let me know what I owe you."

A steady stream of construction and repair work was one thing Garrett hadn't counted on when he'd moved to Mirabelle. Since the job of police chief was only part-time, if that during the winter months, Garrett had taken the position in the hopes of starting up a furniture-building business.

But with a new community pool and an eighteen-hole golf course opening in another couple of weeks, the islanders were gearing up for what promised to be one of the busiest summers they'd had in decades. Everyone seemed to need this or that done sooner rather than later, so he'd made the conscious decision to help the people of this island—his island now—get ready. His own business could wait.

He took a deep breath of cool, crisp air. Although it couldn't be much past eight, it was already dark. The night was quiet. Only a slight breeze ruffled the leaves still clinging to the odd oak tree. He was about to head up the hill toward his own house on the outskirts out of town when he heard a muffled feminine voice. From the tone he could tell the person was upset.

Leaving the cart propped against the nearest building, he walked toward the sound, keeping in the shadows, and slowed the moment he could make out actual words.

"I know it's only been a couple of days."

Pause.

"Nothing? There's no sign of her?"

It was Erica. She had to be on the pay phone near the corner.

"You have to keep looking," she said.

Wasn't there a phone in her apartment? What about a cell phone? She didn't want the call traced. That wasn't good. She was someone who didn't want to be found. The question was why not?

"She met with a divorce attorney?" she went on. "No, she was not having an affair."

Who's she?

"No!" Erica cried, then stopped as if becoming aware of her surroundings. "No, no, no, no," she whispered. "I don't want to think about that. Or talk about it."

"Teddy." She was still whispering, but her voice had taken on a desperate tone. "You're all I've got. If you can't find her, what am I going to do?"

Pause.

"I can't go to the police. You know that."

Pause.

"I'll pay you. I don't have the money right now, but I'll get it. Please. You have to keep looking."

A private investigator?

"Call me when you find anything. Anything."

Pause.

"No, it's better you don't know where I am."

Then silence. She'd hung up the phone. The only sound was crickets chirping in the brush. He was about to turn back to his cart when he heard it, one sniff, then two. A couple sharp intakes of breath. Was she crying? Trying her damnedest not to, if nothing else.

Great. Tough, bristly skin outside, marshmallow center inside. He was so screwed.

CHAPTER SEVEN

SOMEONE WAS COMING. Footsteps up the stairs sounded from outside in the alley. Erica dropped her toothbrush in the bathroom sink, grabbed the bat she'd purchased yesterday for protection and ran into the kitchen. With the barest hints of a pale sunrise filtering through the windows, the footsteps stopped outside her door.

When no one knocked, she snuck to the window and peeked between two slats in the blind. Garrett Taylor. Thank God. She never thought she'd be so happy to see any man, let alone this one. She opened the door and found him buckling a tool belt around his waist. A waist that she had no doubt carried a nicely defined six-pack.

He glanced up and took in her full length before settling on the bat in her hand. "Expecting someone?"

"Sorry." She leaned the bat against the kitchen counter. "When you said last night that you were coming back today, I didn't realize you meant this early."

The moment he and his big frame stepped into the apartment, the space seemed to shrink, and she became fully aware of the fact that she was still in her pajamas, a baggy shirt—without a bra—and a pair of boxers.

"Did I wake you?" he asked.

"No." She wiped the toothpaste from her mouth.

"I figured if I got going early, I might be able to finish

the other apartment, too, before my shift at the station." He closed the door behind him. "Is Zach still sleeping?"

"Yeah."

"Then I'll be as quiet as I can." He reached toward her head and she instinctively backed away. "Hold on there." He held her still while he smoothed his hand over her head. "Your hair was sticking straight up."

Bedhead. Great. His hand stayed on her arm a little longer than seemed necessary, but for some reason she didn't feel the urge to pull away. She had to distract herself. Quickly. She went to the counter and filled the coffeepot. "You want coffee?"

"Sure. If you were planning on making it anyway."

He went over to the supplies he had stacked in the storm-damaged corner, climbed the ladder and nailed in— more quietly than she'd believed possible—a piece of drywall cut to the size of the open area in the ceiling. He taped up the edges and then moved to the wall. While he moved with purpose and coordination, he had amazing grace for such a big man.

"Have you had breakfast?" she asked.

"Bowl of cereal." He glanced back at her with a grin on his face. "But if you're cooking, I'm eating."

While he went back to work, installing the drywall, taping and patching, Erica made them both toast and scrambled eggs with cheese, chopped peppers and onions. "Hey?" Not wanting to wake Jason, she'd walked over and tapped him on the leg. "If you can break from what you're doing, this is ready."

He washed his hands at the sink and ate the breakfast as if he were starving. "Don't you ever cook for yourself?" she asked.

"I'm pretty inept in the kitchen."

She wondered how he was in the bedroom.

As if sensing her thoughts, he glanced down at his plate

and quickly finished his eggs and toast. "Thank you," he said, rinsing his plate in the sink.

Clearly, he was restraining himself, and for some reason that irked her, making her want to provoke him. "So why aren't you married?"

He glanced back at her. "Maybe I've never found a woman who'll put up with me."

"Now, why doesn't that surprise me?"

"You trying to pick a fight with me?"

"What if I am?"

"What if I don't want to fight?" He stepped toward her. "If I want to…?"

Erica glared at him. "You—"

A noise by the door made her glance around him. Jason stood in the doorway, looking as frightened as she'd ever seen him. "What is it?" She ran to him, knelt down. "What happened?"

He wouldn't take his eyes off Garrett.

"Honey, tell me what's wrong."

"Is he going to…hit you?"

"Garrett? Are you talking about Garrett?"

Jason nodded.

She heard Garrett growl behind her. That sound sure wasn't making her nephew feel any better. "No, Zach. He wasn't going to hit me. He would never do that."

"How do you know?" Jason whispered.

She didn't know, but she knew. Somehow she knew. How did one go about explaining that to a kid? "I—"

"Can I say something?" Garrett asked, but before she had the chance to respond he butted right in. "Have you ever gotten mad, Zach? At a friend, a teacher. Your mom?"

Jason nodded.

"Have you ever hit anyone?"

Vehemently, he shook his head back and forth.

"That's right. People get mad. It's a fact. It's human nature. But it's never okay to hit." He knelt down, keeping his distance from Jason. "A man never hits a woman. Never."

Erica's throat nearly closed with emotion as she watched Jason assimilate what Garrett was telling him.

"Can Erica hit you?" Jason asked.

"No." Garrett shook his head. "It's not okay to hit kids, either." He paused, and then asked tentatively, "Has anyone ever…hurt you?"

While Erica held her breath, Jason nodded. The kind of anger she'd never felt before hit her in the chest, sucking out the air. Who hit you? She wanted to scream. *Who?* But she knew it was Billy.

"That was wrong," Garrett whispered.

"Even if it was my fault? Even if I left the car door open? It's my fault the light stayed on."

"It doesn't matter. Hitting is never the right answer."

Jason looked from Garrett to Erica.

Why did kids always think they'd done something to deserve the abuse they received? "Never," Erica whispered. "Even if you left the door open. Even if you break something, or get in trouble at school or make any kind of mistake. There's never an excuse to hit a child."

As a child, she remembered too well thinking there had to be something wrong with her. If she'd just do this or that, or not do this or that, then maybe everything would be better. "The adults in your life are responsible for their own behavior, Zach. Not you. They're grown-ups and they should know better." How many times had she had to tell herself that before she'd believed it?

As if the weight of the world had been lifted off Jason's small shoulders, he stepped back. "Can I watch TV now?"

"Sure." Erica stood. "I'll make you some breakfast."

As Jason wandered into the living room, she could feel

Garrett's unanswered questions boring holes into her back. She turned around and whispered, "I never have and never would hit Zach."

Garrett clenched his jaw. "I want to know who did."

"I can't tell you that," she said, but even she could hear her conviction wavering.

"LAST BUT NOT LEAST, this is my office," Lynn said, after having given Erica and Jason a complete tour of the bar area, storerooms and kitchen. "Such as it is." She stepped into a small room off the kitchen housing a paper-strewn desk and several file cabinets.

A computer and printer of relatively new design sat on a credenza and were covered with a thin layer of dust as if neither had been used in months. Erica wished she could ask to log on to the Internet to see if there was any news yet from Chicago about Marie or Jason, but she already felt beholden enough to Lynn.

Erica let go of Jason's hand and was happy that he didn't immediately reach for her again. Giving him some time to acclimate to the island had been a good idea. Already, he seemed less tense and clingy, although he hated having to wear a baseball cap everywhere.

"Now you know everything there is to know about the inner workings of one of the oldest establishments on Mirabelle Island," Lynn said with a smile.

"So…how long has this pub been here?" Erica asked. She wasn't a small-talk kind of person, but she was standing next to the stairway leading to her and Jason's new apartment and needed to ask if they could unlock it at night after Jason went to bed. It was the only way she could see her way clear to bartending on a regular basis, but she hated asking for favors.

Lynn sat down at her desk. "Well, this particular brick

building's only about a hundred fifty years old, but there's been a pub on this spot since the early 1800s."

"Did you grow up on Mirabelle?"

"You betcha. My parents moved here from Detroit right after they got married. Arlo and I have known each other since we were babies. We got married right after high school and raised two sons here, Ben and Adam."

Jason walked around Lynn's office, looking at family photographs littering the walls and every flat surface, showing Arlo and Lynn with two clean-cut looking boys in various stages of development. "Do they live here, too?" he asked, pointing at two young men in one of the pictures.

"Nope." Lynn's smile disappeared. "One lives in Chicago. The other in D.C. Haven't seen either one of them in years. They're both so busy, I barely get the chance to talk to them these days."

"You should e-mail them," Erica said, pointing at the computer. "It's fast. They probably check messages several times a day at work."

"E-mail? That'd be the day. Arlo pushed me into buying this, but neither one of us knows how to use it. The dang thing crashed on me a couple months ago and I haven't turned it on since."

"I could show you." Erica felt, in a way, as if she owed Lynn, and if being helpful smoothed the way for that door getting unlocked for Jason, all the better. Then there was always access to the Internet.

"We'll see," Lynn said.

Erica hesitated in the doorway.

"All right." Lynn cocked her head. "What do you need?" Erica tried looking innocent, but Lynn only chuckled. "Running a bar and restaurant for as long as I have, you get to know how to read people."

"Can I ask you a favor?"

"You can *ask* anything. Whether or not I can accommodate is an entirely different matter."

Erica motioned to the dead-bolted door on her right. "Does that lead up to the apartment we're renting?"

Lynn nodded. "Sure does."

"Can we unlock it and leave it open while I'm working down here? I mean, when J—" She stopped. "I mean, after Zach goes up to sleep? That way, he can slip down here if he needs me. You can lock it again before you close down for the night."

Lynn considered Erica for a moment. When she glanced over at Jason, her features softened. "Sure. Why not? Sounds like a good solution."

"What do you think, Zach?" Erica asked, opening the door. "Let's check it out."

He climbed the stairs behind her and waited while she unlocked the door leading into their apartment.

"Cool, huh?" She swung the door wide.

He looked around. "We live in a restaurant."

"Almost."

Leaving the door open for Jason, she went back down to Lynn's office and stood awkwardly in the doorway.

"Now what?" Lynn asked.

"Thank you." Erica forced it out. "I think that's going to work great."

"By the way." Lynn nodded toward a large bag of clothes on the floor. "One of the college kids from last summer left some stuff in one of the apartments and never returned my calls. You look about her size. You can borrow all that. If you want."

Erica's gut reaction was to pass on the offer. She'd always hated the way her mother had accepted handouts as if they were the most normal things in the world but the coat sitting atop the pile looked warm. Her leather jacket wasn't doing much by way of protecting her from the biting wind that had been coming in off the lake all morning. The less money she had to spend on herself meant all the more for Jason.

"Warm weather's still a few weeks away," Lynn said, "so some of that stuff won't do you any good for now, but the black pants and red shirts will come in handy."

"Is that the Duffy uniform?"

"Yep."

Well, that settled that. All Erica had were jeans in her suitcase. What she wouldn't have done in that moment for a decent clothing store. She bit down on her pride. Again. "I appreciate it, Lynn."

"Well, I need to pay a few bills before heading back to the kitchen for the lunch crowd."

"Lynn?" Glynnis, the waitress Erica had met earlier, came into the kitchen from the dining area. "Debbie called in sick. Said she's got pneumonia and isn't sure when she'll be on her feet again."

Lynn sighed and turned to Erica. "Well? You said you knew how to waitress, right?"

"Sure." Erica was already looking forward to lunch hour tips.

"Better be careful, or you might make yourself a little too useful around here."

"Put a few of my Italian recipes on the menu and I'll become indispensable."

Lynn burst out with a hearty laugh. "Dearie, we haven't changed the menu in more than five years."

Erica raised her eyebrows. "Exactly."

CHAPTER EIGHT

"Garrett, you in there?" A moment after the knock sounded, Herman poked his head inside the unoccupied apartment in the Duffys' building.

Garrett had finished repairs at Erica's and was now wrapping it up next door. "Over here," he called from the corner of the living room.

"You want to grab some lunch?"

Was it that late already? "Sure." He climbed down from the ladder and put away his tools. "First let me wash up and change into my uniform." He brushed spackling off his insulated flannel shirt, grabbed his bag and went into the bathroom.

By the time he'd finished, Herman was standing outside on the landing, whistling, his face toward the April sun still high in the sky. Garrett's first impression of the man had been spot-on. He was too gentle and kindhearted a soul to be a cop, let alone a police chief. No wonder Jim Bennett had looked off the island for a replacement.

"So where do you want to go today for lunch?" Herman asked.

Great food was tough to come by on this island. Of course there weren't many places that could compete with Chicago on that front, so he didn't bother complaining. Generally, he and Herman alternated between all the restaurants in town, not wanting to play favorites. They hadn't been out to the Mirabelle Island Inn for a while, but that was a long walk.

"Let's go downstairs to Duffy's." Their food wasn't the greatest, but with any luck Erica would be around and he could put a few more pieces together.

Herman grinned and chuckled. "Yeah, all right."

"What?"

"Nothing. I didn't say nothing."

During the short jaunt down the alleyway and out to Main Street, they talked about the upcoming tourist season and whether or not they'd hired enough temporary officers for the holidays. It was a perfectly sunny spring day, making the entrance into the pub all the more disappointing. Garrett hated the dungeonlike feel of Duffy's Pub. At night, it was fine, even gave the place a cozy feeling, but during the day he much preferred the openness of Delores's café.

A sign at the entrance told them to seat themselves. Normally, he came here for dinner and sat at the bar. A few folks were taking lunch in the main dining room. Lynn was in the kitchen. He glanced into the dining room and spotted Erica delivering water to Ron and Jan Setterberg. Ron owned the equipment rental place in town and Jan managed the Mirabelle Island Inn for Marty Rousseau. Dressed in black pants and a red Duffy's T-shirt, Erica was taking their orders.

"I can see you're going to want to sit in the main dining room," Herman said.

"It's too damned dark out here in the bar."

"If you say so."

As they walked toward the lakefront windows Garrett noticed Erica's son sitting by the kitchen. His table was strewn with papers, markers and video games. When Erica glanced up from taking the Setterbergs' orders and noticed them, she faltered.

Garrett smiled and flicked a hand toward the group.

"Afternoon, Ron. Jan," Herman said, smiling at Erica. The Setterbergs returned the greetings to Herman and Garrett.

"Let's go sit by the boy," Garrett said, heading to the table next to him. "Hey, there, Zach. How you doing today?"

"Good." He barely looked up from coloring on a piece of paper.

"Aren't you supposed to be in school?"

"I don't have to go until tomorrow."

"Well, that's cool." He sat down.

Erica spun toward them. "I'll be right with you guys." Turning in the order at the kitchen and dropping off drinks at another table of island residents, she seemed nothing if not efficient. When she brought Zach a glass of chocolate milk and a plate of chicken fingers and French fries and set two glasses of water down in front of them along with their menus, her hands trembled slightly.

He would've liked to think her nervousness had more to do with him being a man than a cop, but he wasn't about to delude himself.

"So what would you like, Chief Taylor?"

"Call me Garrett. I'll take a grilled cheese." Tough to screw that one up. He handed her the menu he hadn't bothered to open. Personally, he liked Lynn a lot, but she was a much better bartender than cook.

"What would you like, officer?" She smiled at Herman.

"Call me Herman, and I'll take a hot beef and a glass of milk."

"I thought you were going to be bartending," Garrett said.

"Why do you care?"

Herman grinned and raised his eyebrows at Garrett. "Just making small talk," Garrett said.

"Sure you are." She took Herman's menu. "One of the waitresses called in sick, so I'm filling in this morning."

"Probably Debbie," Herman said.

Without any further acknowledgment, she turned to her son. "Zach, you doing okay?"

"Mmm-hmm."

She headed toward the kitchen to put in their orders. Zach picked up a couple of fries and seemed to be looking around for something in which to dip. Without saying a word, he walked over to the waitress station and grabbed a bottle of ketchup. Erica ushered Zach carefully back toward the table. "You have to stay over here, okay?"

"But I needed some ketchup."

"We can't have you getting in the other waitresses' way. If you need anything, wave me down."

Erica might be as prickly as all get-out with the rest of the world, him in particular, but with Zach she was calm and gentle, not at all grouchy. She went back to work, but her attention never seemed to waver far from what was happening at their tables. If not watching them, she seemed tuned to their conversation. If not at their table, she was walking by them to get bits and pieces of what they were saying.

It didn't take long for Erica to deliver their lunch orders. As soon as she moved out of earshot, Garrett casually glanced at the kid. For an apparently healthy young boy, he was awfully quiet. He had a marker in one hand and a chicken strip in the other, from which he occasionally took a bite.

"So, Zach, what're you drawing?" There was a picture of what looked like the Mirabelle ferry, the shoreline with trees and two people with gray hair holding hands. "Who's that?"

"Lynn and Arlo." The boy didn't bother glancing up, merely kept coloring blue waves in the water.

"They're nice together, aren't they?" Herman said, leaning forward and setting his elbows on the table. "Kind of like grandparents, huh?"

"Mmm-hmm."

"Do you have grandparents?" Garrett asked.

Herman shook his head.

"Yeah, but my grandma has black hair," Zach said, still not looking up. "She wears lots of necklaces and big earrings and brings me presents."

As if she knew what they were talking about, Erica started toward them but an order came up and she had to deliver it to one of her tables. Suddenly, Garrett felt bad pumping the boy for information. "Do you miss your grandma?"

"Not really."

"The place where you used to live?"

"Yeah."

"You never know. You might end up liking Mirabelle more than you'd think," Garrett said. "There's snowshoeing, sledding and snowmobiling in the winter. As soon as it warms up, there'll be horseback riding and biking."

"I don't have a bike."

"Do you like to fish?"

No response.

"Ever been sailing?"

"No."

"Me, neither. Until I moved here."

Zach glanced up with a questioning look.

"I came here last fall, and it was the best thing I've ever done. Could end up being the best thing that ever happened to you, too."

As if he wasn't convinced, Zach frowned and returned to his coloring. Garrett decided to give it a rest and began an innocuous conversation with Herman. While they discussed summer shifts and vacation time, Garrett studied the boy and his mom, but mostly his mom.

The absence of that leather jacket and boots certainly made her look less intimidating. With three silver rings between her two hands, both ears pierced multiple times and a leather band around her neck, she obviously liked jewelry. She had a nice walk, purposeful and confident, not too fast, not too slow. It could've been the black apron that accented her waist, but he wasn't sure he'd ever seen nicer curves on a woman. The distance seemed perfect from her shoulders to her waist, waist to hips, hips to thighs and on down her legs. Her lines reminded him of the graceful grain of that burled black walnut he had back in his workshop.

Herman whistled. "Earth to Garrett." He waved in front of his face.

"Sorry."

"You ready to go?"

"Yeah." Garrett grabbed his jacket and shrugged into it. The moment Erica moved out of earshot, he whispered, "You have a good day in school tomorrow, okay, Zach? Only two days until the weekend."

"Yeah. Erica says anyone can do two days."

Erica, huh? What happened to Mom? He leaned down to Zach. "And if there's ever anything I can do for you, let me know. That's what police officers are here for. To help."

Zach looked at the badge clipped to the outside of Garrett's jacket. "My dad keeps his badge in his pocket."

Garrett glanced at Herman, and even he showed interest in that comment. Garrett squatted down so he was eye level with the boy. "So he's a detective, huh?"

Zach nodded. "He carries a gun. Do you?"

"Yep. So does Herman." Garrett flipped his jacket open to show the boy his shoulder holster. "What city does your dad work?" he whispered.

"Chicago."

Bingo. He'd been right on the money. He could feel Erica's eyes on him as she made a beeline toward them.

He stood. "Well, have fun at school tomorrow, Zach."

"Thanks."

As they walked outside after paying their bill, Herman said, "Didn't see that coming. A cop, huh?"

"Interesting, isn't it?" But what bothered Garrett more than anything else was that Erica might not be Zach's mom.

The minute Garrett got to his office at the Mirabelle police station, he called the island ferry office and asked them to notify him immediately should Erica Jackson purchase a ticket to get off the island, and then he searched through the national database of missing children, focusing on the Chicago area. Two hours later, he'd turned up no matches.

None of this was making sense.

"YOU DID ALL RIGHT," Lynn said to Erica as she stood at the waitress stand, refilling her coffee cup.

"Thanks." Uncomfortable with the looks of that last exchange between Jason and Garrett Taylor, Erica watched the cops head outside as the lunch crowd thinned out. The front door closed behind the two men, and finally she felt as if she could breathe. "Waitressing is like riding a bike." She turned back to Lynn and noticed the older woman's skin had turned ghost pale. "You okay?"

"Fine. Just a bit queasy."

"Could be you're coming down with something."

"I don't get sick." Lynn straightened her shoulders into a stubborn line and headed back to the kitchen.

More like Lynn couldn't afford to get sick. The more time Erica spent around the restaurant, the more she realized the aging décor had more to do with waning business than anything.

Erica went to Jason's table and sat down across from him. "You and Chief Taylor sure did talk a lot."

"Yeah," he said, absently.

She'd heard some of their conversation, and if she were honest with herself she'd admit he seemed like a decent guy, the way he'd tried to ease Jason's concerns about a new place to live. But she didn't want to be honest, and she didn't want her thoughts preoccupied with Chief Garrett Taylor any more than necessary. Besides, there were moments here and there when she hadn't been able to hear what he'd been saying to Jason, and his expression had been fairly serious.

Jason had finished with his lunch, but he was still drawing. She pushed back his bangs and noticed his naturally blond hair already showing through at the root line. She was going to have to dye it again soon. She stilled his hand and, when he looked up at her, asked, "Do you remember what you and Garrett talked about?"

"Huh?"

"You know, you and the chief. Do you remember what he said?"

"No."

"Think, kiddo. Hard. I need to know." *Whether or not we're going to have to pack up tomorrow and leave.*

Jason concentrated. "He asked me about this picture." He pointed to a couple of stick figures with gray hair. "The one of Lynn and Arlo. Asked me if I had grandparents."

She was right. He had been fishing. "What did you tell him?"

"That my grandma doesn't have gray hair." His eyes turned worried. "Did I do something wrong?"

"No." Vehemently, she shook her head. "You didn't do anything wrong, Zach. It's okay."

Enough was enough. Cop or no cop, she was going to have to set Chief Taylor straight on a thing or two.

CHAPTER NINE

"HOT BEEF. BURGER AND FRIES." Erica put her table's order up. After walking Jason to school Thursday morning, she'd come back to the pub to work through lunch, since Debbie had called in sick again. When she didn't see Lynn at the grill, Erica glanced into the kitchen. Her new boss was leaning over the prep counter with her eyes closed. "You look terrible."

Lynn groaned. "I feel like I took a nasty spin on a carnival ride."

"Is there someone who can fill in for you?"

"Our summer cook was supposed to show up yesterday. I'm guessing he won't be coming at all."

"There's no one else, like for when you get sick?"

"I told you. I—"

"Don't get sick. Because when you do, the pub closes down." Erica got it. Small business owners were never cut any slack, and the restaurant business was brutal.

She glanced into the dining area. It wasn't too busy. If Glynnis could handle this lunch crowd, Erica could cook. Still, she hesitated, hating the thought of doing anyone a favor for no particular reason. Next, Lynn would be doing Erica favors. Then back and forth until things were all cozy and she expected Erica to be her best friend.

Then again, the winter jacket Lynn had given her yesterday had felt awfully warm this morning, not to mention there'd been another jacket, one that had looked suspiciously new, at the bottom of that bag of castoff clothing for Jason.

Oh, hell. She stalked into the kitchen. "Go sit down," she told Lynn. "I'll take care of the orders."

"You don't know your way around this kitchen."

"It's a kitchen, and cooking is what I do best. If it makes you feel any better, you can give me a raise."

Lynn sat down on the stool behind the counter while Erica quickly oriented herself. She glanced at the board, finished with Glynnis's order in process, popped it up under the heat lamps and went to fill the next one.

When Glynnis came to get her order, Erica said, "Lynn's sick. I'll take care of the two tables I've already waited on, but can you get the rest?"

"Sure."

Erica would've much preferred making her favorite Italian dishes, but at least she was back at a stove and grill. An hour or so later, the lunch crowd had been served and Erica spun around to find Lynn watching her through tired eyes. "Well, you weren't lying," the older woman whispered. "You *can* cook."

Erica shrugged.

"I'm going home to take a nap and I'll try to be back before happy hour." Lynn trudged into her office and Erica followed her.

Now was the perfect time to ask to use the computer. "If you want, I could try to get your computer up and running while you're gone. Show you how to e-mail your sons when you get back."

"Go for it." Lynn grabbed the coat she'd hung on a hook by the door.

"Do you have Internet access?"

"The island's got something called WiFi, whatever that

is, and the setup I bought was supposed to work here. What do I know?"

Erica booted up the computer. Immediately, it connected to the Internet and busied itself updating the security systems. "It's working. Do you mind if I see what I can do?"

"It's all yours. See you later."

After Lynn left, Erica ran various updates and scans. The programs found several smaller security issues that had somehow infiltrated Lynn's system and were bogging down the flow. While the computer was chugging away, cleaning things up, she logged onto the Internet and searched the Chicago news for any mention of Marie or Jason. Still nothing out there. Billy was up to something. No missing persons report meant no cops looking for Marie.

Someone came into the kitchen and called, "Lynn?" Garrett Taylor. She'd have known that deep voice anywhere.

Suddenly, the day that had been going so well soured within the blink of an eye. She quickly clicked off the page of Chicago news she'd been scanning and called back, "She went home sick."

Dressed in tan carpenter pants and a worn plaid shirt outlining his broad chest and beefy arms, Garrett came to the office doorway carrying a large metal tool chest. He narrowed those pale gray eyes of his. "She said you could work on her computer? Alone?"

The statement was filled with concern, if not outright hostility, and Erica was sorely tempted to not give the man the satisfaction of an answer. "Her computer needed some debugging and I told her I'd see what I could do to help. That okay with you, Chief?"

"Awfully trusting, aren't they, these islanders?" he said, holding her gaze. "Maybe that's why I like them so much."

Don't mess with my people, or else. She found her feelings oddly hurt by the suspicion and not so subtle threat behind his words and couldn't seem to form an appropriately smart-mouthed comment.

He pointed up the steps. "Arlo asked me to put a chain on your apartment door."

"Go ahead," Erica said. "But first I've got something to say to you." She stood and walked toward him.

Confrontation had never been easy for her. Men were the hardest, but even facing down a woman could make her palms sweat and her face turn hot. A part of her always seemed to be waiting for that hand to strike. To this day, the sound of a man pulling off his leather belt still sent a twinge of fear skittering down her spine.

"I'm listening," he said.

She was so close she was forced to tilt her head back to look into his eyes. She waited for the telltale fear to strike her gut, but it never came. He towered over her, and yet she was not frightened of him. It didn't make any sense.

"Yesterday when you sat with Zach at lunch," she started.

"What about it?" His stance was relaxed, his features calm, as if he were telling her to do her worst. He could take it.

"I don't care if you're the chief of police or the head of the FBI, I don't want you interrogating my...son. Ever again."

"Your son."

"Yeah."

He didn't say another word, merely studied her, making her feel for a moment like a bug under a microscope. Then his gaze traveled and his pale eyes darkened with something damned close to awareness and she became intensely focused on the broadness of his shoulders, the squareness of his jaw, the look of surprising softness to his lips.

Something was going on between them, something heady and sensual, something that had her tuning in to his every movement. Suddenly there seemed to be little question in her mind that they were going to happen. The only question seemed to be how far they'd go once they started.

She tilted her chin higher and glared at him. "From now on, if you've got a question you ask *me*. Not Zach. Got it?"

"Fair enough."

Fair enough? That was it? Not quite.

He took a step toward her, almost touching her. "I don't know what it is yet, but you're hiding something."

"I don't know what you're talking about." Her voice sounded just a little breathless even to her own ears.

As if they were magnets drawn together, he leaned closer. "I'll find out what it is."

The subtle challenge in his eyes held her in limbo for a moment. *Move first.*

No, you.

You want it.

So do you.

No! She stepped back and made a pretense of looking at the kitchen clock. "Is it that time already?" She headed for the kitchen door. "I have to pick up Zach from school."

He glanced away and pointed up the steps as if nothing out of the ordinary had passed between them. "The chain on your door will only take me a few minutes."

"Great. Then you'll be gone when I get back."

"So we're clear, Erica," he whispered, "I don't trust you."

"So we're clear, *Chief Taylor*—" she pushed backward through the kitchen door "—I haven't done anything wrong."

THE MOMENT SHE WAS out of sight, Garrett turned away from the swinging kitchen doors, closed his eyes and regained control of himself. *Sonofabitch.* He'd almost kissed her, a woman who was almost a complete stranger.

He ran a hand over his face and took a deep breath. Whether it was the way she smelled or cooked or the way her eyes seemed to be inviting him to do his worst, that woman was driving him crazy, making him forget he was first and foremost a cop.

One minute she was in his face, all pouty lips and attitude, telling him how things were going to be as if she was the one with the gun and badge and the next minute, her eyes softened with the knowledge that she was only a woman and he was only a man. She knew, same as him, that their bodies would join perfectly. Size didn't matter. One big, one petite, they'd fit like dovetail joints, slide together as if they'd always belonged. The thought of it made him groan aloud.

It'd been too damned long since he'd been with a woman. Simple as that. But Erica was not the right kind of woman. What he needed was soft and giving, sunshine and blue skies, a woman whose light shined so brightly her smiles would obliterate every shadow inside him. He needed a woman who instead of reminding him of who he was could help him forget everything he wasn't. Was there anyone on the island even close?

A blond-haired, blue-eyed schoolteacher came to mind. Hannah Johnson. What do you know? There wasn't a mean bone in that woman's body. She was positive and light-hearted, happy and uncomplicated. With that angel by his side, he could get all this Erica nonsense out of his system and move forward. He flipped open his cell phone, dialed the school's number and was surprised when the receptionist put him through to Hannah's room.

"This is Miss Johnson."

Her sweet voice alone sent waves of peace through him. "Hey, there, it's Garrett."

"Garrett?" She paused. "Oh, Garrett! Hi!"

"Are you free for dinner tomorrow night?"

"Um. Um." There was a slight pause. "Sure. That sounds nice."

"How does Duffy's sound?"

"Great," she said. "I usually get together with Sarah and Missy for happy hour on Fridays, so I'll meet you there."

"Sounds good." Garrett already felt better.

"THAT'S ALL THERE IS to it." Erica stepped back from Lynn's now smoothly running computer. The Friday lunch crowd had diminished to a slow trickle and Lynn was feeling better. "Now you try it."

Lynn rolled her chair up to the keyboard and after only a few missteps successfully sent an e-mail message off to her oldest son. "So that message goes all the way to Chicago and there aren't any long-distance charges?"

"That's right. It's fast and cheap."

"When will Adam get the message in D.C.?"

"It only takes a few minutes. If he's on his computer."

"I don't believe it." A moment later, the computer dinged. "What was that?"

"You've got mail," Erica explained. "Probably from Son One already."

"That quick?"

"Yep."

Sure enough, her oldest had already sent his mom a response. Lynn giggled as she read his message. He was ecstatic that his mother had finally gotten online. Her other son also responded relatively quickly. "This is amazing." She smiled at Erica, and then, much to Erica's consternation, Lynn leaned over and hugged her.

"It's not a big deal," Erica said, sloughing it off.

"It is to me." Lynn patted Erica's cheek. "We better be careful, or you won't become indispensable, you'll turn into just-like-family."

A normal person might have found that statement heart-warming, but the mere thought of what Lynn was thinking set off Erica's warning bells. "Okay, then." She backed up and glanced at her watch. "I have to go pick up Zach."

CHAPTER TEN

"AN AMBER ALERT?" THE chief stared at Billy. "That means you believe your son to be in imminent danger. You sure you want to take this that far?"

This was going to be a balancing act. Billy could get away with turning the tables on Marie, but there were cops here who knew her. He'd have to push just hard enough to get all the troops roused and looking for Jason, but if he pushed too hard they might start talking, worse, linking him to the disappearance of his wife and son.

"No." Billy sighed. "You're right. Marie wouldn't hurt Jason."

"So what do you want us to do?"

"She told me she wanted a divorce, Chief, and was going to fight for full custody." Billy hesitated. This would set the stage. "She more or less kidnapped my son."

"Then we need to issue a warrant for her arrest."

"So be it." Billy nodded. Just find 'em, Chief. I want my family back." He left the chief's office and went to his desk. Within moments, his fellow detectives, having heard the news, gathered, sitting nearby or propping themselves on his desk. "How you doing?" one of them asked.

"As well as can be expected."

"Do you have a clue where she might've gone?"

"No. But I'll tell you what I do know." Billy glanced around the circle. "The morning she disappeared, we got into a fight. I'll be the first one to admit our marriage wasn't perfect, but, dammit, I told her I'd do anything to make her happy, go to counseling, change jobs." He jabbed his fingers through his hair. "She told me she was going to file for a divorce anyway."

"Damn."

"Sucks."

"Why would she disappear? And take Jason?"

Billy hated what he had to say next, but these were the guys to spur on, the men who were going to find his son. "I don't like airing dirty laundry, but Marie had been…drinking a lot. I caught her smacking Jason around." He looked away. "So I told her I was going to fight for full custody."

"Marie?"

"That doesn't sound like her."

"I know. Hard to believe. But after her mother died… she went through a bad spell."

"So she took the kid and left?"

"No. The school said her sister, Erica, picked up Jason." Billy stood and paced. "She was always filling Marie full of all kinds of crazy ideas. I think they've been planning this for a long time. I think…" He paused, put his face in his hands for a moment or two, pretending to gather himself. "I'm worried they might hurt Jason. Just to get at me."

The face of every single detective around him filled with barely suppressed rage. "What do you want us to do?" one of them asked.

"Get the word out," Billy said softly. "I need to find my son before they hurt him."

WITH THE SUNSHINE HITTING her face and a cool breeze at her back, Erica hiked up the hill to the elementary school to pick up Jason. On her way, in an attempt to put Lynn's hug out of her mind, she mentally revised Duffy's old-fashioned menu.

There were too many options, but not enough diversity. If it were her pub, she'd pick the top eight to ten favorite entrees off the current menu and drop everything else. Then she'd add several Mexican, Italian and updated American selections.

But, then, it wasn't her pub.

She reached the school and waited by the office for Jason. When he rounded the corner, her heart lifted, that is until his sadness registered. "It couldn't have been that bad, could it?"

"It was okay."

No, it wasn't, but she could tell that just like after his first day of school he didn't want to trouble her. Well, that wasn't going to cut it today. "You can tell me all about it on the way to the grocery store." She held the door open for him and they took off outside. When he still didn't offer anything, she asked, "Was that boy you met, Brian, in your class?"

"Yeah."

"What's he like?"

"We played together at recess."

"So he's nice?"

Jason nodded.

"Good. What's your teacher like?"

"She's okay."

She asked one question after another. Getting him to talk was like pulling teeth. Open-ended questions, she'd heard somewhere, were supposed to encourage conversation. Well, whoever had come up with that marvelous advice had never met this six-year-old. The kid barely opened his mouth. Is this what he'd been like with Marie, or was it just her?

By the time they reached Newman's grocery store, Erica was out of questions. "Okay, here we are."

She grabbed a cart and for the next fifteen minutes they zipped through the aisles, snapping up staples. The produce was fresh, but the herbs selections limited. She stood in front of the olives for several minutes wishing for a more eclectic assortment. The cheeses offered in the dairy case didn't amount to much past the standard cheddars and Colby. But what could she expect from a small store in the Midwest boonies?

Suddenly, it dawned on her that she had no clue what Jason liked to eat, other than the standard burger and fries he'd been ordering from every restaurant they'd eaten at these past several days.

She stopped the cart. "What kind of food do you like, Ja—Zach?"

He shrugged.

"Pizza? Spaghetti? Lasagna? We're Italian, you know? You and I."

"Whatever. I don't care."

It wasn't right for a kid to be so damned agreeable. Before checking out, they stopped in the toy aisle and Erica let Jason select several things. He picked out little army figures and some oozy, goozy playdough. Erica grabbed markers, paper and coloring books to keep him busy while she worked. As they made their way to the checkout, Erica turned the corner with her cart and almost ran into a gray-haired man wearing wire-rimmed glasses.

His maroon-colored apron identified him as a store employee. "Afternoon, miss," he said.

She nodded.

"You finding everything you need?"

"Actually, no. Hasn't anyone in this store ever heard of Asiago or feta?" At his taken-aback look, she added, "Those are types of cheeses."

"I know. We don't have much call for specialty items." He chuckled and held out his hand. "Dan Newman."

As in Newman's Groceries. Must be the owner. "Erica Jackson." Reluctantly, she shook his hand. "Can I special order a few things?"

"What did you have in mind?"

"Other than cheeses, a particular brand of olives, fresh artichokes. Stuff like that."

"Why don't you give me a list? I'll see what I can do."

"Really?"

"New on the island, huh?"

She nodded. "I'm bartending at Duffy's."

"Well, then, I'll see you tonight, and there happens to be a brand of imported beer I've been asking Lynn to stock for a while now."

She shook her head and laughed. "I'll see what I can do."

"You do that."

Once she and Jason got back to the apartment, Erica asked, "Do you want to watch TV while I make you dinner?"

Jason shook his head. "I can help."

Meaning he didn't want to leave her side. She set him up at the kitchen counter, gave him a dull knife and set him to chopping basil. A while later, her penne *arrabiata* with garlic, basil and red chilies was ready. "You hungry?" she asked, scooping up a bowl of pasta.

"Not yet."

After eating quickly, she said, "Well, I gotta get back to work. You want to come with me, or we could call Brian's mom and see if you two could play?" It was time for the Friday happy hour crowd downstairs. Tonight she was bartending.

"I want to go with you."

Why did that not surprise her? "Okay. Off to the salt mines." She scooped some penne pasta into a couple of bowls and headed downstairs. She found Lynn in the kitchen and handed her the dish filled with still steaming pasta. "Try this."

"What is it?" Lynn took a bite and chewed.

"Easy and inexpensive. A change of pace. You make vats of the sauce ahead of time. Pasta cooks up in minutes. Sprinkle it with some grated cheese, serve it with a salad and crusty bread and you can charge more than anything else you have on the menu."

"Mmm," Lynn murmured. "You made this?"

"After I picked up…Zach from school."

"I helped," Jason added.

"You sure did." Erica smiled at him, then looked back at Lynn. "Well?"

"It's a little too hot for my tastes, but it has good flavor. What makes it spicy?"

"Red chilies."

"You have a recipe for this?"

"It's all up here." Erica tapped her temple.

"Not sharing your secrets, eh?" Lynn chuckled. "Can you tone the heat down?"

"Absolutely."

She took another bite. "The islanders don't like changes."

"So you leave their favorites on the menu and you add some new and interesting things for the summer tourists. Specials. What do you say?"

"I'll think about it."

"Can Zach hang out at the bar? Just for this weekend?"

"Bribing me, huh?"

Erica grinned. She was actually starting to like Lynn. "You caught me."

"Sure." Lynn took another bite of pasta. "As long he stays out of the way."

Erica took Jason's hand and led him out of the kitchen and into the bar where Arlo was filling one of the stainless steel bar coolers with beer. "I'm going to need to walk around back here without tripping over you. So you have to sit over here and keep yourself busy, okay?"

She moved one of the tall stools to the end of the bar, helped him up, and plopped a root beer and the new toys they'd purchased from the grocery store in front of him. She turned around and took a deep breath. She was going to be bartending for the first time in years.

Within fifteen minutes, no fewer than five people had walked through the door and come to sit at the bar, and several couples and a small family had been escorted to tables in the restaurant. Someone put money in the jukebox and the sound of classic rock songs filled the air. Friday night happy hour had begun, and it turned out she hadn't forgotten nearly as much as she'd thought.

Erica was in full swing when someone called her name, "Hey, Erica!" Sarah came toward the bar, her smile wide and sincere. Tonight, she looked stunning in a cashmere sweater and black dress pants. "How are you doing?"

"Good."

Sarah was soon joined by Jason's teacher, Hannah Johnson, and another young woman introduced as Missy Charms.

"We usually meet for happy hour on Fridays," Sarah explained. "But tonight Hannah's deserting us."

"For a man," Missy added.

Hannah blushed and looked away.

"I'd love to stay and chat," Erica lied. It was really the last thing she'd like to do. "But I'm kind of busy."

"That's okay. We won't bother you."

"Would you ladies like anything to drink?"

After they gave her their orders, Sarah asked, "So how's your new job going?"

"Good." So far working in a pub on Mirabelle wasn't all that different than the blue-collar joints she'd worked at back home, especially from a bartending standpoint. Given this was a well-known vacation destination in the Midwest, she'd expected Cosmopolitans, Appletinis, or froufrou blender drinks, but these people were turning out to be salt of the earth. With only a few exceptions, they drank beer, wine and regular mixed cocktails.

"The Duffys are nice people," Missy said.

"I hope you'll like it here," Hannah added before she walked over to the end of the bar where Jason was sitting and patted him on the back. "Hey, Zach. How're you?"

"Fine," he said without glancing away from his game.

"What're you playing?"

"Super Mario Brothers."

"Hey, Zach," Sarah called. "You should come over to our house some time and play Brian's Xbox 360."

"Really?" At that he looked up, his eyes wide. It was the first excitement Erica had seen on Jason's face all day. "Sweet."

"Maybe even tomorrow while your mom is working?" Sarah offered.

"Okay." He was back to his game.

"That all right with you?" Sarah glanced at Erica.

It wasn't a half-bad idea. It was Saturday, so Jason wouldn't have school. "Maybe Zach and I can watch Brian the next day I have off?"

"Sounds like a plan."

"A good plan." Hannah patted Zach's shoulder. "See you at school on Monday." She rejoined the other two women.

As Erica set a glass of chardonnay in front of Hannah, Garrett Taylor was walking straight for the bar.

CHAPTER ELEVEN

DAMMIT. HERE WE GO AGAIN. The man was going to ruin a perfectly good night. Why wouldn't he leave Erica alone? Still, she couldn't stop herself from checking him out. In a soft-looking leather jacket and dark gray dress shirt, he sure cleaned up nicely.

"Hey, there." He sat on the bar stool next to Hannah.

"Hi!" She smiled at him, a shy smile that said he was all hers and she couldn't be happier about it.

Figures. Opposites attract. Every night needed a day. Beauty and the beast. Now that Erica saw them together, she couldn't believe she hadn't expected them to be dating. Two attractive people move to an island this size and bang, they're going to hook up.

So what had happened in Lynn's office yesterday? He may not have made the slightest move to do anything about the obvious attraction between them, but that didn't change the fact that it'd been there.

"Hello, Garrett," Sarah said with a teasing lilt.

Garrett glanced at the other two women. "Sarah. Missy."

"Sarah, let's go get a table for dinner," Missy said, standing up from the bar.

"See you guys later." Sarah waved as she followed Missy.

"Sorry, I'm a little late." Garrett returned his attention to Hannah. "A game warden stopped by with some paperwork."

"That's okay." Hannah glanced up at Erica. "Garrett, this is Erica."

"We've met."

"You have?"

Erica barely caught herself from rolling her eyes. "What can I get for you?" she asked.

"A beer. Anything from the tap'll do."

Too bad this tap didn't pour arsenic. She filled a chilled mug with beer and set it in front of him.

He reached for it with his big hands, workman's hands, rough and calloused, but clean with neatly trimmed nails. His fingertips accidentally brushed against hers as he reached for the handle, and he quickly glanced at her. "Thanks."

"No problem."

There were those pale gray eyes again looking at her as if they couldn't decide whether or not they liked the view. "So how's it going here at Duffy's?" he asked.

"Good." She washed a few glasses.

"Zach do okay in school today?"

She was surprised he cared, but then maybe he was only making small talk for Hannah's sake. "He likes Hannah, and Brian's in the class."

"Every little bit helps."

There was something in his subtle accent that reminded Erica of home. "What area of Chicago are you from?" She would've put money on the South Side, maybe Armour Square.

"Kenwood. Near Washington Park. Know the area?"

"Not really," she lied, but Armour Square was a cakewalk compared to Kenwood. She'd worked there for a while, until a coworker had been murdered in the parking lot after closing one night. The next day, she'd quit. "Did you work in that precinct?"

At first, he didn't answer. "No. Englewood."

He glared at her as if angry she'd made him remember,

and no wonder. That district was one of the worst neighborhoods in Chicago. The kind of place it was sometimes hard to tell the cops from the criminals.

Garrett Taylor. Suddenly his name rang a bell. This guy had been in the news last year related to a police brutality case. What was he doing on Mirabelle?

As if the conversation had turned sour, he stood. "Ready to get a table, Hannah?"

"Sure."

"There's one by the window overlooking the water." He placed his hand at the small of Hannah's back.

"See you later, Erica."

"Bye, Hannah. Chief."

Much to her surprise, he stopped next to Jason and let Hannah go on alone to their table. "Hey, Zach. How you doing?" she heard him ask.

"Okay."

"So what do you think of Miss Johnson?" he whispered.

"She's okay."

"Was I right about the candy?"

"Uh-huh." Jason's eyes lit up. "She even lets us chew *gum* after lunch."

"No way."

Jason nodded quickly, excited now. He went into a long-winded, for a kid anyway, explanation of every nice thing Hannah had done to make him feel at home. "I even got to pick who I wanted to sit next to in class."

"Who?"

"Brian."

"I should've known that. Duh." Garrett chuckled.

"It's even better than my old school."

"Good. I'm glad you like it here," Garrett said. "Well, I gotta go eat dinner. See you around."

"Bye."

Erica would've breathed a sigh of relief after they'd left the bar if Garrett hadn't ended up directly in her line of vision every time she went to the waitress stand for orders. Hannah's back was to the bar, but more often than not, Garrett was watching her, making her wonder if he'd chosen that location on purpose.

Part of her was irritated by his constant scrutiny, but another part of her, a part she couldn't deny, was intensely aware of him. Curiously, the more she watched him with Hannah, the more she realized they didn't really fit together. Hannah was pleasant and easy. He was stiff and edgy and seemed barely able to keep his focus on what Hannah was saying. He might've traded the pumped-up streets of Chicago for the comfy, relaxed lifestyle of Smallsville, Wisconsin, but there was nothing soft or tranquil about him. He didn't fit on Mirabelle any more than she did.

Two older men came to sit at the bar. "Well, lookie here," the tall, big-boned one said. "It's fresh meat—er—a new bartender."

She glanced at the man, ready to snap back at him, but the guy looked harmless enough. "Erica Jackson."

"Pleasure to meet you, Erica dear. Doc Welinski. Everyone calls me Doc." He stuck out his hand, and Erica couldn't very well ignore him. She pulled back the second she had the chance. "This old coot's Bob Henderson," Doc said, tilting his head to the man on his left. "He and his wife run the drugstore."

"Hi, Bob."

Bob, thankfully, had no interest in being friendly. He nodded and quietly ordered a whiskey and water.

"I'll take a club soda," Doc said. "You might as well pour one of them foreign beers off the tap for a friend of mine."

She was delivering their drinks when Dan Newman came

to sit next to Doc. "This must be for you." She set the beer in front of him.

"You betcha." He grinned and flicked his head toward his friends. "I see you've met the other two stooges."

She nodded. "You guys come here often?"

"Every Friday for the last ten years."

"That your son over there?" Doc asked.

"Yeah."

"Looks very well behaved."

A woman named Sally McGregor with short salt-and-pepper hair ordered a gin and tonic. "None of that cheap gut-rot stuff, either," she said, sitting down one stool away from Dan. "Top-shelf gin. Got me?"

Finally someone who spoke Erica's language. "Coming right up."

Then the couple who had been in the restaurant for lunch the other day, Jan and Ron Setterberg, came in and sat not too far from Jason. They greeted Erica and the woman chatted, thankfully, in a friendly way with Jason. From there the bar came close to filling up. Between tending to the waitresses and her own customers, Erica barely had a moment to stop by and check on Jason. At one point, Lynn came over and surprised Erica by setting a burger and fries in front of Jason. "Got an extra one. You hungry, Zach?"

"Yes!" He set his game down and dug in.

The bowl of penne she'd brought down earlier for him sat virtually untouched. "You didn't like the pasta?"

"Too spicy," he said, before gulping down the burger.

She should've known a kid his age might not like the red chili heat. "Thanks, Lynn."

"No problem. How's it going?"

"Good."

The glasses had been washed, trays stacked, and the liquor

bottles well organized, exactly as they had been. "Well, it sure looks like you've got everything under control."

"I haven't had to strike up the blender once tonight."

Lynn laughed. "Well, that won't last. You got nothing but locals in here tonight. Once the tourist season hits, you'll have a blender in one hand and the martini shaker in the other."

"Thanks for the warning." She paused. "How am I doing?"

"I don't know." Lynn walked farther into the bar area and called out, "How's our new bartender doing?"

"Peachy," Dan said.

Doc held up two thumbs. "She's keeping 'em coming."

Bob nodded quietly.

"Too much ice in my drink," Sally McGregor said.

Lynn turned around. "If Sally McGregor didn't complain," she whispered, "then I'd worry."

Surprisingly, Erica felt rather relieved. She was starting to like this place, despite the fact that working around a kid's schedule was tough.

"But I've been watching you," Lynn whispered, leaning in toward Erica.

"And?"

"Would it kill you to loosen up and smile every once in a while? They won't bite, you know."

"I'll try." Erica sighed. "Could you watch the bar for a few minutes while I get Zach up to bed?"

"No problem. By the way, I unlocked the door in the kitchen."

"Thanks." She packed up Jason's things. "Come on, kiddo. Let's get you up to bed."

"Good night there, Zach," Jan said. "Will you be back next Friday night?"

"Dunno."

"We're working that out," Erica said.

A round of good-nights came from everyone else close

enough to hear as the two of them headed into the kitchen. Erica showed Jason the staircase up to the apartment. "This'll work out great, don't you think?"

"I guess," he said, hesitantly. Once in their apartment, Jason got ready for bed and climbed under the covers. "You can't stay, can you?"

"I have to get back to work." She brushed his bangs back off his forehead.

"What if…what if someone comes to the apartment?"

She saw the fear in his eyes. "That's not going to happen."

"How do you know?"

"Remember all that driving we did?"

He nodded.

"No one's going to find us here."

"Promise?"

"I promise." She planted a kiss at his temple, feeling more comfortable with how quickly she'd fallen into the strange routines of psuedo-motherhood. "If you need me, all you have to do is run downstairs, through the kitchen and find me at the bar. Okay?"

"Okay." He was being such a trooper. "Will you come in and sleep with me when you get off work?"

"Tonight and every night, kiddo. For as long as you need me." Her heart sank as she left the apartment, and her misgivings must have shown when she came back to the bar.

"How's he doing?" Lynn asked.

"New apartment. New school. It's a lot for a kid."

Lynn sighed, seeming to consider something. "If it'd help, I could sit with him until he falls asleep. The kitchen's closed, and you're much more efficient in the bar than I am. If you want, that is."

Erica glanced at Lynn and felt emotion tighten her throat. "You'd do that?"

"I've been bugging my boys for years for grandkids. It's

nice having a little boy around." She smiled. "We're glad to have you here, Erica."

Erica didn't know to say, let alone how to say it. *Oh, hell.* "I'm glad to be here, Lynn."

As Lynn disappeared into the kitchen, Erica made her way to the other side of the bar, passing beneath the TV mounted overhead. A lull in the conversation made the sound audible.

The Chicago Police Department is urging anyone with information regarding missing six-year-old Jason Samson...

At the mention of Jason's name, Erica quickly glanced up and breathed a sigh of relief that Garrett had left the restaurant, and no one in the bar seemed to be paying a lick of attention to the broadcast. Even so, it was only a matter of time before someone figured out Erica and Jason's true identities. Then what?

She tuned back in to the TV newscaster as a picture of Marie, smiling and holding a blond-haired Jason, flashed up on the screen. Erica's heart felt ripped apart.

...an arrest warrant has been issued for Jason's mother, twenty-five-year-old Marie Samson. The boy and his mother were last seen by a neighbor the morning of their disappearance.

An arrest warrant? Erica would've bet anything Marie had asked Billy for a divorce. Now he was getting ready for a custody battle.

The screen switched from a shot of the national news correspondent to previously filmed footage in Chicago of investigators going in and out of a small, white house. Erica had only been there a few times, but it was unmistakably Marie's. Billy, surrounded by detectives—his friends—came out through the side door and reporters crowded around him, asking him questions.

"Do you have ideas where your wife and son may have gone?" one of the reporters asked.

"No," Billy murmured, stopping for a moment. "I'll tell you, like I told the detectives, this is all Marie's sister's doing. That woman has always been trouble. A couple days before Marie disappeared, she called and—" He clamped his mouth shut and headed toward his car. "I can't say any more."

Always been trouble? What the hell? Erica *had* called to talk to Marie a few days before Marie's frantic message, but Billy had answered, and that had been the end of asking Marie out to lunch. Billy was lying and trying to deflect suspicion onto Erica and Marie.

"I promise you this," one of the detectives who'd been standing next to Billy said to the reporter. "We're going to find them. You can count on that."

The detective looked angry, as if he'd shoot first and ask questions later. Now there was no way Erica could go back to Chicago to look for Marie. Not when every cop in the city was looking for her and thinking she'd wronged one of their own. For the first time in a very long time, Erica felt frightened. Of Billy. Of his cop friends.

She was alone on this one.

CHAPTER TWELVE

GARRETT KEPT STEP WITH Hannah as they walked to her house, a pale blue Cape Cod a block off Main. She talked a mile a minute about her teaching career. Turned out this apparently shy and reserved daisy of a woman became a chatterbox once she was away from Sarah and Missy. By the time they reached the steps to her house, he was all small-talked out.

"Do you want to come in?" She put her hand on the step rail and moonlight twinkled in her eyes. "I've got a bottle of wine, and we could make a fire."

The intent behind her suggestion was clear, and Garrett hesitated. Hannah's backyard was adjacent to Sarah's, and he wouldn't have put it past the wedding planner to be peeking out the back windows of her apartment over her floral shop.

"Hannah, I don't want to rush things." They had all the time in the world for what she had in mind. Neither one of them was going anywhere.

"I get it. I do. It's just…"

Just that she wanted to force the issue because she could sense he might not be interested in her sexually? She might be right. Her mouth was a short dip of his head away, but he felt not one urge to kiss her pink, glossy lips.

What the hell was wrong with him? She was everything he wanted. Sweet, beautiful, a homebody, like him. She talked a lot, but was easy to be around. Comfortable. Best of all, she was an innocent. Nothing at all like him. When Hannah smiled, the world smiled with her. Chipper. That's what she was.

Unfortunately, even formulating the word *chipper* in his mind made his teeth hurt from the sweetness. Still, being around all that sunshine had to eventually rub off on him. When he was around her, he could be the man he wanted to be. An upstanding cop. A man filled with integrity and goodness.

A man whose mind was filled with visions of a certain dark-haired woman with intense brown eyes. He thought of how Erica had looked behind Duffy's bar tonight, slinging bottles of booze around and filling up beer mugs like a pro. Any woman that comfortable around a beer tap couldn't possibly be the woman for him.

It was a lot to ask, a fairy-tale life, but people made their dreams come true every day. Why not him? "I want to do things right between us," he said. "Okay?"

Her eyes softened. "Okay." She put a hand on his chest. "Good night, Garrett."

He and Hannah were new to each other. It'd come. "Night, Hannah."

She went through her front door, the interior lights flicked on, and Garrett turned toward the lake for a quick walk by the shore before heading home. He walked slowly so as not to disturb the silence of the night. One of his favorite things about Mirabelle was the quiet, no chatter from crowds, no honking horns and, best of all, no police sirens.

The air felt cold and the sky was clear. A quarter moon was already partway through its trek across the sky. He kept his head up and his gaze out toward open water, focusing on the way the light flickered off the turbulent surface of the black water.

The muted sound of laughter and music rolled down the

shore from Duffy's Pub. Garrett glanced upward. He could imagine Erica tending the bar as she had when he and Hannah had been eating dinner. She'd loosened up as the evening had worn on and by now she might even be laughing with the patrons. She was a complete unknown, possibly even a criminal, and that woman could very well have the entire town wrapped around her pinky in no time.

Dammit to hell. He might as well head home. A short jaunt all the way up the hill, past the stables and into the woods at the outskirts of town would take him to his house and its secluded ten acres or so of forest. He climbed the steps leading toward the street level and headed down the alley toward Main.

When the silhouette of a woman—a very curvy woman—took shape, head down and leaning against the outside brick wall of Duffy's Pub, he stopped. "What are you doing out here?" the cop in him asked.

Erica started as if she hadn't heard him approach, then gathered herself. "Why do you care?"

Two feet away and he could still smell her. "I think it's time we settle a few things between us."

"There's nothing between us to settle." She pushed away from the wall and walked toward the door to Duffy's.

Against his better judgment, he followed. "What do you got against cops, anyway?"

"Nothing."

"Bullshit."

"What about you?" she said, turning on him. "You've had it in for me from the moment we first met on the sidewalk outside the Bayside Café."

"It was the badge. And you know it."

"Maybe there's just something about you that rubs me the wrong way."

At the moment, all that seemed to matter was that he got to rub her at all, and that was the problem. She made him lose control, messed with his balance, threw a buzz saw at his plans. There was only one solution. "I want you off my island."

A look of surprise and something else flashed in her eyes. She backed up and hit the brick behind her. "You want me off your island?"

"Tomorrow isn't soon enough."

"*Your* island?" The angry bite edging into her voice said more than anything that she'd recovered from her initial shock. Now on the offensive, she stepped toward him. "That's funny 'cause I heard you haven't even been here a year. This isn't your island any more than it's mine."

"I've got a badge that says it's mine." He closed the short distance between them, trying like hell to intimidate. Maybe if he upset her enough, she'd spill something, anything, giving him reason to put her on the next ferry off Mirabelle.

When she thrust her chin out, something told him it wasn't going to happen. "You think I'm not good enough for Mirabelle, don't you?" she whispered.

"I didn't say that. I just don't trust you."

"You know what? You're right. I'm not good enough. Even I know it. This place is all lollypops, tiaras and fairy tales. Me?" She shook her head and chuckled. "I sure as hell am not a princess." Her smile disappeared. "You and me, Garrett, we're two peas in a pod. I may not be a princess, but you're not even close to being a knight in shining armor—"

"Don't—"

"Garrett Taylor, a cop from the wrong side of the tracks."

"Don't do this—"

"One foot in the gutter—"

"Stop it!" He grabbed her wrists and pressed her back against the brick wall.

"You think if you stay here long enough," she whispered, "this place, these people will clean you off. Don't you? All I do is remind you that it's not going to be that easy."

She was right. She'd hit the nail on the head. Hard. She stirred something low and deep inside him, something he'd long ago tried to put away. She brought out the worst in him, lit his fuse and make him feel like a bomb hot to explode.

"Every time you look in my eyes," she said, as if she could read his mind, "you see yourself."

Somehow, some way, as if she'd cast a spell on him, he forgot about Hannah, forgot about the kind of woman he was trying to convince himself he needed and moved toward her. He pressed against her, from her knees to her breasts, pulsed his hips against her and instantly went rigid with need.

He wanted inside her. Here. Now. "Who are you?" he growled.

"What you see is what you get," she whispered.

He wanted to see, all right, and feel every part of her. He lifted her shirt and splayed his hand over her stomach, lost himself in the feel of her, all soft and firm at the same time, under his hands. Her lips parted and her warm breath mingled with his in the cold night air. His mouth hovered a hairsbreadth from hers. One of them moved and their lips touched, softly, then harder and harder still. Their teeth clicked and their tongues clashed.

Then he scraped his knee against the rough brick, piercing his awareness. In a back alley, he was pressing a woman up against a wall like no more than a rutting deer. She had his number, all right.

He jumped away and threw his hands up in the air. She fell back, looking as dazed as he felt. He would've expected her to smile, to leer at him, triumphant in her victory. Instead, she wouldn't meet his gaze.

He took a deep breath of cold night air, clearing what felt like a fog from his brain. "I'm sorry—"

"Don't!" She turned away and, before slamming the back

door to Duffy's in his face, whispered, "You're like every cop I've ever known. Taking what you want without giving a shit who gets hurt."

"WELL, THAT SHOULD about do it." Lynn put her hands on her hips and glanced around. "Let's call it a night."

Erica had done her best for the remainder of her shift to put what had happened between her and Garrett out of her mind, but now that everyone had left the bar, it all came back to her in a rush. Lust. That's all it was. Two hot bodies. Close quarters. It was bound to happen.

She hung the washrag she'd been using to wipe down the bar stools over a rod in the utility room off the kitchen and switched off the light. She'd been helping Lynn close down the bar and restaurant for the night, and the last step was walking up the steps to Erica's apartment so that Lynn could bolt the door from inside the restaurant and then head home herself.

"Do you think you'd ever feel comfortable locking up by yourself?" Lynn asked as she followed Erica up the steps.

"Sure." She'd closed up at several of her previous restaurants and bars. She could do it here.

They reached the top and Erica went into her apartment. The light above the sink and a night-light in the bathroom lent a soft glow to the apartment.

"You okay?" Lynn asked. "You've been awfully quiet for the past couple of hours."

I want you off my island.

Though Erica was past doubting Lynn's concern as genuine, she wasn't ready to confide in a stranger. "Just tired, I guess."

"I've been thinking…let's list a couple of your Italian dishes as specials this next week. See how they go over."

"You sure?"

Lynn nodded. "All the businesses on the island are gearing up for a busy summer. I'm afraid Duffy's without some changes will get lost in the shuffle."

"How 'bout one red and one white dish?" Erica asked. "I mean, one tomato and one cream base."

"Sounds good to me. Order what you need from Dan Newman and have him put it on my account."

"Can I use your computer to type up some menu inserts?"

"You know how to do that?"

Erica nodded. "Good night, Lynn."

"Night, Erica."

Erica closed the door, listened to Lynn turn the dead bolt, then she attached the chain Garrett had installed. She leaned back and, immediately, the remembered feel of Garrett assaulted her senses. His lips. His taste. The hard feel of his muscles pressing against her. His work roughened hands stroking her stomach. The sound of his voice.

I want you off my island.

She never would've believed anything a stranger said would hurt so much, but with one sentence this man had managed to cut a swath so deeply through her that she couldn't seem to catch her breath. She'd let her guard down. Tonight, in the bar, she'd started wanting to fit in, almost yearned to find a place with these people.

Pipe dreams. Garrett was right. She didn't fit on Mirabelle, and the way she'd reacted to him, like an animal in heat, proved it.

Hurt turned to anger, an emotion that had never let her down. So what if she didn't fit in this fantasyland? She didn't have a choice. There was no place else to go. No place to run. Not yet. Unless they were discovered sooner, the day she had enough cash she and Jason would be gone. Then Garrett Taylor would have his precious island all to himself again.

CHAPTER THIRTEEN

GARRETT PARKED THE brand-new boy's bike at the bottom of the steps leading to Erica's apartment. Regardless of the truth behind Erica's situation, he felt like a heel for what he'd said—and done—last night and could think of no other way to make it right. He taped a note for Erica to the handlebar with a simple *I'm sorry* written inside and headed for the police station.

While the building itself was an old white clapboard structure built around the turn of the century and on the state's historic registry, his corner office with a new computer, plush carpeting and a fresh coat of paint could've been in any business building in the suburbs of Chicago.

He greeted the receptionist, went back to his office and immediately flipped on his computer and TV, hoping for some news about Zach. And Erica. Half an hour later, he sat back in his chair, the pictures flashing across the TV screen of Marie and Jason Samson and Erica Corelli burning into his brain.

Corelli. He had to admit that name fit her better than Jackson. So now what? Arrest her? For what? The warrant issued by the CPD had been for Marie Samson, not Erica Corelli. Bring her in for questioning? Something told him that could be a bad move. There was more going on here than he was going to get from the news.

But you're a cop, Garrett. Act like one. He picked up the phone and was dialing when Lynn came into his office.

"I need to talk to you," she said.

"Can it wait a few minutes?"

She glanced at the TV on his credenza where photos of Zach and Erica were splashing across the screen and closed the door behind her. "No, it can't. You know why I'm here."

He hung up the phone and glared at her.

"Arlo and I both saw the news this morning," she said. "I want to know what you're planning on doing about it."

He sat back in his chair. "There's only one thing I can do. Your Erica may have kidnapped a child."

"He's her nephew. Not a stranger. And chances are she's here for a damned good reason."

There was no doubt Zach wasn't afraid of Erica. Garrett couldn't help but remember the look of fear on the kid's face that morning he'd thought Garrett was going to hit Erica. "Lynn—"

"You don't know what's happened to Erica's sister. That boy's real mother. What harm is there in waiting to see how these chips fall? Those two aren't going anywhere unless she gets spooked."

"I've got a duty as a police officer."

"Your first duty is to the residents of this island. She's one of us now. Hardworking and a good person. And she loves that little boy. She would never, ever hurt him."

"That's not the point—"

"Don't tell me you've never broken any rules." Lynn flattened her hands on his desk and leveled her gaze at him. "Jim said one of the reasons he hired you was because you never let anyone else tell you right from wrong."

Did he?

"So help me, Garrett, if you turn her in, I'll never forgive you. And neither will Doc, Dan or Bob."

"They know, too?"

"Wouldn't surprise me."

"You're threatening a police officer, Lynn."

"So what are you going to do? Arrest me, too?"

They glared at each other.

"You've seen Erica with that boy. Does it look like she's kidnapped him?"

No. Not even close. "Does she have any clue you know the truth?"

Lynn shook her head. "And I don't intend on telling her."

"All right." He took a deep breath. "For now I'll hold off on making that call. But no one says anything to anyone. I don't want her running scared. You got me?"

She nodded.

"Why?" he asked. "Why are you sticking your neck out for her?"

Lynn looked away and didn't say anything for a few moments. "I lost a daughter many years ago. She was five. She got pneumonia one winter and like that she was gone. My youngest." She took a deep breath. "Every once in a while, I see something in Erica's eyes. Something stubborn and full of fire that reminds me of my Charlotte. Even Arlo noticed it that first day she came into the bar."

"I'm not promising anything, Lynn, but she tries to leave this island and I'll crack down on her so fast heads will spin."

"Fine by me." She patted his hand. "I have a feeling you won't regret this."

As she left his office, Garrett had a feeling he most certainly would, but there was one thing he could do to make sure this wasn't going to be the biggest mistake of his career. He picked up the phone and dialed.

"Wilmes here."

"John, it's G.T."

"Hey. I was reaching for the phone to call you."

Garrett leaned back and let the picturesque view of the

marina calm him. "So you found something, huh?" Before he gave up anything, he wanted what John knew.

"Nothing under the name of Erica Jackson," John said. "But then we had a missing persons report filed for a six-year-old kid. The dad's claiming the mother abducted his son. There's a connection to a woman named Erica Corelli. The half sister of the missing mother."

"So what's the story?" Garrett asked.

"A kid and his mom disappeared within a few hours of each other last week. The dad is claiming the wife was going to file for a divorce and when he threatened to get full custody she and her sister ran off with his kid. He's a detective in CPD. Our precinct. Billy Samson. Did you know him?"

"No. You?"

"I know *of* him. Checked him out. Grew up here. Made detective a year ago. By all accounts he's an okay cop, but on the hotheaded side."

"What cop isn't?"

"This guy's been suspended without pay. Twice."

That was different. "Any reports of 9-1-1 calls made from his house?"

"None."

Didn't necessarily mean anything.

"I e-mailed you a couple photos. You get them?"

Garrett pulled up e-mail on his computer and despite knowing what he'd find opened the pictures to cover bases. The first photo was the one the news had been flashing of the boy. This picture showed a kid with blond hair, but cut it shorter and dye it brown and Jason turned into Zach. The second photo was Marie Samson. He'd never seen her before. But the third, Erica Corelli, was a long-haired Erica Jackson. No question.

"Recognize any of them?" John asked.

"Yeah. I got the aunt and the kid."

"On your island?"

"Yep."

"No shit. What about the wife?"

"Nope."

"We better let the dad know."

"Hold off on that. Are they considering this a kidnapping?"

"Not yet."

"Do you know for sure this cop is clean?"

"No."

Garrett debated. "Do me a favor and sit tight for a little while. Something about this situation doesn't feel right. Billy Samson is an unknown. If this turns into a custody dispute all the wife has done is sealed the case for the husband. I got my eye on the aunt, so this is the safest place for the kid. That's what's important."

"You sure about this?"

"No, but when has that ever stopped me? Or you?"

John chuckled.

"This is a small island," Garrett said. "They're not going anywhere without me knowing about it. Keep me updated, though, okay? You find out anything that puts this kid in jeopardy, let me know."

"Will do."

After Garrett hung up, he stared at the picture of Erica Corelli and the thought occurred to him that he liked her better with shorter hair. Showed off her long, graceful neck. He ran his hand over his mouth, remembering their rapid-fire encounter last night in the alley. Just thinking about how soft she'd felt under his hands threatened to make him lose focus.

"What are you up to, Erica? Where's your sister?"

So much for trying to kick her off his island. He had to convince her to tell him her side of the story. That meant Erica was going to have to feel as if she could trust him. And for a woman like that to trust a man, any man, let alone a cop, meant he had his work cut out for him.

DURING THE NEXT FEW weeks as the grass greened and the trees leafed out, the breeze coming off the lake turned warm with the promise of summer, and May flowers bloomed in the wrought iron baskets hanging from every lamppost down Main, Erica had the distinct impression Garrett was quietly watching her every move. He would show up at the most unexpected times, in the baking-goods aisle at Newman's, at a checkout lane in Henderson's Drugstore, or on the street as she was walking Jason home from school.

The first time she'd noticed him after finding the bike at the bottom of her apartment stairs was in front of Arlo's stable. Jason had been with her and riding the apology gift, so rather than ignore Garrett, as she would've been otherwise inclined to do, she stopped. "Garrett," she called.

In his uniform and apparently on his way to the station, he'd headed toward them. "What's up?"

"Zach, you wanted to tell Garrett something, right?"

Jason had grinned and nodded. "Thanks, Garrett. This bike is sweet."

"You're very welcome." Garrett had ruffled Jason's hair, and Jason had zipped off down the street, leaving Garrett and Erica alone.

"You shouldn't have done that," she'd said. "The bike, I mean." But after Jason had seen it leaning against the stairs, she hadn't been able to break her nephew's heart, not after all he'd been through.

"No, the bike was completely called for," Garrett had said. "What I shouldn't have done—"

"Can we pretend as if the alley never happened?" She couldn't seem to keep her gaze from searching out his hands.

"Sure." He'd nodded.

Without another word, she'd made herself walk away. She had to focus on more important matters, like the fact that Marie had yet to call or leave a message on Erica's cell phone.

Although Erica had the phone in her apartment reconnected and called Teddy at least every other day, he rarely had news. She kept abreast of the Chicago Police Department's progress in locating her sister through Lynn's computer, but the investigation seemed to have stalled and the attention the case had initially garnered had waned substantially. No one seemed to care any longer about a cop's wife and son disappearing with her troublesome sister.

Except for Erica and Jason.

Despite the fact that their existence on Mirabelle had settled into a relatively predictable, if not comfortable, pattern, Marie was never far from their thoughts. In the mornings, Erica walked Jason to school. Then she went back to the restaurant and prepared whatever sauces and desserts were needed for the lunch and dinner menus. The initial test Lynn had done on Erica's Italian specials had been wildly successful, so Lynn had decided to run specials every week.

After the lunch crowds came and went Erica walked back to the school to pick up Jason. They'd spend several hours together, doing his minimal homework, going for walks exploring the island or running errands before she would head back to the pub for the dinner rush. She would get Jason to bed, close down the bar and head up to the apartment to sleep until the alarm went off the next morning when the routine started all over again. Give or take, Erica was working twelve-hour days. She was exhausted most of the time, but things were working out, and she felt better having some cash stashed away for whatever might come their way.

And she was adjusting to living with a young boy. She'd worked out trade-offs on playdates with Sarah. Erica had Sundays off, so she took Brian all day. He'd stay overnight in their apartment and she got both boys to school on Monday mornings. Sarah took Jason Friday nights and an occasional afternoon until bedtime.

All things considered, Jason was doing okay. He and Erica were getting along the way a close aunt and nephew should. He and Brian were quickly on the road to becoming best friends and riding their bikes all over the main part of town, he was comfortable sleeping over at Sarah's apartment, and he occasionally looked forward to school. Once or twice every week Jason even went up to the stable to hang out with Arlo, and from what Erica could tell they enjoyed each other's company.

Erica and Jason's lives were slowly, irrevocably becoming intertwined with each other and with the people of this island. Nothing brought that point home better than Lynn calling Erica to her office one morning after the lunch crowd had cleared out.

"Yeah, what's up?" She'd been on her way to the walk-in cooler for ingredients to prep the roasted red pepper white sauce.

"The feedback's coming in on your specials."

"And?"

"I've decided I want to do an entirely new menu." Lynn sat back in her chair. "Will you help me?"

It was a loaded question. This wasn't a simple let's-throw-the-noodle-against-the-wall-to-see-if-it-sticks kind of venture. Erica could tell by the look in Lynn's eyes that she could afford neither the financial nor emotional drain of a failure.

What if Marie called, needing help or wanting Jason back home? What if Billy found them and she was forced to leave the island? She'd been living day to day, and tomorrow everything could change.

Even so, Erica didn't want her new—she had to admit it—friend to fail. "Yeah, I'll help."

Lynn smiled and pointed to the chair next to her desk. "Then sit down. Let's do this together."

Over the course of the next hour, she convinced Lynn they needed a smaller, more eclectic menu and an expanded wine and beer list for the tourists, and Lynn helped her understand that sometimes the tourists were looking for down-home cooking, a bit of an escape from the fancy city food. In the end they hashed out a menu together.

"You giving us your recipes this time?" Lynn asked with a smile.

"Ever heard of job security?" Erica laughed. "But I will print the menus off on your computer like I did with the special inserts," she said.

"That'd be nice."

"Now all you need are some renovations in the restaurant or at least a little redecorating, and you'll be set."

Lynn chuckled. "You're about as subtle as a barbed fishing hook, you know that?"

"Sorry." Erica glanced away.

"You're right, though." Lynn sighed heavily. "Mirabelle's had a rough couple of years with a slowdown in tourists. Business has been tough. Arlo and I have been barely breaking even."

"You'll bring in more business with a fresh new look."

"I know."

"I hear talk about two new municipal pools and a golf course opening next week."

"At the last town council meeting, the hotel owners said they were fully booked all the way through *next* summer."

"Then maybe now is the right time to put a small investment into the place. Before the tourists start arriving."

"What were you thinking?"

Erica went through all the plans that had been running through her head these last weeks. "There's a lot I can do myself to keep the costs down."

"We'll get a bid and see what we can manage." Lynn's eyes

lit with excitement. "If Garrett can get his part done for a reasonable investment before the summer season starts, I'm all in."

Garrett? Erica's stomach pitched at the thought of him. Of course, he'd be doing the remodeling. When so much of the rest of her life was in a state of complete and total upheaval, this snag seemed par for the course.

GARRETT'S ESTIMATE ON COSTS for his part of the project came within the amount Lynn felt she could put toward refurbishing the pub, so she closed both the restaurant and bar, despite the locals' fervent protests, until they were finished with all the redecorating and remodeling.

For Lynn's sake, Erica decided to put aside her differences with Garrett and work like crazy to get everything done in time. The next several days were a flurry of activity with people constantly coming and going. Although Erica could hear Garrett gutting the bathrooms, tearing out carpet and pounding this and that, she saw him only in passing and made a point of never being alone with him.

Lynn had given her a tight budget for redecorating, forcing Erica to prioritize. The first thing she did once Lynn had given the go-ahead was to order a variety of plants that would cozy up the atmosphere. Next were new, trendy votive holders for the tables, cloth napkins, new menu covers, a few new light fixtures and small carafes to hold silk greens and flowers. She'd put out the word to every employee to scrounge up various shapes and sizes of frames at garage sales, and she ordered inexpensive posters or printed stock photos off the Internet to fill the frames. All of the updated decorations, she hoped, would give the place the warmth it'd been lacking without turning it *all feminine* as Arlo had warned.

While Erica waited for everything to arrive, she and Lynn pored over the menu, discussing changes, ordering wines and new food items. Once Lynn had made her final decisions, Erica designed new menus and was alone in Lynn's office, printing them out when Garrett poked his head through the doorway.

He hadn't shaved that morning, and the growth of beard covering his face, though heavy, looked quite a bit lighter in color than his hair. Although she still felt emotionally stung by what had happened in the ally, her libido was telling her in no uncertain terms to let it go. She found herself having to resist the urge to reach out and trail her hand along his cheek to find out if his beard was indeed as soft as it looked. This was going to be a long week.

"I need some help with something," he said. "There's no one else here."

Meaning she was a last resort. At least they were in agreement on something. "What do you need?"

Custom windows had been ordered for the new entrance and wouldn't arrive until the end of the week, so he'd started in the bathrooms. "The fixtures in the women's—" He looked down at the menus coming out of the printer. "Did you design these?"

"Yeah. For Lynn."

He began reading one, but the printer kicked out another on top of the first.

"You can pick it up," she said, somewhat reluctantly.

He put his gloved hands in the air. "Even if I took these gloves off, my hands are probably still filthy."

She picked one out of the stack and held it up for him. Why she would care about his opinion was anyone's guess, but she was more than a little worried about this gamble paying off for Lynn.

"Flatbreads. Quesadillas. Garlic shrimp," he read off several selections. "Lasagna. Penne *arrabiata*. Buffalo chicken sandwich. Dry rubbed salmon."

"What do you think?"

He glanced up at her. "You're asking me?"

"Yeah."

"I'm far from an expert on menus," he said. "I'm getting hungry just looking at it, if that helps."

"So you think it's a good menu?"

He read through the rest of it. "I'd order all but a couple things, so you'll get me coming back. I like, too, how you kept some of the island favorites in that Down Home section." The tone of his voice was surprisingly reassuring, his smile comforting.

She looked away, swallowing.

"It'll work. Don't worry."

She glanced at him, her suspicions aroused. "So what's up with the Mr. Nice Guy? Last time I checked," she said, leaning back in Lynn's desk chair, "you were wanting me on a one-way ferry to the mainland."

"Maybe I was wrong."

"Maybe?"

He looked away, apparently forming his words. "The Duffys have needed to do something like this with their pub for a long time. They needed a nudge. What you're doing here for Lynn…is nice. You're good for her."

"So all of a sudden you're—"

"You can quit with the tough-guy business yourself, okay? You and I both know it's an act." He shifted on his feet, clearly uncomfortable. "I thought we'd agreed what happened in the alley a couple weeks ago, didn't happen."

She studied him, trying to figure his angle. That she could tell, he didn't have one. This was for Lynn. "All right. What did you need?"

"Come with me."

She followed him into the women's bathroom. He'd already ripped out the old flooring, replaced the counter and sinks and was in the process of installing the fixtures. Unfortunately, Erica found something oddly sexy about his efficiency.

"The faucets aren't lining up with the pipes." He got down on the floor and scooted under the sink on his back. "I need you to hold them in place while I fit them together down here."

"Okay." Her eyes were glued to his legs sticking out from under the vanity counter. He was wearing loose-fitting jeans, but the line of his thigh muscles were clearly outlined as he lifted one knee. And that bulge in his groin… Oh, lord.

"Erica? What are you doing up there?"

"Oh, sorry." She grabbed the faucet for the first sink and held tight while it vibrated with his movements.

He grunted and his legs shifted. He reached for the pipe wrench on the floor and tightened the pipe. "Let's go to the next one." A few minutes later, the fixtures were installed and he came out from under the counter. "Thank you."

"No problem. How long will the bathroom take?"

"The last thing I have to do in here is lay the tile this afternoon, then I'll finish with the men's by tomorrow night."

"That's fast."

"It's what Lynn needed. I told her I'd take a few days away from the station."

"I hear you put in some additional shelving at Newman's and built a new front desk for one of the inns."

"Make hay while the sun shines."

Maybe she'd been wrong about him, too. Maybe he did fit here on Mirabelle. "What would this island do without you?"

He grinned. "Hire a new police chief."

CHAPTER FOURTEEN

GARRETT FINISHED BOTH bathrooms and started in the next day on building and installing a wine rack for the wall separating the bar from the dining area. A simple box frame with shelves crisscrossing to form storage areas for bottles of wine, he expected to finish by the end of the day. That is, unless he kept getting distracted by a certain female working in the same general area.

Erica didn't have enough time to repaint the entire place, so she was giving the dingy white walls in both the bar and restaurant a wash of heavy cream-colored paint. The end result was a faux-stucco appearance, surprisingly sophisticated for such a simple task. Unfortunately for Garrett, it was this exact process that threatened to turn his one day job into two.

He found himself tuning in to every movement she made. Whether she was bending over for paint, reaching up toward the wall or climbing up and down a ladder, she exhibited grace and control, not to mention the most incredible curves. He was surreptitiously eyeing those exact curves when someone cleared her throat behind him. He spun around to find Lynn standing with her hands on her hips.

"She sure can work wonders with paint," Lynn said, having apparently come up behind him through the kitchen door.

"Yeah." He imaged Erica could work wonders on a lot of things.

"Doesn't look much like trouble now, does she?" Lynn whispered.

"We both know looks can be deceiving," he whispered back. Erica was far enough away in the other room that, as long as they were quiet, she wouldn't be able to hear what they were saying.

"Not actions, Garrett. She's been nothing but helpful since day one." She raised an eyebrow at him. "If you let your guard down for one minute, you might be surprised by the results."

No, he wouldn't. He knew exactly what would happen, and it'd happen pretty damned fast.

Erica finished the last wall and glanced back at them. "Not bad for only a few hundred dollars' worth of paint," she called. "What do you two think?"

"It's beautiful," Lynn said.

"Looks good," Garrett added, nodding his head.

"Well, I'm heading up to the stables to bring Arlo some lunch." Lynn moved toward the entrance. "You two help yourselves to whatever in the kitchen for lunch."

"Will do," Garrett said.

"See you later," Erica added.

The pub's front door closed and they were alone.

Erica walked over to where he stood in front of the wine racks. "They look great. You've really never done these before?"

"Nope."

"Perfectionist, huh?"

"Not really. They're simple."

"Wine racks, tiling, plumbing. How does a cop learn to do all that?"

"My dad."

"You two must have been close."

Hardly. He had to change the subject. "Did you need something?"

"Umm. Yeah. I was going to install new drapery rods in the dining room. Can you help?"

"Sure." He followed her and marveled at how bright the dining room seemed.

She'd stripped down the old, faded curtains before glazing the walls and had marked exactly where she needed him to drill holes for the brackets. As if they'd been working side by side for years, before he could formulate a request for anything, she would put the exact tool or piece of hardware in his hand. In less than half an hour the rods were up on all four windows, and he stood back and watched Erica finish the job.

First she draped a filmy red fabric across, around and over the rods. Then she decorated what she'd called a scarf with a string of leaves and what looked like some type of berry, creating a custom, completely updated look that brought to mind an Italian bistro.

"You've done this before, haven't you?" he asked.

"What?"

"Redecorated restaurants."

"A couple times. I was head chef and manager at the last place I worked."

"Which was?"

"An Italian place in…Minneapolis."

She'd been here almost a month and she was still lying. Instead of getting angry, he found himself feeling oddly hurt by her unwillingness to confide in him. Though he had the feeling she was running from Billy Samson, he wanted to hear the truth from her. He found himself wanting to protect her, help her. Fight for her. Maybe she'd been working on him more than he'd realized.

She came down from the ladder, putting her within only a few inches of him.

"Why are you here?" he asked. "On Mirabelle?"

She looked into his eyes, vulnerable and honest for only

a moment. "I told you. I came here once when I was a little girl with my mom and my sister."

"You're looking for the fairy tale, aren't you?" He saw it flickering hopefully in her brown eyes.

"Yeah. Right."

"Erica, what are you running from?"

Looking away, she folded up the ladder.

"Tell me the truth. Maybe I can help."

"There's nothing to tell." She walked away.

SOMEONE WAS COMING.

Billy! Wake up, Erica. Wake up.

She forced open her eyes. Her heart pounding with fear, she lay in bed for a moment, completely still, listening. Though it was early morning, the apartment was dark, the sky outside heavy with clouds. She'd been sound asleep lying next to Jason when something had woken her. An unfamiliar noise. A tapping on the metal steps. Soft. Creaking. Intermittent.

Slowly, she climbed out of bed. Hoping not to awaken and frighten Jason, she grabbed the bat she'd left leaning against the bedside table, then quietly, but firmly closed the door and padded barefoot out into the kitchen.

She peeked around the edge of the blinds covering the windows, but saw no one. Tightly gripping the bat, she paused, held her breath and listened. A strong burst of wind came in off the water and hit the building like storm waves hit the breakwater outside the Mirabelle marina, and the sound intensified. It wasn't a person. She looked out the window. The sign attached to the rail, declaring this a private staircase, had broken free at the base and was flapping in the wind and hitting the rail.

No one was there. It was only the storm that had woken her. Rain came in sheets pouring down like a violent shower.

The wind gained momentum, gusting in great bursts, rattling the old windowpanes, the door, making the outside metal staircase creak and groan.

She couldn't stifle the feeling that something was very wrong. She picked up the phone and dialed Teddy's number. The call went to his answering machine. "Teddy?" she whispered, not wanting to awaken Jason. "I know it's early, but I just wanted to touch base—"

"Erica!" Teddy had apparently heard her voice and picked up. "I'm glad you called. You need to give me a number where I can get hold of you."

"That's not a good idea. Have you found something?"

"I got some bad news."

"What? Tell me."

"One of Marie's neighbors finally fessed up about something."

Erica waited.

"A week before Marie called you, she went out to lunch with this neighbor and told the woman she was seeing a divorce attorney. Billy had hit Jason."

"I knew it."

"The lawyer wouldn't tell me anything. But Billy found out. That's how he justified the warrant for Marie."

Oh, God. Oh, God. Oh, God. "That neighbor needs to tell the cops."

"She won't. Not yet, anyway. Billy's threatened, in a roundabout way, every single one of Marie's friends. They're all scared the cops are on Billy's side."

And she couldn't blame them.

"I'm still working on this, okay? We'll get there, Erica."

"Thanks, Teddy." She hung up the phone and had no sooner closed her eyes than Jason called from the bedroom.

"Erica!"

"Here!" She ran down the hall and found him sitting up

in bed. "I'm here." She sat on the edge of the bed. "It's just a storm making a lot of noise. Do you want to see?"

"No!" He held his head as if he might block out the sound. "No!"

"Hey. It's okay." She scooted across the bed and wrapped her arms around him. "A little rain. Some wind. It'll be gone before you know it." She fell back with him onto the mattress and drew the comforter over them.

He grew still and then whispered, "What if Mommy never calls us?"

"Don't even think about it. She loves you. She'll call."

"What if Daddy—" He paused. "What if she's hurt?"

"Jason, do you know where your mom is?"

He shook his head.

"Did you see something?"

At first he didn't say anything, and then he whispered, "I didn't want to go to school that morning."

"You mean, that day I picked you up?"

He nodded.

"Were they arguing, your mom and dad?"

He nodded again and several tears dribbled down his cheeks.

"It's not your fault, Jason. I swear, none of this is your fault." She felt him relax.

"Mommy always sings to me when there's a storm," he whispered.

"What does she sing?"

"The song about the bird."

"The mockingbird song?" Erica smiled, remembering her own childhood. Every once in a great while their mother turned amazingly maternal and sang them to sleep with that song. So whenever Erica babysat Marie, which was more often than not, she'd sing the song.

Softly, slowly, Erica sang past the lump in her throat. By

the third verse he was back to sleep, and Erica was wide-awake. For the first time since they'd left Chicago she couldn't shake the terrible thought that she and Jason might never see Marie again.

"I WANT TO HELP YOU finish."

Garrett spun around from where he was working in the restaurant's entryway to find Erica standing behind him, dressed in a pair of paint-spattered jeans and a faded black T-shirt. He was remodeling the entryway, getting ready to install windows and new wainscoting, and the last thing he needed was Erica and her curves in close proximity for the rest of the day. "That's not a good idea."

"Come on. This is it," she said, standing in a swath of bright and cheery sunlight as it gleamed through the area he'd cut out of the exterior walls. "If we can finish the foyer today, we can reopen tomorrow. As planned."

"I can handle it."

"You can get this done? By yourself? Today?"

No. Probably not. Although he'd already framed the opening for the windows and reinforced the lower half of the wall for the extra weight, some help would speed things along. "All right, fine, but only if you do what I tell you when I tell you to do it without any back talk."

"When have I—"

"Zip!"

She stifled a smile, but to her credit kept her mouth shut.

"All I need is for you to hold the windows in place while I attach them to the frame."

"Where do you want me?"

A few obvious places other than the pub quickly came to mind. "Come here." He indicated she stand next to him, but she hesitated. "Scared? Of me?"

"No," she said, a surprised look on her face. "I'm really not."

"Come on then. Let's go." He could feel her gaze on him as he squatted, grabbed the window off the ground and lifted, placing it inside the hole in the wall and positioning it. The damned thing was heavy and he sure didn't want it to fall on her. "Okay," he said. "You hold the right side steady. I'll screw the left side into the frame."

She grabbed hold of the window.

"I'm going to let go now. You got it?"

"Yep."

He went around with his drill, screwing the window into the frame. As he got closer to her, he could smell that sweet citrusy scent in her hair. He turned around, caught her looking at his neck, and she seemed to lean toward him.

"Are we finished?" she asked.

"Not yet." His gaze shifted from her eyes to her lips. "We have two more windows."

By the time they'd finished, his body was on fire and he'd inadvertently backed her into the far corner of the foyer. As he worked his way toward her, he could feel her gaze fixated on him. The muscles of his forearms. His fingers. He could almost hear her imagining what his hands would feel like roaming her body. He could see it on her face, hear it in the quickening of her breath.

He glanced at her, and she didn't bother to look away. "Can I let go now?" she said softly.

"Please," he whispered. "Let go anytime you want."

"In your dreams."

"Every one of them." There was less than a foot between them when he stepped toward her.

Her breath came fast. "You have bits of wood in your…" She reached up and brushed at the sides of his hair.

He couldn't—didn't want to—stop himself. Setting his hands on her waist he lifted her up, held her to him as she wrapped her legs around him and quickly lowered her mouth to his. It wasn't a kiss. Not even close. This was a collision of need and want, two people taking, no one giving. Their tongues tangled, their bodies interlocked. She nipped at his lower lip and neck and he nipped back.

He dipped his hands under her shirt, caressed her back and flicked open the clasp on her bra. When he cupped her breast, felt the velvety softness, the glorious weight, his knees nearly buckled. He staggered back against the wall.

"Holy cow!" Lynn's voice came from the inside of the restaurant. "Look at that." They both stilled. Lynn couldn't see them. "I can't wait to put up the green-and-white striped awnings like all the other businesses along Main."

Garrett slid Erica slowly down the front of him, cringing at the sweet agony of her pressing against his erection until her feet touched the ground. She backed away, swallowed and was smoothing her hair when Lynn stepped into the entryway.

"I can't believe what a difference this makes in the whole feeling in the bar," Lynn said.

Garrett cleared his throat, and for Erica's sake tried to make conversation. "Like it, huh?"

"Garrett." Lynn set her hands on her hips. "You do beautiful work."

"Thanks. Erica was holding the windows in place for me."

"I see," Lynn said.

How could she not? Erica's lips were deep red and swollen, almost bruised. "I've got to get back to putting those menus together." She crossed her arms over her chest and headed for the kitchen. "Or we won't be ready for the grand reopening tomorrow."

Sonofabitch. He'd been feeling her up in broad daylight for the entire island to see. "Lynn—"

"Go." Lynn flicked her head in the direction Erica had disappeared. "Talk to her. I only interrupted you because I could see you two from the street. I love the windows, but…"

"Anyone else see—"

"No."

He took off and found Erica in Lynn's office, pulling her shirt back down after very likely having rehooked her bra. "Erica." He still felt drugged by her kisses. "I'm sorry."

"For what?"

"For…that."

She looked away. "You're an asshole."

"That's what I've been trying to tell you."

"Not for the kiss, you idiot." She ran past him. "For being sorry for wanting me."

CHAPTER FIFTEEN

GRAND REOPENING NIGHT had arrived.

Erica had printed flyers up and the staff had posted the notices on every board throughout town letting the locals know Lynn was offering a buy-one-entrée-get-one-free opening weekend simply for stopping by and testing out their new menu before tourist season began.

Butterflies fluttered in Erica's stomach as she and Lynn hustled here and there with last-minute preparations of food, adjustments to décor, and directions for the staff, including the bunch of college kids who had arrived to work for the summer. Tonight was Erica's big night. She was cooking from the updated menu with the help of a newly hired assistant cook, and Lynn and Arlo were manning the bar.

Erica glanced at the clock. Ten minutes to their first new and improved happy hour.

Jason bounded into the kitchen. "Lynn is unlocking the door," he said. "Right now! There are people outside waiting. I saw them through the new windows."

"No kidding?" Erica was pleased Lynn had told her that Jason, as long as he didn't cause any trouble, could continue to hang out at the bar on occasion.

"Go look."

She peeked through the swinging doors. Sure enough, a small crowd of friendly and familiar faces had gathered and they were filing past Lynn.

"Aren't you excited?" Jason asked, bouncing up and down.

"Yes!" She laughed. "I'm glad you're here to help out. 'Cause I'm going to need it."

He straightened his shoulders and a glow of pride brightened his face. "Can I stay up late?"

"For a night like this? Absolutely."

When several people she'd never met were among the first big group to arrive, she headed out toward Lynn in the bar. She pointed to the tall man and his pregnant wife, a couple she recognized from lunch several weeks back. "Who are those people coming in with Marty and Brittany Rousseau?"

"Oh, that's Marty's sister, Sophie, and her husband, Noah Bennett. They live in Rhode Island during the school year and got back yesterday for the summer season." Sophie was very pregnant, looking as if she might pop at the sound of a loud noise. "That's Noah's dad, Jim Bennett, our old chief of police and his wife, Josie," Lynn went on to explain and then pointed at the two teenagers. "That's Lauren and Kurt. Sophie's kids. I've heard a rumor she's pregnant with another set of twins."

"Hey, Lynn!" Noah said. "Your place looks great."

"Thanks." She swung a thumb toward Erica. "It's all her doing. Our new chef."

Chef? A person who'd learned the culinary arts at Al's Diner? Hardly.

The Rousseau group came over to the bar and Lynn made introductions. "Welcome to Mirabelle," Sophie said, smiling.

"Thank you."

With two teenagers and a baby on the way, the family looked happy. Erica was suddenly struck with a deep sense of loneliness and was so grateful for Jason's presence. She drew him in front of her and rested her hands on his shoulder. "This is my...son, Zach." She felt like a traitor introducing him that way, but there was no help for it.

There was another round of hellos, and Jason smiled.

"Sarah said you were looking for a babysitter," Lauren said.

"I'll watch Zach for you," Kurt said.

"Hey!" Lauren flicked her fingers against his shoulder. "Get your own client."

"You've already got Brian. Zach is mine!"

"Hey, hey, hey," Noah said. "I'm sure you can work out a schedule with Sarah and Erica."

"But, Dad!" Lauren said.

"Take turns," Sophie added.

"Sarah and I are going to have a busy summer," Erica said. "I have no doubt we'll have enough hours for both of you. Consider yourselves hired."

Sophie and Noah smiled at her. Heck, maybe this parenting gig wasn't all that hard after all. After thanking everyone for coming, Erica steered Jason back into the kitchen. She kept one eye on the front entrance as the food orders came in and was surprised that she knew everyone who came through the doors. The three stooges, Doc, Bob and Dan, came, as well as the Setterbergs, the Andersens, Charlotte Day and Mary Gilbert, and…great. Wonderful. Just what she needed to set tonight's tone. Garrett and Hannah came through the door.

She hadn't seen Garrett since that terribly wonderful kiss in the new entryway, and, even now, the remembered feeling of his hand on her breast made her nipples harden and a heat that had nothing to do with the kitchen stove pool low in her belly.

Erica wished she could fault Hannah, but she couldn't. The woman was a wonderfully compassionate teacher and gorgeous. Even her blond hair was natural. Her only flaw was being innocent enough to date a two-timing jerk like Garrett Taylor. That man didn't deserve her.

Their new hostess showed Garrett and Hannah to a table,

and a few minutes later Glynnis stuck an order up on the board. "Linguini, rigatoni."

"What table?"

"Seven."

Garrett and Hannah's table. So he was sorry he'd kissed her, was he? The light shrimp linguini was most likely for Hannah. "Is the rigatoni for Garrett?"

"Yeah, why?" Glynnis asked.

"Just curious." Erica was going to give him one tasty dish, all right.

GARRETT GLANCED UP AS Glynnis brought the entrees he and Hannah had ordered to their table. What the hell was he doing here? Oh, yeah. Hannah had called and asked him to give it one more shot. He owed her that at least.

"That smells so good." Hannah set down her glass of white wine and took a whiff through that dainty little nose of hers.

Garrett sat back and took a swig from his bottle of beer. "Thank you, Glynnis." The steamy scent of garlic and sweet Italian sausage rose in waves off his tomato-based rigatoni.

"You're welcome, Chief."

As their waitress walked away, Hannah twirled several strands of linguini around her fork and took a bite. She closed her eyes and moaned. "I don't know how we got so lucky, but this island so needed Erica Jackson."

The island be damned. He could tell himself he didn't trust her, that she was hiding something and all he cared about was the safety of Mirabelle's tourists and residents, but the truth was becoming harder and harder to ignore. He wanted her. In his arms. In his bed. *He* needed Erica.

Feeling desperate, he watched Hannah nip off a piece of shrimp, hoping the look of her pink lips wet with a creamy garlic sauce might put his mind where it was supposed to be. His tactic didn't seem to be working.

"I've never tasted shrimp this perfectly prepared," she murmured. "Erica is a goddess."

He should've been physically moved by the beautiful woman sitting across the table from him nearly having an orgasm over her pasta. Instead, all he wanted was to head into that kitchen, take Erica into his arms and kiss her basil-scented skin up one side and down the other.

"Aren't you going to eat?" Hannah asked.

He forced a smile. "I'm having fun watching you." He set down his beer, poked several tubes of pasta with his fork and stuffed them in his mouth. At first, the flavors of basil and garlic, sausage and cheeses combined in savory splendor until the heat hit him. His mouth turned to fire. He forced the bite down his throat and his eyes watered uncontrollably.

"Are you okay?" Hannah asked.

"Fine," he managed to choke out. His tongue, throat and lips burned as if they might blister. "Went down the wrong pipe." He glanced more carefully at the dish. Crushed hot peppers. Everywhere. *I'll be damned.* He glanced into the kitchen and found Erica watching him with a grin on her face. To spite her, he stabbed another forkful and shoved it in his mouth. "Mmm, mmm, mmm." In truth he couldn't blame her. He'd been a cad.

"It's good, isn't it?"

"Never tasted better."

From that moment on, the restaurant filled to the brim. Garrett glanced into the kitchen a few times, but it was clear Erica was crazy busy keeping up with the orders.

When he only finished half his plate, Hannah asked, "Didn't you like it?"

"It was great. I guess I ate too much bread." He dumped it into a takeout container, paid the bill and they took off for Hannah's house.

When they got to the front steps, she turned toward him. "Why don't you come in?"

He hesitated, thinking he should end it right here, right now.

"Look," Hannah said. "I'm getting the impression you're not that into me. That's fine, but wanting you to come inside doesn't mean I want a commitment."

"Commitment's not the problem."

"You don't like…men, do you?"

He laughed. "No. I like women."

"Just not this woman."

She deserved to know about Erica. "Hannah, I need to tell you—"

"No." She shook her head. "No confessions. Nothing serious. Not tonight. I want to have some fun." She grabbed his hand. "Come on. Let's see if we can make this work."

One last shot. He followed her through the front door and glanced around. The place was meticulously decorated. Every chic and stylish detail had clearly been planned out, from the furniture to the rugs and framed art. The trendy golds, browns and greens all melded together, creating a seamless transition from one room to the next.

Garrett occupied himself in the kitchen, opening a bottle of wine and pouring two glasses while Hannah went into the living room and turned on soft music and lit several candles. She came up behind him and put her arms around his waist. The heat from her skin felt nice through the fabric of his shirt.

He turned around and handed her a glass of wine. "Cheers."

She clinked her glass with his, took a sip and then drew him toward the sofa in the family room. He sat down next to her and set his wineglass on the coffee table. Leaning forward, he kissed her. "Is this what you had in mind?"

"Mmm-hmm." She drew him back with her and kissed him again.

Nothing. They had absolutely no chemistry. He gripped her waist, trying one more time, and let his fingers inch under her shirt to touch her skin. Still nothing.

She pulled back and her shoulders slumped.

He looked away.

"This isn't working for you, either, is it?" she said.

Either? At least he wasn't the only one unaffected. "I'm sorry, Hannah."

"It's not your fault we're not right for each other."

"I thought maybe something would develop." But every time he looked into her eyes, he ached to see brown instead of blue, dark, short hair, rather than long blond strands.

"Well, at least now we know for sure." She smiled. "We were probably trying too hard. It's not as if there are droves of available singles on Mirabelle. Maybe if we let things develop on their own…"

Unconvinced, he glanced at her.

"You're right." She laughed. "If things were going to happen, they would've happened by now." She put some distance between them on the couch and took a sip of wine. "I like you, though."

"Friends?"

"Yeah." She patted his hand. "You know there is someone on this island I think you would connect—"

"No." He picked up his wine.

"But Erica—"

"Trust me, Hannah, it wouldn't work."

"Maybe the fact that you're fighting the obvious so much," she said, swirling the wine in her glass, "is a sign it would. Maybe too well?"

CHAPTER SIXTEEN

"WE BROKE UP," HANNAH said with a careless shrug.

Sarah and Erica had been in Sarah's backyard getting their two boys ready for a day at the pool with the Rousseau twins when Hannah had walked over to visit.

"That sucks." Erica did her best to feign disinterest, but she had a feeling it wasn't working

School was officially out and it was Saturday, the busiest day of the week for both Sarah—weddings galore—and Erica—lunch and dinner crowds—and Kurt and Lauren had agreed to babysit on this hot June day.

"Well, I guess you can't call it a real breakup since we hadn't been a real couple."

"Two dates," Sarah said, handing Brian a beach towel and a bottle of sunscreen. "Doesn't technically qualify you as a couple."

"When?" Erica asked.

"A few weeks ago," Hannah said.. "The night you guys reopened Duffys."

Erica had seen Garrett at least every day since then, but him being back to his distant watchful self, they'd barely said a word to each other.

"You guys have your swimsuits on?" Lauren asked Jason and Brian.

"Yeah," they said in unison.

"Then let's hit it," Kurt said.

The four kids took off with towels in hand.

"See you later, Zach," Erica called. "Have fun."

"Behave, Brian," Sarah added.

Erica turned back to Hannah. "You seem like you're okay with it? Are you?"

"Oh, sure," Hannah said, apparently unfazed. "Breaking things off was very definitely a mutual thing. We're still friends."

"Walk with us, Hannah," Sarah said. "I've got to get my shop opened."

"So what happened?" Erica asked, falling in step with the other women.

"Nothing," Hannah said. "That was the problem."

"Nothing?" Sarah unlocked the glass-paneled front door to her floral shop. "As in no zing?"

"I don't get it." Erica shrugged.

"Nothing," Hannah said again. "From the beginning, we never really clicked."

She had to be joking.

The three women walked into Sarah's shop where half the space was dedicated to her wedding planning business, displaying such things as invitations and table décor. The other half held the typical trappings of a flower shop.

"I mean, we could talk, carry on a conversation," Hannah said, flipping on lights. "He's a great guy, but when we kissed…there was…absolutely nothing there."

"Did you ever try, you know," Sarah asked with a grin, "doing it?"

Erica put her head down and corrected the placement of a potted plant.

"God, no," Hannah said. "Garrett's the most prudish man I've ever known."

Garrett Taylor? Were they talking about the same man?

"He wouldn't even kiss me on our first date. Wanted to

take it slow, he said. From the start, we really didn't have a connection."

"Seriously? You didn't feel anything?"

"Kissing Garrett was like kissing a good friend. Kind of interesting, but…yeah. You know what I mean?"

Erica looked away. She couldn't imagine a woman not being turned on by the most fundamentally sexual man she'd ever met.

"Maybe he'd be different with another woman," Sarah mused. "You should go out with him, Erica."

"Me?"

"That's a great idea," Hannah said. "You two are perfect for each other."

She headed toward the door. "I'm not interested in a relationship, and Garrett's definitely not interested in me."

Sarah laughed. "Right."

"Who said anything about a relationship?" Hannah called after her. "A little fun never hurt anyone."

Fun? Garrett Taylor? Hardly.

"TIME TO CALL IT A DAY," Herman said, stopping by Garrett's office door. "You up for a beer?"

It was almost six. Between full-time shifts at the police station and the work he was wrapping up for some of the locals in his shop, he'd been burning the midnight oil for a few weeks now. "Sounds good to me."

"Some guys are heading to Duffy's."

Damn. Garrett rubbed his tired eyes. Although Erica had rarely been far from his thoughts, hanging around her in a social setting was asking for trouble. "On second thought—"

"Aw, come on. This group is worth it. Jim, Noah, Marty. They're all good guys."

He'd been hoping to visit with Jim Bennett, Mirabelle's

ex-chief of police. Now was as good a time as any. "Okay, let's go."

The tourist season was in full swing, so the place was crowded and noisy with the jukebox playing an old '60s song. Hannah, Sarah and Missy had nabbed a booth and were clearly flirting with a table full of fishermen. Even Hannah. Garrett grinned and gave a short wave in greeting. He and Herman found the men in the bar side of Duffy's along with several other locals, the table loaded down with pitchers of beer, burgers, fries and baskets of various appetizers.

"Looks like we're late," Garrett said.

"There's still room at the table."

Garrett glanced around, looking for Erica and found her behind the bar. She nodded at him and then went back to work. Looked like she was taking a break from cooking tonight and training in a new bartender, some young college kid.

Garrett walked toward the end of one of the tables and held out his hand. "Hey, Jim, how are you doing?"

"Good. Good." He shook hands and motioned toward the chair next to him. "You can sit here if you promise not to talk shop."

"Well, that'll be tough, but I'll manage."

"Garrett, this is my son, Noah."

Noah reached out. "So I hear you're from Chicago."

Garrett nodded and poured himself a mug of beer.

"How're you liking Mirabelle so far?"

"Love it. Exactly what I was looking for."

Noah laughed. "You're a better man than me."

The conversation around the table was lively and varied, and Garrett found himself relaxing for the first time in weeks. When the waitress stopped by, he ordered one of Erica's pasta dishes, guessing she'd prepped all the sauces

earlier in the day. He was right. The Alfredo sauce with pro-
sciutto and some exotic-sounding mushrooms was like
liquid velvet over the fettuccine.

At one point, he looked up to see if Erica was still at the
bar and saw a familiar picture of a woman with long hair
flashing across the TV screen. Erica Corelli. The song on
the jukebox ended and he could just make out the voice of
the Chicago newscaster.

"…recent developments in the Jason and Marie Samson
case. If anyone has information with regard to the whereabouts of Erica Corelli, please contact the Chicago police."

The screen flashed to a detective answering questions.
"No, an arrest warrant has not been issued at this time. We
believe she may be able to shed some light on the disappearance of Marie and Jason Samson. At this point, Erica
Corelli is considered a person of interest and only wanted
for questioning."

She was one step away from a suspect. Maybe Garrett had
been wrong about Erica. Maybe she was hiding something.

"Look." A clearly agitated Billy Samson appeared on
the TV screen. "The morning Marie disappeared, she'd
asked for a divorce. I told her we'd work it out, but I'm
sure her sister talked her into leaving with Jason." Then
he stared directly into the camera. "Marie, if you're out
there, listening, I just want you to come home. Everything will be fine."

"You okay?" Jim Bennett grabbed Garrett's arm.

"Yeah. Fine." He searched the bar for Erica. She was in
the shadows, her back to him, as she watched the TV screen.

A PERSON OF INTEREST? What the hell did that mean?

Erica stared, dumbfounded, as a picture of her, long-haired
and frowning, flashed across the screen. Billy had no doubt
picked that particular photo in the hopes of eliciting public

sympathy. She hoped the cops weren't buying whatever lie he was selling. They couldn't all be idiots, could they?

Everything will be fine.

Billy was clearly doing what he could to deflect the investigation away from him. Her fist clenched around the cleaning rag. *Oh, God, Marie. Please be safe. Please be alive.*

Suddenly, she remembered where she was, behind the bar with a room full of people surrounding her. Slowly, she glanced around. No one was paying the slightest bit of attention to the TV screen.

She glanced out toward the tables. Garrett was watching her. As if he were impassively waiting for something, anything. *My God.* He knew. Even more startling was his reaction. Or rather his lack of one. What did that mean?

Lynn came out of the kitchen and glanced up at the TV. "Damned news," she muttered, picking up the remote and switching to a sports channel. "Too depressing."

Did Lynn know, too? Erica panicked. What if one of them had already called the Chicago police? She had to get out of here. "Lynn, I need to go home."

"You okay?" Lynn said. "You don't look so good."

"I feel like crap."

"Okay." Lynn rubbed her shoulders. "Let me know if you need anything."

Erica ran upstairs two steps at a time and picked up her phone. She hadn't checked her messages for a few days. She said a prayer as she dialed into her voice mail. *Please, Marie. Please, please, please. Talk to me.*

There was only one message that began with a long moment of silence. She sensed someone on the line and was about to delete it when a man's voice sounded. "Erica. I know you have Jason." Billy. "Better you bring him home, before I find you myself."

It wasn't the words themselves that raised goose bumps

on her arms and caused her to lose her breath. It was the menacing tone of his voice. He wasn't merely angry. He was raging. Erica had seen this kind of uncontrolled anger before in some of the men her mother had dated. She'd sworn that kind of abuse would never, never, ever happen to her. How Marie had fallen into it, she couldn't understand, but her sister must have lived with that, day in and day out.

With trembling fingers, Erica called Teddy's number.

"Yo, this is Teddy."

"Teddy, it's Erica," she whispered. "They're calling me a person of interest."

"Yeah, I found out about that a couple days ago, but since you won't give me a number—"

"What's going on?"

A long, slow sigh buffeted the phone receiver. "I called the son of an old friend. A cop. To see what I could find out."

"And?"

"You told me you left spur-of-the-moment. Never went home. Never packed anything."

"I didn't."

"Then why were your suitcases gone? Your clothes. Toiletries? Your car's missing, too. The cops are saying it looks like you planned to be gone for a long time."

"I don't… I didn't— Billy. He must've made look as if I'd packed." She hung her head, feeling desperate and so alone. "So now what?"

"You sit tight. The cops on this case are good men and good detectives."

"I want to come home, Teddy. I need to find Marie."

"That's a bad idea. You come back and he'll take Jason away from you."

"But I—"

"Erica, there's nothing you can do here." He paused. "I'm sticking with this until the end. Okay? I promise."

"Thanks." As Erica hung up the phone the little hope she'd been harboring that Marie might still be alive dwindled to near nothing. She slumped against the wall in the hallway of her apartment and cried.

"Erica." Suddenly Garrett was there, steadying her. "What happened?"

Another place, another time, another man, and she would've rubbed her eyes dry and stood on her own two feet. So far she'd handled everything life had thrown in her face, and this was no different. Except that Garrett was different. Except that she was more frightened than she'd ever been in her life.

One look into her eyes and he pulled her into his arms and held her while she cried. Held her without a word, without question, and she completely let go. Finally exhausted, she drew in a shaky breath and leaned back. "I'm sorry." She touched the big wet spot she'd left on his shirt.

He grabbed her hand and gripped it tightly. "I can't help you unless you tell me what's going on."

"I can't do that. It's not safe."

"You can trust me. You know it."

She shook her head and rubbed her cheeks dry.

"Erica Corelli," he whispered her real name.

She stared at him. He had known. "What do you want from me?"

"The truth."

"You won't believe me."

"Try me."

"There's too much at risk, Garrett."

"I've known who you are for weeks now. You don't start talking and I'll be putting in a call to the Chicago PD."

Still, she didn't say anything.

He grabbed her arms. "Tell me the truth, Erica, or I'll be making that call."

"If I tell you everything, what then? You're a cop. I'm a *person of interest.*"

"I can't help you if you don't tell me the truth."

She yanked away from him.

He reached into his pocket and pulled out his cell phone.

"No!" She put her hand over his and pushed the phone down. "Okay. The truth." She paced back and forth, calculating, measuring, looking for any possible escape. There wasn't one.

"I'm all you got, Erica. You have nothing to lose by telling me the truth and everything to gain."

"My name is Erica Corelli." Relief in letting go washed over her in great waves. Until now, she hadn't realized the toll all the lying and withholding of information had been taking. As tears trailed down her cheeks, she told him everything from the very beginning. The truth.

"You never went back to your apartment?"

"No. As soon as I got Marie's message I went to Jason's school. When she didn't meet us at the restaurant, I left town with Jason."

He had his cop face on. Brusquely, he wiped her tears away. "Do you know where she is now? Marie?"

"No. She'd call my cell if she could."

"Not necessarily. Cops can get those records. Billy could potentially see your in and outgoing calls."

"Can he find me here?"

"If you've used your cell phone." He nodded. "Have you?"

"No."

"Where is she? What do you think happened?"

"I don't know, but there *are* bad cops, you know."

He was silent a moment. "Yeah, I know."

"What if she's dead?"

"You don't know that."

"I'm starting to feel it. In here." She tapped her chest. "I might've been able to do something. If I'd gone to their house, if I'd stayed and confronted him. She needed me and I didn't do anything."

"You did what she asked. You protected Jason."

She rubbed her face dry. "You going to call the Chicago PD?"

He nodded.

"You can't! I trusted you—"

He grabbed her by the shoulders and held her still. "I need to find out what the detectives on the case know. If you're telling me the truth, you've got nothing to worry about."

CHAPTER SEVENTEEN

ERICA LAY IN BED, LETTING the morning breeze from the open window blow over her bare arms. Lynn had made her take the day off, claiming that next week, the first week of July, would be the busiest of the entire summer and she wanted Erica fresh and revived.

She glanced over at Jason, sleeping soundly on his side with his mouth wide-open. As she pulled the covers up and over his shoulders, she wondered if he was ever going to be comfortable sleeping alone in his own bed before they had to leave Mirabelle. The thought of having to pull up stakes and move depressed her more than she'd expected.

Rolling out of bed, she tiptoed down the hall and snuck into the kitchen. After starting a pot of coffee, she jotted down another one of her recipes in a notebook she'd started for Lynn. After all Lynn had done, the least Erica could do is make sure business at the pub wouldn't be interrupted if Erica had to leave quickly.

She cracked open the kitchen window and glanced out at the view of the water, letting her sleepy mind wander. It was early, the sun barely rising over that big water, but she could hear a boat motoring around the marina. Most likely, it was the ex-police chief, Jim Bennett, who apparently wintered in Florida and ran a charter fishing operation during the summer months. Nice life.

Waves rolling ashore, boat motors and gulls cawing, the

marina sounds were so different from the drone of traffic, horns honking and sirens wailing. A city the size of Chicago was never quiet, and it was a lonely place. So many people, but no one Erica had called friend. Not once had she really missed the big city, the clubs, nightlife or restaurants.

The realization that she might actually like living here on Mirabelle shocked her. This island's slow pace, the peace and quiet and, more than anything, the people, everything seemed to have come together to create an experience Erica hadn't expected. She'd imagined the islanders would be close-knit and exclusionary, but instead of shutting her out, each and every one of the people she'd met had welcomed her with open arms. Except for Garrett.

Her sense of tranquility dissolved at the thought of him. *Cop.* But it wasn't that simple. He'd promised to help her, and although a part of her was wary, a bigger part of her was beginning to trust him. And that, more than anything, scared her.

Her feelings toward Garrett were a jumble of conflicting emotions. One minute she felt like smacking his arm and the next she wanted to smack his lips. Without saying a word, he managed to rattle something deep inside her, roused something primal and visceral. Could that be all there was to it? Sex? Could it be as simple as getting laid and then all would be well? Unfortunately, there was only one man on this island in whom she was interested.

"Erica?" The soft and sleepy voice came from behind, interrupting her thoughts. Jason.

"Hey, there." She lifted him up and set him on the counter. "How you doing this morning?"

"Okay."

"Guess what? I have the day off."

"Can I still play with Brian?"

"I don't think so." Sarah's parents had come to help out with Brian since Sarah had three weddings this weekend.

This was the first time Erica had Jason to herself for an entire day since they'd come to the island. "He's doing something with his grandparents."

From the frown on Jason's face, he wasn't as excited about spending the day with her as she was about time with him. "Ah, come on." Erica nudged his arm. "It's my first day off in a long time and I want to do something with you."

"All right." That was a lackluster response if she'd ever heard one. He jumped down from the counter, wandered into the living room and picked up his video game.

"So what should we do? Jason?"

Not bothering to look up, he said, "I don't know."

"Oh, come on. You must have something in mind."

At that, he glanced at her, looking angry. "Why do you want to do something with me anyway?"

"Because… well, because I like you."

He went back to the game. "You're stuck with me, that's all."

"Hey."

"It's true." Without taking his fingers off the handheld device, or his gaze off the small screen, he kept talking. "The minute Mom comes to get me I won't see you again. Just like I didn't see you before. You don't want me. You'd rather work."

Some of what he'd said was right, the perceptive little stinker, but she'd been getting better at this mothering thing. She sat down on the coffee table in front of him. "Can you put the game away for a minute, so we can talk?"

He didn't say anything.

She waited.

Finally, he set it aside and stared at her.

"You're right. I have been working a lot. We needed the money."

Jason picked at the sofa cushion.

"Okay, I'll be honest. I wasn't sure what to do with you. How to act. How to be. What to say, do, not do. I'm not a mom."

"Is that why you never came to my house in Chicago?"

Erica had purposefully steered clear of bad-mouthing Billy, but—Billy be damned—the record needed some straightening. "The reason I didn't see you much back home didn't have anything to do with me not wanting to."

He looked away.

"I'm going to be straight with you." She paused. "I came to the hospital when you were born. Your dad took my gift and told you and your mom were sleeping. I didn't get it at the time, but that was the beginning of your dad keeping me away from you and your mom.

"I'd call Marie and suggest for us to get together for holidays or weekends here and there, but your dad usually had a reason why it wouldn't work. I always called on your birthdays. Did you know that?"

He didn't respond.

"Your dad always had an excuse why I couldn't talk to you," she said. "I sent cards and gifts, but I'm going to guess you didn't know that, did you?"

This time he shook his head.

She tapped the video game device he'd been playing. "I gave you this for your last birthday."

"My dad gave it to me."

"The wrapping paper. Did it have all different kinds of balls on it?"

"I don't—" He stopped, thinking. "Yeah. It did."

"I picked that paper because I didn't know your favorite sport."

"I remember." He looked up. As understanding dawned, tears glistened in his eyes. "It had footballs and soccer balls. Basketballs and baseballs."

She nodded. "I tried, Jason. I did."

"My dad is mean."

She let him come to his own conclusions.

"He hits my mom."

"Well, you don't have to worry about him anymore, okay?" She pulled him into a hug. "From now on, no matter what happens, nothing and no one will keep me away from you. I promise."

She'd do anything and everything possible to keep Billy away from Jason. Along with that realization came another. The day was going to come when she would have to leave Mirabelle. She'd miss it, the island, the people. She'd miss Garrett.

She let Jason go and smiled. "So what do you want to do today?"

He thought for a moment and then grinned up at her. "I've never gone horseback riding."

"There's a first time for everything!"

GARRETT HAD RETURNED Mrs. Gilbert's rolltop desk many weeks ago, only to have her drag out an old cedar chest in dire need of refinishing. She said she wanted it for one of the guest rooms and there was absolutely no hurry, and he hadn't the heart to refuse. Refinishing was a nice change from building or repairing, and the hand-carved scrollwork on the front of the chest had intrigued him.

Working from top to bottom, it'd taken him a few days to strip the entire piece and he was now sanding it, working from bottom to top. Pulling the sanding block away, he blew at the wood dust and ran his fingertips along the dry surface. Smooth as a baby's bottom. The finish was as good as it was going to get. He vacuumed up all the wood particles on the chest and the floor around him, and then went about rubbing on a light stain over the entire surface of the chest.

This was his favorite part, bringing out the grain on a good piece of wood. Slowly, with every stroke the chest morphed from pale nondescript chunks of wood into a work of art. The only thing he liked better was designing his own pieces with exactly the right types of wood. He'd been stockpiling some cherry, hoping to design something worthy of the fine wood.

When he finished staining Mrs. Gilbert's chest, he stood back and examined every square inch. All was even. He cleaned up and decided to head into the house for something to eat. As he stepped out of his workshop and into his yard, he heard voices coming up his drive.

"I want to see where this road goes." It was a child. A boy. "Come on. Please."

"I'm sure it's private." That was Erica.

Jason must be with her.

Garrett peered through the thickly leaved trees and discovered them on horseback. Walking to the top of the drive, he called out, "Hey, there."

"Garrett!" Jason and his old gray appaloosa trotted into the yard. "Is this where you live?"

"Yep. This is it." Garrett nodded, feeling a surprising sense of pride. His ten acres, loaded with a variety of thick old pines and hardwoods, was located on the outskirts of town and away from the typical tourist track. Although he'd paid a pretty penny for the place, by Chicago standards it'd been a steal. He wondered what they—Erica in particular— would think of it.

"We're exploring the island," Jason said.

"Well, it's about time."

Erica directed her horse, a chestnut mare with a white stripe down the center of its face and white stockings, next to Jason's. "Garrett. I'm sorry—"

"I'm glad you're here." He waved it off. "Sally McGregor's place is about the only property on the island you have to worry about trespassing on. Except for maybe one of the houses on the uninhabited side of the island. I've heard that guy gets prickly about visitors, but you two won't be making it all the way down there."

He grabbed the reins and held the horses still. "So Arlo let you take the horses out alone, huh?" he said, trying for some normalcy.

"I've been helping him in the stables, so the horses know me," Jason said. "We promised not to gallop."

"I was a little leery, but Arlo said these two are as gentle as they come." Erica grinned. "And know their own way home in case we fall off."

"Well, that's good to know."

Erica looked over his yard and home. "This is beautiful. I saw a painting once of a big log cabin just like your house at a store in the mall. You know, one of those places with bird feeders and cheesy mailboxes that look like fish?"

He nodded. "Do you want to come inside? Get a snack or something?" He glanced up at her. "Lord knows you've fed me enough."

She looked hesitant, as if entering his home would be too personal, as if it might change things between them. She was probably right. Things between them had changed enough already. A woman couldn't cry on a man's shoulder for damned close to a half an hour without things changing.

"You don't have to come in," he offered quickly. "That is, if you don't want. I can bring something outside. Something to drink?"

"I don't think—"

"I'm thirsty," Jason said.

"The least I can do is get you some water or a soda."

"All right."

They dismounted and Garrett tied the horse's reins to a tree branch in the shade near the edge of the yard. "I'll be right back." He went into the house, grabbed some water and a couple cans of soda and headed back outside. Erica was sitting on the porch steps and Jason was climbing onto an

A-framed wooden patio swing Garrett had made for the Rock Point Lodge.

"Is it okay if he swings on that?" she asked.

"Sure." He held out his selection of beverages. "He can test it out for me."

She grabbed a bottle of water. "You made it?"

He nodded. "Carl Andersen ordered ten of them for his hotel. That's one of the last two." He brought a can of soda to Jason and returned to sit next to Erica on the steps.

"It's beautiful."

"It's okay. A little too rustic for my tastes."

"You live in a log cabin."

"I'm a city boy, remember?"

She laughed. "So what are the winters like on Mirabelle? For a city boy?"

"Quiet. Peaceful. No traffic sounds. No trains." He looked away, remembering. "You can step outside your front door and hear the snow falling on the ground."

"Sounds nice."

"It's better than nice. It's like heaven."

"Heaven." An emotion he couldn't quite put his finger on passed over her features. "You don't mind the cold?"

"It's colder longer than in Chicago, but, no, I don't mind. Why? You thinking of staying past summer?"

She looked away. "I don't think so."

Strange, how the thought of her leaving didn't set well. Not anymore.

"Did you call the Chicago police?" she asked.

Although Garrett hadn't talked directly to Dave Hatcher or Gary Gable—two seasoned cops he'd collaborated with on a couple cases—he'd breathed a long sigh of relief when he'd found out several weeks ago the powers that be had put these two very smart and honest cops on the case.

"Mmm-hmm."

"And?"

"I've left a couple messages. We're playing phone tag."

"I don't want you to get into trouble."

"You don't need to worry about that. You have enough on your mind."

"What's in that building?" Jason asked, and pointed to his right.

"That's my workshop."

"Can we see it?"

"Sure."

Garrett walked across the yard and held open the door. This workshop for him had been a dream come true. In Chicago, he'd made do by parking in the driveway and using his one-car garage for woodworking, and he'd never had enough room to do the kinds of projects he'd wanted. Here, he could do whatever his heart desired.

"Don't touch anything, kiddo," Erica said.

"I won't."

As she glanced around, Garrett noticed her hair had grown, giving the ends a softer look. She seemed calmer, less likely to bolt at the slightest trouble. More and more, she was looking as if she was settling on Mirabelle.

"So this is where you build all your furniture, huh?" she asked.

"Mmm-hmm."

"Can I make something?" Jason asked.

"Sure," Garrett said. "If it's okay with Erica."

"Not today, kiddo. Garrett was probably in the middle of something and we've taken up enough of his time." She set her half-empty bottle of water on one of the workbenches as if she suddenly couldn't get out of there quickly enough.

Jason picked up a hammer off one of the workbenches and spun around in search of something to pound.

"Jason, don't touch any—"

He knocked the end of a board of cherry lying across two sawhorses and spun it toward the cement floor. Erica grabbed for the wood at the same time as Garrett and he bumped into her, knocking her off balance. He reached out to steady her, his hands landing on her waist, and held her up as she managed to catch the piece of cherrywood before it hit the cement floor.

"I'm sorry!" Jason cried.

"It's okay." Erica set the wood back on the sawhorses, turned around, and her gaze connected with his.

"Good save," he whispered, absorbing the feeling of the curve to her hips. For a moment he breathed in the scent of her hair. Sweet like oranges. No. Tangerines. "Thank you."

"I'm going back outside," Jason said, but Garrett barely heard him.

"It's a pretty piece of wood," she whispered. "What is it?"

He didn't want to let her go. Not yet. "Cherry."

"I thought cherry was dark," she said, an almost breathy quality to her voice.

"That's the stain."

"Oh."

His hands were still on her waist. Jason was outside and Garrett's back was to the door with Erica in front of him. If he pushed upward, he would no doubt drag her T-shirt along, baring her skin and no one would see except him. Before he could stop himself, his rough fingertips connected with warm soft skin. Upward even more and he'd hit the lower swell of her breasts. He wanted to feel her again, the weight of her in his hand.

The sound of his own breath puffing from his chest in a short burst snapped him out of it. "I'm sorry."

"There you go again." She picked up his hand and ran her fingers over his rough calluses. "Why is this so wrong?"

"You make me lose control." He looked into her eyes. "I touch you and I can't think. All I know is want. Need. You. Now."

"And that's bad?"

"For me it is. You have no idea what could happen."

"I think I have an idea." She pressed his hand to her breast. "And I'm not the least bit sorry. Or frightened."

He closed his eyes and grew instantly hard for her. She was killing him. Bending his head, he leaned toward her. Those lips. Just a quick kiss and—

The door creaked and they jumped away from each other.

"Erica, are you coming?" Jason asked. Clearly, he hadn't seen them touching.

"I'll be right there." She stepped away from Garrett.

Garrett ran a hand over his face, as if that would clear his head.

"We have to go." There she was again, that skittish colt. "Thanks for the…water." She dashed out of his workshop and into the yard.

"Yeah, thanks, Garrett."

Garrett took a moment to regroup, let his body settle back down and then followed them out. "No problem," he said, walking across the yard.

Erica went to her horse and stood there, looking at the stirrups.

"Need some help?" He came up behind her.

"No, I can—"

He held her at the waist and lifted her up into the saddle. She was so light he could probably do a few bicep curls with her on his arms.

None too gently, she shoved her feet in the stirrups and turned her horse toward the driveway. "We have to go, Jason."

Garrett turned toward the boy and helped him onto his saddle.

"Thank you," Jason said, turning his horse to follow Erica. "No problem."

With a deep sense of loss, he watched them trot back down his drive and out of sight. What was he going to do about her? Them?

He went back to his shop and glanced at the cherry lying there, waiting to be put to use. He ran his hands along the smooth grain and closed his eyes, remembering the feel of Erica's skin. He imagined her naked. On her side. Showing off her wonderful curves.

A bed. He was going to make a bed. With a headboard as smooth and curvy and beautiful as he knew Erica would be lying on her side. If all that work didn't drive her from his system, then he might have to do something about this crazy, all-consuming obsession for her. That's all it could be. A crazy, sure to be short-lived obsession.

CHAPTER EIGHTEEN

BETWEEN THE UPDATED décor and the new menu, business almost tripled at Duffy's Pub during the month of June. Some of the regulars were upset with the crowds destroying their favorite local haunt, but Lynn offered resident discounts for everything on the menu and at the bar, and all was well again.

Once the summer college crew had arrived, several servers, a couple more bartenders and cooks, Erica's role of head cook evolved into more of a general manager. She helped with scheduling and ordering and stocking, and when the kitchen closed down at ten, Lynn usually went home, leaving Erica to lock up.

Tonight, though, was the Fourth of July, and they'd been nonstop busy. After the kitchen closed, both Arlo and Lynn stayed to help Erica out at the bar. Although the island fireworks display over the marina had long since been played out, and the families with kids had gone home to bed, Duffy's Pub was still crowded and didn't look to be clearing out anytime soon.

Erica was busy getting one of the waitresses several rounds of drinks for her tables when three rough-looking characters, for Mirabelle at least, sat down at the bar. From their sunburns and T-shirts, they looked like fishermen who'd had a long day of too much fun. Little except their hairiness and size distinguished one from the other. The biggest one sported a goatee and also happened to be balding. The other two were cleanly shaven with full heads of hair, one graying, the other still dark.

She walked toward them. "What can I get for you boys?"

"Well, sugar," the balding one with the goatee said, "I'm sure there's a lot you could do for us."

The other two guys laughed. None of the three looked as if he was experiencing any pain, but it was hard to tell whether or not they'd already reached their limits at one of the other restaurants or bars on the island. If Erica had been back in Chicago, she may not have served them, but here on Mirabelle she didn't need to worry about any of them jumping behind the wheel of a car. "You boys staying on the island?"

"We're sleeping it off on my boat docked in the marina, sugar, so gimme a martini. So dry I only want you to look at the bottle of vermouth." Baldy chuckled.

"I'll take a beer," dark hair said.

"Same here," said gray guy.

Erica prepped the drinks and set them down in front of the men. "You want a tab?"

"That I would," Baldy said. "And I'd like a smile to go with my cocktail." He grabbed Erica's wrist. "Lemme see a big one. Come on, sugar."

She couldn't help sizing him up. If push came to shove, she couldn't take this guy. He was too damned big. She gave him as tolerant a smile as she could muster. "Let go of me."

"Oh, but you feel so good." He ran his hand up her forearm, sending prickles of warning up through her shoulder and down her spine.

"Hey, fellas." Arlo came over. "Why don't you just enjoy your drinks?"

She tugged again and the hulk let her go, but she couldn't shake the feeling that she needed to wash her arm. She glanced up at Arlo and, by unspoken agreement, they switched stations. Arlo took the loudmouth and his two friends and she stayed on the other side of the bar.

Less than half an hour later, Arlo was busy at the waitress station when from the corner of her eye she saw Baldy waving his arm. "Hey, Erica!"

Dammit. One of the servers had probably given him her name. She walked over, making sure to keep away from his reach.

"What's it gonna take to get another martini?"

"What about you two?" She glanced at the other men.

"I'll take another beer."

"Me, too."

She glanced at Arlo and he nodded, letting her know he hadn't served them, and she prepped another round of drinks. She noticed the hulk get up from his stool and breathed a sigh of relief that she would be able to deliver the drinks without having to hassle with him again.

There was movement at the end of the bar and something touched her arm. Before she realized what was happening, the hulk had tugged her out from behind the bar and was towering over her.

"Look at you. Sexiest thing on this island."

That ugly face moved toward hers and Erica reacted. She smashed her knee into his midsection and pushed his shoulders. He was too tall. She'd missed his groin, pissed him off and forced his two buddies to cover his back.

"Now that—" he grabbed her wrists and pressed her back against the wall "—wasn't very nice."

FINALLY, AFTER A VERY LONG day monitoring and shutting down the more disruptive of the island's Fourth of July revelry, Garrett was off duty. He'd changed out of his uniform and into khakis and a T-shirt and was about to head home and relax when the call from Duffy's Pub came into dispatch. At the mention of Erica's name, he immediately switched gears.

"I'll send someone right over," the dispatcher said.

"I'm going, too," he called, grabbing his gun, cuffs and badge.

After running full out the six blocks to the pub, he was right behind Herman and one of their part-time officers as they rushed through the door. Quickly, he glanced around. Most of the pub's patrons were still at their dinner tables, so things couldn't have gotten too far out of hand.

He glanced toward the bar. Three men surrounded Erica, not a one of them less than a foot taller than she. The sight of her, scared, but stubborn as hell, sent an immediate jet fuel-like shot of adrenaline pumping through him. If they hurt her, manhandled her in any way…

He held himself back. Barely. *Settle down, G.T. Settle.* He wasn't in uniform and in his current state of mind and body any involvement on his part wouldn't be pretty. Better to let his officers defuse things while he hung back and surveyed the situation. Let his boiling blood cool to a simmer.

"Police!" Herman yelled. "Leave the lady alone, boys."

The biggest asshole was standing right in front of Erica, looking extremely pissed. The other two seemed appeared ready to back up their man. Arlo and Lynn were behind the bar. A couple of waitresses were standing by, staring. The people at the tables closest to the action were quickly becoming aware something was wrong.

"If you need help," a man whispered behind Garrett. "I'm a cop with the Chicago PD, and I got your back."

"I'll let you know," Garrett said, without taking his eyes off the disturbance.

"Now everyone settle down," Herman said. "Okay?"

One of the three men turned around and moved fast. Two swings and Herman was down for the count. The other guy moved toward the part-time officer. The young man freaked. He sputtered and fumbled for his gun. The man swung, hit him solid in the gut, and the officer doubled over and fell to the ground. Sucking air.

Three against one. Garrett had faced worse odds.

The big guy laughed and leaned in toward Erica. "Now how 'bout that kiss?"

Erica remained perfectly still. *Good girl.*

Arlo picked up a chair and went at one of the men. Garrett used the distraction to make his first move.

"Don't even try it, old man!" One of the men whipped out a hand and yanked the chair out of Arlo's hands.

Garrett surprised the other one with a kick to the gut. As he went down, Garrett grabbed Herman's cuffs and swiftly secured the man's wrist to the bar railing.

One down, two to go.

The other guy came at Garrett with the chair he'd taken from Arlo. He swung. Garrett ducked. The chair smashed to pieces on the bar. He came up, grabbed asshole number two's shoulders, yanked him down and kneed him in the face. The satisfying sound of bone breaking echoed through the suddenly quiet bar. A solid punch to the kidneys had the man groaning on the floor.

"Lynn! Cuff him." Garrett tossed her his cuffs and then focused on the big guy.

He watched Garrett, gripping Erica's wrist in his beefy hand. "You come any closer, and I might have to hurt her." The guy whipped Erica in front of him and cinched an arm around her neck.

"Let her go," Garrett bit out. "Then—maybe—I won't *kill* you."

"I'm going to make my way outside." The guy dragged Erica with him down the back hallway toward the emergency exit. "Let me get to the marina. And I'll let her go."

Arlo came to as the man was moving past him. He grabbed the guy's leg, making him stumble. Garrett moved. He shoved Erica out of the way and rammed the man. The guy threw a couple punches at Garrett, connecting once or twice. Garrett tried to subdue him, but it wasn't happening. Time to get tough. He pushed the guy backward down the hall and outside through the emergency exit.

The minute the idiot charged Garrett, grabbing him around the waist and smashing him into the wall, that was it. Garrett let loose. He punched the man in the gut, the face, the gut again. "So you like to pick on women, huh?" He hit him again, and again and again.

Vaguely, Garrett was aware of someone coming through the back door. "Garrett." The whisper barely penetrated the sound of blood rushing through his brain.

The guy fell to his knees.

"Not such a big man anymore, are you?" Garrett said, air pumping in and out of his lungs. He felt like an animal. Enraged and mindless.

"Stop." Erica. Her hand on his arm was soft, but insistent. "It's over."

The jerk staggered to his feet, made one last lunge toward Garrett. Garrett backed up and let him fall on his face.

"You all right?" she asked. "Garrett?"

He turned around and swallowed. "*You're* all right. That's all that matters." If this man had hurt her, no one would've been able to keep Garrett from ripping him apart. His hands shook. He glanced down at the blood, his mixed with the other guy's, covering his knuckles. He'd almost killed a man. Again.

"Garrett." She touched his arm.

He pulled away, couldn't look at her. Shame, dark and heavy, closed over him. "Get up!" He yanked the guy to his feet and pushed him toward the street. "Let's see how you like sleeping it off behind bars."

CHAPTER NINETEEN

IN HIS WORKSHOP, Garrett sanded the cherry, one long sweep after another. He might not be able to deny the fury he'd felt last night, but he could work it off. He could use the wood, use the easy comfort of the mindless routine to lose himself, to forget the world and its ugliness. Only this ugliness wasn't going away.

The all-consuming rage that had jolted through him when the jerk had grabbed Erica had clung to him through the night, infusing his dreams with darkness, charging his body with tension. Sanding wasn't going to cut it this morning. The reality that he had no business becoming a husband to any woman, let alone a father, sat on his shoulders like a four-hundred-pound barbell. He may not have killed that man, but he, and he alone, had killed his dream last night.

He stalked over to his table saw, flicked on the power switch and grabbed a length of pine. No way was he risking ruining his inventory of cherry or black walnut, not this morning. He measured as little as possible, cut, drilled and hammered as much as possible, and at the end of a good hour of focused concentration, he had a pine bookcase.

By no means was it a perfect piece of furniture. He'd pounded the soft wood too much in most places, denting it. They made trendy lamps out of pounded metal, why not furniture out of pounded wood. He grabbed his mallet and whacked it a few more times. It made him feel better and might even make for an interesting look. He'd probably stain it up and varnish it for the hell of it.

He pounded. Pounded. Pounded. When a hand touched his shoulder he spun around, his mallet in the air. Erica stood, looking at him.

"What do you want?" He was growling at her, but that's what she got for sneaking up on him.

She didn't even back away. "I brought you something to eat." She held a thick pizza box in her hands.

The smell alone made his mouth water and his stomach grumble. He hadn't eaten since dinnertime yesterday. "I'm not hungry."

"You're not hungry for a homemade Chicago-style pizza?" *Damn.*

"Fine." She set it down on the workbench. "I'll leave. You can eat later." Her gaze shifted to his hands and she reached out, pulling one toward her.

He pulled back, but her grip was surprisingly firm.

"You should get something on these cuts," she whispered.

"And you should be frightened of me."

"I'm not." She pulled his hand to her lips and gently kissed each busted-up knuckle.

"Erica, I could've killed that ma—"

"That man was big and mean and drunk. He scared me to death. I don't know what he was planning on doing and I'm glad I didn't have to find out."

"If you hadn't stopped—"

"No." She shook her head. "You would've stopped yourself."

"You don't know that." He tried to pull his hand away, but still she wouldn't let go. "You can never know what's inside a man."

"I think I understand what's inside you."

"You think—"

"I've known blackhearted men," she said. "My mother dated more than I care to remember. Some made her promises they never kept. Some said horrible things to her. Some beat her. And Marie and me." She placed his hand against her cheek and flattened her own hand against his, and all he could think about was how he might scratch her soft skin. "The one who knocked her around the most was a cop."

That explained a lot.

"He only lived with us for a couple of months, but it was enough. One night, Marie and I woke up in the middle of the night and heard him hitting her. I couldn't stand it. I hopped up, made Marie slide under the bed and wait for me, then I tiptoed down the stairs. He had her cornered in the kitchen. He backhanded her and then punched her in the gut. I stood there on the steps, paralyzed. I never did anything to make him stop. I was eight, and I've never gotten that uniform out of my mind."

Well, he'd wanted the truth and he'd sure as hell gotten it. "I'm sorry," he said, as if that could make up for the fact that he'd been born a man.

"*You* have nothing to be sorry for." She glanced up at him, the challenge back in her eyes. "Because you are not that kind of man."

Maybe not, but he was close.

"You know what the worst part was about seeing my own mother getting beaten?"

He swallowed, unable to imagine. His father had used a heavy hand, spanking him and his brothers now and again, but he'd never hit their mother.

"The worst part was being too scared to do anything about it." Tears fell down her pale cheeks. "You, Garrett, you don't stand back. You don't wait. You're not scared mindless. You protect. You defend."

There was nothing he could say, nothing that would help her understand.

"A while back, you told Jason that it was never okay to hit. Well, that advice needs an amendment. It's never okay to hit, unless you're protecting yourself or someone else." Reaching up on her toes, she kissed his chin, in a touch as soft as it was sweet.

He stood, ramrod straight, trying not to lean into her, but when she wrapped her hands around his neck and drew him down to her he let her kiss his mouth.

Her lips were gentle and loving, and he kissed her back softly, slowly, but then their tongues met and her breathing quickened and he felt the current of need she stirred up deep in his soul. The strength of that need scared the shit out of him. "You need to go."

"Garrett—"

"Go!" he yelled, wanting to frighten her, wanting to turn her away from him as his dreams of a happy, contented life here on Mirabelle shattered to pieces.

She didn't jump, just stood there, looking at him with tenderness in her eyes.

He couldn't stand it. "Don't you get it? I could be that cop who beat your mother."

"Never."

"Tell that to the guy I almost killed in Chicago. Tell that to his family. I almost kill a man and all I got was a suspension. With pay. They cheered my first day back at the precinct. Patted me on the back, gave me high fives. A man—no, a husband and a son—was paralyzed because of me and they cheered."

"You were doing your job."

"But no one understands what was going through my mind that day."

"Tell me."

"I wanted to kill him. One less problem on this earth."

"Don't you think every single one of us has had those kinds of thoughts? I know I have."

"Yeah. The difference is that you don't carry a gun." He ran his hands through his hair. "That's why I came to Mirabelle. I wanted the Chicago cop I'd become…gone. Out of my life. I didn't ever want to think like him again. You know what? I'd done a damned good job of getting rid of him until you showed up. You brought him back, Erica. One look at you and my thoughts go wild. I want you every which way but Sunday. Even now." He closed his eyes. "It's everything I can do to keep my hands off you."

"What's wrong with feeling that way? Why is that so bad?"

"Because I'd tear someone apart if I thought he was keeping me from you. You bring out the worst in me. You bring out a man I don't want to be." Mirabelle had changed him, but what he felt for Erica had thrown him back to square one. "So I'm asking you… please. Stay away from me."

ERICA STALKED DOWN THE hill, Garrett's words raging through her mind like gasoline on a fire. She had never, in her life, been this agitated over a man. He made her feel so angry, so frustrated, so…small.

She stopped and hung her head, tears popping up from nowhere. She could stand a lot of abuse from people. Her skin had gotten pretty damned thick through the years, but to have the first man in a very long while she'd grown to respect, a man she almost trusted, a man she was actually starting to have feelings for turn on her in this way was too much.

She charged into the pub's kitchen and stopped outside Lynn's office. "Can I use your computer?"

Lynn glanced up from some paperwork on her desk. "Sure. What's the matter?"

"I need to search for something."

"Search? What do you mean?"

"Boy, you really don't know much about computers."

Erica moved past Lynn's chair, knelt in front of the keyboard and screen, and showed Lynn how to perform a search. "You can find out almost anything. Phone numbers, answers to trivia questions that are driving you nuts, old friends even."

"What are you looking for?"

"Old news articles on something." Erica hesitated. "Garrett. He said he almost killed a man in Chicago."

"Oh, that." Lynn waved her hand dismissively. "Our last police chief, Jim Bennett, looked into that before he hired Garrett. That guy was connected to a murderer."

"Garrett said he paralyzed the man."

"Well, that's not the whole story, but I don't remember the specifics. That guy was all drugged up on something when he attacked Garrett's partner."

With Lynn looking over her shoulder, Erica ran a search on Garrett and found several news articles on alleged police brutality in Chicago, one on Garrett in particular. She remembered hearing about it on the news, seeing the photos in the paper and immediately dismissing the situation as another bad cop practically getting away with murder.

Now, she read the articles in an entirely new light. Garrett and his partner were looking to question a man about a murder that had taken place the night before. He wasn't a suspect, but there were eyewitness accounts that he'd been with the suspect around the time of the crime.

When they approached the man at his house with a search warrant, the guy bolted upstairs. While the man's wife pleaded with them to come back another time, that her husband was ill and would calm down if they left, they had no choice but to corner the guy in the second floor of the home. High on meth, the man attacked Garrett's partner. Garrett had beaten the guy and the man had fallen through a window in front of the wife and three children, breaking his back.

Garrett's partner was later found to have two broken ribs and bruised kidneys from the altercation, and after several weeks Garrett was cleared through an internal investigation and fully reinstated. The man who had attacked them was permanently paralyzed.

There was a picture of Garrett dressed in a black suit and tie coming out of a courthouse with, most likely, an attorney. Garrett, with gaunt cheeks and dark circles under his eyes, looked as if he hadn't slept or eaten for weeks.

"Bad cops don't agonize over hurting someone," Erica whispered.

"No, they don't," Lynn said. "If Garrett hadn't been here last night, I'm not sure what would've happened."

"He's a good man," Erica said softly. How could she get him to believe that if he kept pushing her away?

LATE MONDAY, BILLY SAT at his desk, listening to his voice mail. One of the other detectives came in and sat down a few desks away. "So how'd your vacation go?" Billy asked the man, only half listening to some woman involved in one his cases blubbering away on the message left on his phone.

"Perfect. I love that place. Any news on your wife?"

"Eh. Naw." Billy was so sick of people asking him. "Where'd you go again?" He deleted the message and went on to the next.

"Wisconsin. Mirabelle Island on Lake Superior."

Since the time Al Capone and his cronies had built rustic hideouts in northern Wisconsin, the state had been considered Chicago's playground, but Billy had never understood people's fascination for the woods.

"It's a straight shot north on Highway 51," the detective went on. "Feels like it takes forever to get there, but once you do, it's all relaxation."

"Sounds boring."

"Exactly what I need. Except for this time. There was a real nasty bar fight on the Fourth. As good as any you get down here, that's for sure."

"You break it up?"

"Didn't get the chance. Their police chief nailed the guy. Normally, Mirabelle's the quietest place on earth."

"Vegas, baby. That's my style."

"Not me, man. The wife and I been going to Mirabelle every year since the kids moved out. Now they've got a golf course, pools, and some of the best food I've ever eaten. Better Italian than anyplace down here."

"You're so full of shit."

"I swear." He put his hand on his chest. "Some Chicago chef is taking a walk on the quiet side."

"No way."

"Cheryl had fettuccini with the creamiest white sauce. Different than anything I've had down here. A little sweet-ness to cut that rich, heavy flavor, you know."

"Yeah. I've had something like that before." For Marie's last birthday, her sister had brought over some new recipe she'd concocted. "Did it have scotch in it?"

"How would I know? I like what I had better. Some tomatoey dish with peppers, artichokes, olives and…"

"Eggplant?"

"Yeah! That was it."

Well, I'll be damned. Erica went to Mirabelle. That's where that Polaroid picture had been taken of Marie with her sister and mother. Billy pushed back from his desk and grabbed his suit coat.

"Where you going?"

"All this talk of food has me hungry. See you later." Billy walked away from the detective's desk.

Time for a road trip.

CHAPTER TWENTY

THE NIGHT WAS RAINY and too cold for the likes of July, so business was slow in the pub. The kitchen was closed, Erica was helping Lynn out at the bar, and Jason was sound asleep upstairs. Given how busy the bar had become, the three stooges had elected to switch their customary gathering night from Fridays to Mondays. Erica set a couple beers down on the bar in front of Bob Henderson and Dan Newman, and was freshening Doc's club soda when the front door opened, letting in a blast of cool, wet air.

With a smile on her face, she glanced up ready to welcome whoever had decided to brave the elements. A man, his head down and wearing a baseball cap, stepped in and shook the dampness off his jacket. The second he looked up she felt the blood drain from her face. Billy Samson. He caught her gaze and the beer mug slipped from her hand, smashing onto the floor. He headed straight for the bar.

"Whoa!" Lynn said. "Can't believe you haven't done that before tonight, but I guess there's a first time for everything."

Erica bent down and picked up a large chunk of broken glass, a thick bottom piece with one edge rounded and the other jagged and pointed.

Lynn watched her put it in the front pocket of her apron, then glanced into her face. "You okay?"

"Call Garrett," Erica whispered, clenching her jaw. She

did not want Lynn, or anyone else for that matter in this bar to get hurt, but if push came to shove, she wasn't going to be backing away from trouble.

Billy took one of the empty stools directly in front of her and nodded at the three older men on the other side of the bar. "A little chilly out there."

"Ah, that's nothing," Bob said. "Wait a couple months."

Billy turned his full attention on her. "Hello, Erica."

"Billy."

Lynn glanced between the two of them. "I'll go get a broom and dustpan." As Lynn slipped into the kitchen, Erica hoped her friend understood the direness of this situation.

"Gimme a beer," Billy said.

Erica popped the cap off the nearest bottle and set it in front of him. "What are you doing here, Billy?"

"Oh, I think you know."

She glared at him. "Where's Marie?"

"I was hoping you might be able to tell me."

"Liar." He was only saying that for the benefit of everyone else at the bar. Erica swallowed and leaned over the bar. "If you've hurt one hair on her head, I swear, I'm going to come after you."

He laughed. "I'd like to see that," he said, and then took a long pull off the bottle. "Now, where's my son?"

"I don't know what you're talking about."

Lynn came back with a broom and swept up the broken glass. "Still pretty wet outside, huh?" she said. "Is it looking like it might clear up?"

"Oh, I think it's going to get worse," Billy said. "Before it gets better."

While Billy drank his beer, Lynn, for some reason, started up with some inane small talk, and it was all Erica could do to not lunge over the bar at him. Her nerves had had about all they could take when Garrett walked through the door. Without bothering to shake the rain off his shoulders, his gaze darted back and forth, assessing the situation. He sat down a few stools away from Billy.

Anyone who didn't know him wouldn't have noticed his slight shortness of breath or the sheen of sweat on his upper lip, but it was clear to Erica that he'd run all the way down the hill. He'd also managed to put on his uniform jacket with his badge clearly displayed on the outside pocket. Erica had never been so happy to see a man, any man, before. She could've kissed him, right then and there.

"Hey, Erica. Lynn," he said, sounding surprisingly calm. "How's it going tonight?"

"So far, so good," Erica said. "What can I get for you, *Chief?*"

He gave her a slight, reassuring smile. "Water's fine."

Billy glanced back and forth between Erica and Garrett, and then settled on Erica. "Made some new friends, I see."

Erica let Garrett's badge speak for itself.

"I got one of those, too." Billy stuffed his hand into his back pocket and threw his own shield onto the bar.

Garrett made a show of studying the ID. "Detective. Chicago PD. Good for you. What are you doing on Mirabelle?"

"She's got my son, Jason."

The couple tourists at the bar seemed oblivious to the building tension, but at the tone of Garrett's voice, Dan, Doc and Bob quieted and focused on their conversation.

"Who does?" Garrett asked calmly.

"Her." Billy stabbed a finger in Erica's direction.

"What makes you think that?"

"Couple months ago, Jason disappeared from school the same day she did."

"Hmph." Garrett grunted. "That doesn't sound like a lot of evidence to go on. How long you been a detective?"

"Look. She's got Jason. I know it."

"Why would she have your son?"

"How the hell should I know? Can't have one of her own, has to take someone else's. I know she's got him. Somewhere on this island."

Garrett held the man's gaze. "Lynn, you ever seen a kid with Erica?"

Lynn held Billy's gaze for a moment before shifting to Garrett. "A kid?" she said. "With Erica? No, sir."

"Bob, Dan, Doc? Did Erica move to Mirabelle with a kid?"

They all shook their heads.

"Naw."

"She doesn't have a kid."

"No, siree."

It was all Erica could do to hold back the sudden rush of tears. These people who hardly knew her and Jason were protecting them.

"I know everyone who comes and goes on this island," Garrett said. "She isn't hiding anyone."

Billy glanced from one face to the next and nodded. "I get it. You've made lots of friends, Erica." Then he stared at Garrett. "I want to see her place."

"You got a *valid* search warrant?"

Billy remained silent for a moment. "I can get one."

"Erica, you want to show Billy your apartment?"

"No."

"Why, you—" He made a show of lunging across the bar.

Lynn stepped protectively in front of Erica, but Erica put her hands gently on the older woman's shoulders and moved her aside. "Thanks, Lynn, but Billy only beats up women in private."

Garrett slammed his gun onto the bar. "This how you want to handle the situation?"

The tourists at the bar backed away, and everyone in the restaurant seemed to turn toward the commotion. The only sound was the jukebox playing in the background.

Billy glanced at the gun and went still. "I got one of those, too, but I know how to use mine."

"Good for you."

"I'd be willing to bet a cop in a town this size doesn't have much of an occasion for a gun. You know how to use that, Chief?"

"Fifteen years on the Chicago PD, the last seven in Homicide," Garrett said softly, "would indicate, yes. Maybe you've heard of me. Garrett Taylor."

Recognition dawned in Billy's eyes. "I remember. You were in the news a while back."

"Yes, I was."

Billy leaned back, keeping his hands on the bar.

"Now that we understand each other." Garrett holstered his gun. "You get a *valid* warrant, Detective Samson, and then you can see Erica's apartment. Until then, you get off my island. Now."

Dan stood. "Want some help there, Garrett?"

"Making sure that asshole gets on a boat?" Bob added.

"If you boys are offering, I won't turn you down."

"We're right behind you." Doc had already made it to the other side of the bar.

Never taking his eyes off Billy, Garrett got on his radio and told his dispatch to arrange for a water taxi. Then he stood and, keeping his distance, signaled for the door. "Time to go."

Slowly, Billy stood and finished his beer, flipped a five spot onto the counter and focused in on Erica. "This isn't over, *sis*. I'll be back."

WHATEVER YOU DO, TAKE care of Jason.

Marie had left a lot of unanswered questions in the wake of her disappearance, but one thing had been clear; she believed Billy would hurt Jason. And since they'd been on Mirabelle, Jason had admitted to the abuse. There was no way Erica could stand back and let Billy take back his son. Garrett had no sooner escorted Billy out the door than Erica untied her apron and threw it onto the counter. "I'm sorry, Lynn, I have to leave."

"No, you don't," Lynn said, clearly concerned.

"I don't have time to explain now, but I'll call you."

"Erica." Lynn grabbed her arms and held for a moment. "Whatever's going on, you can count on us to help."

Erica had already seen the proof, the way the islanders had stood up for her with Billy, but she couldn't risk anything happening to Jason. "I know, Lynn. I can't tell you how much it means to me, but this is…bad, and I don't have time—"

"I know enough for now."

"I've been lying. You don't know anything."

"I know Zach's real name is Jason. I know you're his aunt not his mother."

Erica's heart raced.

"I know you love Jason. I know that man who was in here is not a good person. As far as I'm concerned, the rest of the story can wait for another time. For right now, I trust you've had a good reason for doing what you've done. All you need to do is trust back."

"I…I…can't."

Erica ran double-time all the way up the steps to their apartment. She couldn't help Marie, wherever she was, but she was going to make damned sure that Billy Samson never hurt Jason again. She pushed open the door, ran down the hall to Jason's room and shook him awake. "Jason?" She grabbed her nephew's hand.

Groggy with sleep, he rolled over. "What?"

"We have to leave the island."

"Why?"

"I can't explain right now. We have to go."

Jason's eyes turned round with fear. "It's my dad, isn't it?"

Erica didn't know how to tell him.

"You said he wouldn't find us."

"I did my best, Jason, I'm sorry."

"But I like it here. I don't want to leave."

"We don't have time to waste." She pulled his suitcase from under the bed and opened it. "Pack what you can fit in there. Only the most important things."

While Jason packed, Erica ran into her room, grabbed her bag from the closet and pulled out all the cash she'd been saving since she'd arrived on Mirabelle and the set of fake driver's licenses she'd had made before leaving Chicago. When a knock sounded on the outside apartment door, she jumped and nearly fell over backward.

"Erica!"

She never thought she'd be so happy to hear Garrett's gruff voice. She ran to the door and called out, "Is he gone?"

"I put him on a water taxi."

She yanked open the door.

"Herman's watching to make sure he doesn't come back."

"Oh, he'll be back, all right."

Garrett glanced down at the cash in her hands and the fake IDs. "You don't need to run."

"Yes, I do." She ran down to her bedroom, pulled the suitcase out from under the bed and threw things inside.

"I've dealt with plenty of guys like him before," Garrett said. "You'll be okay."

She glanced into Jason's bedroom. "I wouldn't put it past him to kill me," she whispered.

"Erica," he said, holding her shoulders. "I won't let anything happen to you, or Jason. I *will* protect you. Both. The people of this island will not let that man get to either of you."

Erica wanted to believe him. With everything inside her, she'd grown to care for the Mirabelle residents, especially the Duffys, but she couldn't take this last step. "I have to go."

"This is exactly what he wants you to do," Garrett whispered. "You better believe he'll be watching and waiting."

"Then I won't dock at Bayfield. I'll go to Washburn."

"That won't make a difference. When he finds out you're not on the island, and he will find out, he'll track you down. And Jason. Then what?"

"I can take care of us."

"You'll do your damnedest, I know." The respect and admiration in his eyes nearly broke her resolve. "You've eluded a cop for months. That's some feat. Eventually he'll find you. You'll have to run again. And again. He won't stop. You know it."

Hadn't she told her sister the exact same thing? And where had it gotten Marie? Hopefully, not dead.

"What kind of life is that for Jason? For you?" He reached for her arms and held her still. "You always looking over your shoulder and that boy always afraid. Is that what you want? For him?"

Erica had seen the fear in Jason's eyes. That little boy deserved to laugh and have fun, deserved to grow up without fear. She had to be honest. She was frightened. "I don't know what to do."

"Make your last stand here on Mirabelle. With me. With other people who've grown to care about you. People who will protect you."

"I can't—"

"Erica, you saw the way Lynn, Doc, Bob and Dan stood

up for you in the bar. No one on this island is going to let anything happen to you. I won't let anything happen to you. Or Jason." He made her look into his eyes. "Trust me."

Trust him. What he was asking her to do defied her nature. She'd been alone so long, fending for herself, how was she supposed to step aside and let someone else take over? "I don't know how."

"I'm not asking you to stop fighting. I'm asking you to fight back. With help. You stay ready. You stay strong and you watch for him."

Jason had to come first.

"Erica?" Her nephew stood in the doorway, looking frightened. "I don't want to leave."

"I know, kiddo." She held out her arms and he ran into them, almost knocking her over.

Garrett looked down at them. "All you have to do is believe, trust, that I've got your back."

Amazingly, she did. This stubborn, tough as nails, cynical cop was exactly like her. And he had a big gun. No one was going to get through him. "Okay." One word had never been so hard to say. "What do you want us to do?"

"Finish packing your things. You can't stay here."

"You said we shouldn't leave."

"You have to leave this apartment. Not the island. I can't protect you and Jason here. Can't see the windows. Too close to shore."

"Then where do we go?"

"With me. You're staying with me."

For a moment, Erica could only stare at him. "Jason, why don't you go finish packing?" After he'd left the room, she turned toward Garrett, shaking her head. "The two of us sleeping under the same roof is *not* a good idea."

"You think I'm not aware of the inherent complication in this plan?" He looked away. "We don't have a choice."

"*You* have a choice. You don't want to do this. You don't need—"

"Yes, I do."

"Arlo and Lynn? Sarah and Brian? Hannah? They all have room. I can stay with one of them."

"You want to put any of them at risk?" Garrett whispered. "Billy won't be coming back during the day. He'll come at night when Jason is sleeping. The only place I can ensure your safety is at my house."

He was right, and she knew it.

"I won't touch you, I swear," he whispered.

Unfortunately, she wasn't sure she could make the same promise.

CHAPTER TWENTY-ONE

WITH ERICA AND GARRETT each holding one of Jason's hands, Garrett led the way to his house. Once they'd left the relative security of the town center, Erica seemed spooked by every sound, a rustling in the bushes, the hooting of an owl, branches swaying in the wind. After the events of the evening, he couldn't blame her, but he knew Samson wouldn't be stupid enough to try anything tonight.

Finally, they reached his yard where golden yellow light streamed from his kitchen window. They'd taken no more than a few steps when a corner porch light flicked on.

Erica quickly pulled back.

"It's okay. That's a motion detector, and I left the house in a hurry, so the lights are still on." He climbed the porch steps, unlocked his front door, and went in first to make sure they were alone. "Come on." As they followed him inside, he tried not to watch Erica's reaction. Normally, he wouldn't have cared what anyone thought of his home, but he wanted her to like the place.

Jason looked around, and his gaze, albeit a bit of a sleepy one, landed on the big-screen TV in the family room. "Wow," was all he said.

Erica stepped through the threshold and stopped.

With knotty pine walls and a dark plank floor, the place was rustic. Granite countertops and new appliances softened the cabin-y feel, but the brown leather furniture, a big-screen

TV and lack of anything even remotely resembling a knick-knack made it look, he supposed, like a man's house.

"Things are a little messy." Shutting the door and locking it, he went around picking up magazines and mail, a coffee cup here or a water glass there. "I wasn't expecting visitors."

"It's beautiful."

"It is what it is."

"Did you do the remodeling?"

He shook his head. "The people that owned it before me gutted the place and started from scratch. I've made all the furniture, though, except for the upholstered pieces."

Jason yawned and headed for the couch.

"Jason, let's get you back to bed," Garrett said.

"Good idea," Erica agreed. "You can watch TV in the morning, okay?"

He nodded.

"Where to?" Erica asked.

"Upstairs." Garrett led the way through the kitchen and pointed toward the guest bedrooms in the back of the house. "I'll be sleeping back there in case either of you need me." Then they went up the wide staircase and into the larger of the two upstairs bedrooms. "You guys are in here." He had a king-sized bed, so Erica would sleep more comfortably here than in the double bed in the other room. "I changed the sheets the other day, so they should be okay for the night anyway."

He set their suitcases near the bed.

"This is your room." Erica glanced around. "We can't stay here."

"This is where I want you." In more ways than one, he thought ruefully.

"Why?"

"Because I need to be downstairs. I need to know what's going on at the entry level."

She turned toward him. "Garrett—"

"That's an order."

Jason had already climbed into the big bed and was snuggling in. No doubt he'd be down for the count within minutes.

"Do you need anything?"

"No," she said, but she didn't look pleased.

Too bad. "One more thing." He pulled her into the hallway. "I didn't want to say anything before, but you're going to have to talk to the Chicago police."

She looked away. "Billy will tell the detectives on the case where I am, won't he?"

Garrett nodded. "You'll have some explaining to do."

"I don't have anything to hide, but I won't leave Jason alone and I won't take him back to Chicago."

"I'll make a few calls. See if I can get the detective assigned to the case to come here." He turned to go.

"Garrett?"

He stopped.

"I won't tell them Jason is here. I won't let them take him away from me. If you can't deal with that, then maybe he and I had better leave."

"I can deal with that. For now."

She reached up and touched his cheek. "Thank you. For everything."

He stepped back, putting distance between them. "It's no more than I'd do for anyone else." He knew that wasn't true. Before he succumbed to the urge to touch her back in a lot of places much more intimate than her cheek, he hightailed it down the stairs.

ERICA AWOKE THE NEXT morning to the sounds of someone quietly moving around downstairs. After a momentary sense of panic passed, she calmed herself with the sounds of water running, cabinets softly closing, and the morning news on the TV. Garrett was awake, and she was in his bedroom, safe and sound, with the scent of his hair—a blend of some spicy shampoo and fresh-cut wood—on his pillow. Smiling, she buried her nose into its downy softness. Good thing Jason was still asleep or he'd giggle at her strange behavior.

Last night, the room had been quite dark, but this morning sunlight streamed through the wall of windows opposite the bed. After a few minutes, she sat up and glanced around the room. The furniture, unlike what she'd seen of the rest of the house, was a mishmash of unmatched pieces. The space was large, simple and uncluttered, and the décor was early male monotonous. The carpet, walls and furniture were varying shades of brown. Everything else, the drapes, comforter and sheets and lampshades were black. About the only personal item in the room was a photo on his dresser.

Moving quietly across the plush carpet, she picked up the frame. Four men, all of them broad-shouldered and built and dressed in black tuxes, stood surrounding a sturdy-looking woman in a pale blue dress, a corsage around her wrist. Garrett was the tallest and in the back. It must've been one of his brothers' weddings and looked to have taken place relatively recently.

They looked comfortable with one another, as if the moment the photographer had finished taking the picture they'd all taken a swig out of the bottles of beer they were hiding behind their backs.

Setting the photo back down, she padded out into the hall and stood at the railing at the top of the stairs looking down below. Garrett was standing at the counter, dressed in a white shirt and boxers, looking down at a newspaper with a coffee mug in his hand. He looked so comfortable, so at home in this setting, a setting vaguely reminiscent of the rustic cottage she'd stayed in on Mirabelle as a little girl with her mother and sister, a rustic cottage that had hung forever in her memory as a dream house. Garrett's house fit her grownup dream to a tee. With a contented sigh, she went down the stairs in her oversized T-shirt and boxers.

He glanced up, his hair mussed on one side and heavy stubble shading his cheeks. So this was what he looked like fresh from sleep. If only she could curl under his arm and wrap her arms around his waist. "Morning." He yawned.

"Did you sleep all right?"

"Sure."

"I'd feel better if you'd—"

"Nope. We talked about this last night." He shook his head. "If that asshole finds out you're here and decides to get cocky, he's going to have to go through me to get to you and Jason."

"Garrett—"

"That's the way it's going to be. I'd appreciate it if you'd make yourself at home while you're here. I'm not much of a host."

She wandered over to the cabinets, searching for a cup. He reached behind her, opening the door to her left, his breath buffeting the top of her head. She closed her eyes and barely kept herself from leaning back against him. More than anything, she wanted his arms around her, reassuring, comforting. Arousing, if she were being completely honest with herself.

He held out a mug and stepped back. "Help yourself to whatever, whenever. Same goes for Jason."

She poured some coffee. "Can I make you breakfast?"

"You don't need to do that."

"I know…I just…" She hated being a burden, hated imposing or having to lean on anyone for anything, but she was scared for Jason and worried more than ever about Marie. Cooking would make her feel somewhat useful.

"It's going to be all right." He reached out and touched her shoulder.

She could almost feel the layers of her thick, tough hide

falling away one flake at a time. This island, these people, Lynn, Arlo and Garrett reaching out, protecting, caring, helping for no reason.

"Every islander will know what's going on by the end of the day. Just to be safe, I'll be circulating a picture of Samson. He won't be able to set foot anywhere on this island during the daytime hours without someone blowing the whistle. Mirabelle is the safest place for you and Jason."

"I know." The only safer place would be in his arms.

AFTER WATCHING ERICA COOK breakfast in nothing more than a T-shirt and a pair of boxers, Garrett had to get out of the house. The look of her hair, mussed up from sleep, and her clean, unmade-up face, had taken everything out of him. Today was his day off, so he'd gone out to his shop to work on the quickly progressing bed frame for his own bedroom.

After a few hours, he heard Erica call his name as he was dovetailing the end of a long board of cherrywood for the side panel of the frame. He shut off the machine and spun around to find Erica and Jason behind him.

"I have to go to work," she said. "I'm taking Jason with me."

Garrett glanced at her, knowing full well the safest place for the boy was right here, at his side, but he wasn't sure he'd know what to do with the kid for an entire day. He sure as hell had gotten himself in over his head this time.

"I'd rather he stays with me." He glanced down at Jason. "If that's okay."

"Can I?" Jason grinned.

"You're sure?" Erica asked.

Garrett nodded. "It'll be nice to spend some time with him." He walked out with Erica. "Don't worry about him. Okay?"

"I won't." She took off down the hill.

Garrett went back into his workshop and studied Jason. "So what do you want to do?"

"I dunno."

"How 'bout we put together a toolbox for you?" Garrett found a small metal box still in good shape that he hadn't used in years. "Here." He handed it to Jason. "Now we need to fill it up."

From his myriad spare tools, he selected a light hammer, screwdrivers, a wrench set and a small measuring tape. Then he put together a box of various nails, bolts and nuts. Odds and ends came next. A carpenter's pencil, a small square with a level attached.

"There you go."

Jason had been placing each item into the box, organizing and reorganizing as he went. "Do I get to keep this?" he asked, his eyes round.

"Absolutely. They're all yours."

"Thanks, Garrett. Can I make something?"

"How 'bout we make you a box or something to put your game cartridges in?"

"Really?"

"Really."

Jason grinned again.

Garrett gave him the smallest pair of shop glasses he could find and let him turn on the table saw. After Garrett cut the sides and bottom for a small box, he gave the boy a practice board and showed him how to pound in nails. "Go to it."

Jason took his hammer out of his toolbox along with a handful of nails and smacked away. "Like this?"

"Get them started before you hit them too hard," Garrett said, and then demonstrated. "That way you won't bend them."

Having Jason with him out in the workshop shed an entirely different light on his work. Teaching the boy was much more fun than he'd expected. Memories flooded in of the time Garrett had spent with his father after he'd come out of prison a different man, calm and peaceful, and full of cancer. Garrett had been more than a little resentful that his mother had forced him to spend so much time helping his father, but now he was thankful for the few short years they'd had together.

"Okay. How's that?" Jason had managed to pound in several nails straight as an arrow.

"Good job." Garrett smiled and patted him on the back. "Before you know it, you'll be making your own furniture."

Jason, so young and vulnerable, smiled up at him.

Garrett couldn't imagine ever putting a hand to that sweet face, let alone putting a bruise on that little body. Maybe he was not as much his father's son as he'd believed all these years. He could never hit a child any more than he could hit a woman. He could be patient and tolerant, loving and forgiving. Maybe Garrett being a father wasn't such a farfetched idea after all.

CHAPTER TWENTY-TWO

"WHY DIDN'T YOU CONTACT us sooner?"

The room was full of cops. True to his word, Garrett had made a couple of calls and pulled in a few favors to get the main detectives on the Samson case here on Mirabelle. Erica now sat at the table in the conference room in the island's police station where distrust hung in the air like a cold, heavy vapor, making her skin crawl.

"You knew we were looking for you, right?" said cop one, a guy named Dave. The guy looked mean, no sense of humor.

"I didn't contact you because I don't know anything."

Cop two—Gary something or another—tapped his pen on the table. "Tell us what you do know."

Erica glanced at Garrett. At first the detectives had insisted on interrogating Erica alone. It was only after Garrett had subtly implied that maybe Erica should get an attorney that they'd allowed his presence.

"Go ahead." Garrett nodded. "Tell them what you can."

Erica began with the day she'd gotten Marie's call.

"Do you still have the message?"

"Yes." She put her cell phone on the table and shoved it toward the detective.

"Why do you think she left?"

"Why do *you* think?" she threw back at them.

"Just answer the question."

"Billy Samson is abusive."

"What makes you believe that?" Gary asked.

"There were no suspicious doctor visits," Dave said. "No domestic dispute calls from the house, the neighbors all say everything was fine."

"He's a cop. What do you expect?"

"Where do you think she went?"

Erica clamped down on her emotions. "I *hope* she found someplace safe, but I can't guess where that would be. She and I hadn't seen each other much for the last several years."

"Why is that?"

"She always had reasons why she couldn't get together, but Billy didn't like her seeing me. He had her convinced I was a bad influence."

"Why would he do that?"

"For God's sake." Now she was getting mad. "Do you know anything about abusive men?"

"If you really thought he was abusing her why didn't you do anything?"

"I tried." Erica looked away.

Was there anything she could have done differently? Should she have orchestrated some kind of intervention? But the truth was that anything short of kidnapping Marie wouldn't have made any difference. Even then, too many women went back to abusive environments. Her own mother had done it over and over again.

She sat forward in her chair. "I got a question for you guys."

They didn't say anything, only looked at her.

"Did you know Marie went to see an attorney about a divorce the week before she disappeared?"

No reaction. She couldn't tell if they'd already known or not.

"Where did you hear that?"

"An old friend of mine used to be a private investigator. He did some digging around for me." She pulled the piece of paper out of her pocket with the name of the attorney and flicked it toward them.

"Where's Jason?"

Erica glanced from one to the other, holding their gazes. "I don't know."

In truth, Jason was out fishing with Jim and Noah Bennett. The ex-police chief had gotten wind of the situation and had come to offer Garrett his assistance. It had been Garrett's idea to keep him somewhere unexpected in case Billy found out about this meeting. The Bennett men had agreed to the plan without asking one question.

"The folks at Jason's school in Chicago say a woman matching your description picked him up on the day Marie disappeared."

"He was already gone when I got to the school."

"So you up and left town for no reason."

"I needed a vacation. Spur-of-the-moment thing."

They didn't believe her and she didn't care. Both cops glanced at Garrett and Erica hoped like hell that he would keep his word and hold off saying anything until after the meeting. When Garrett's expression didn't change, both detectives crossed their arms and sat back in their chairs.

"Didn't look spur-of-the-moment to us."

"Almost every stitch of clothing was gone from your apartment. Even the post office was asked to hold your mail."

She didn't have any answers for that.

"It's okay, Erica. If Marie lied to you to get you to help her, we understand. We do a lot for family."

Erica turned to Garrett. "I never went back to my apartment. I swear. I didn't go to the post office." She didn't care whether or not the other cops believed her, but Garrett was an altogether different story. "I didn't plan any of this."

For an instant, a glimmer of doubt darkened his pale eyes, and then he relaxed. "I know you didn't. So do they."

The detectives ignored him and focused on her. "The sooner you tell us the truth, Erica, the sooner we can get to finding your sister."

"I didn't—"

Garrett put his hand on her shoulder. "What are you guys looking for?"

They glanced at each other and then back at Garrett. "Billy was going to fight for full custody. Apparently, Marie's a heavy drinker. She's the one who hit Jason—"

"He's lying!" Erica shouted.

Garrett squeezed her shoulder. "Have you been able to corroborate anything he's claimed?"

Neither detective said a word.

"Any of her friends say she drank too much?" Garrett asked the detectives. "Anyone ever see her lose her temper?"

Still nothing.

"Look, I know you guys are good cops," he said. "I know you're trying to get to the truth, but you're barking up the wrong tree. And you know it. This isn't about an angry mother trying to get custody of her kid."

"Where's the boy?"

"I told you I don't know," Erica said.

"Erica, we *will* charge you with kidnapping if you don't cooperate," the no-humor cop said.

She glanced at Garrett. He'd promised to protect Jason from Billy, but that was as far as he'd go. "Listen to the voice mail from Marie on my phone," she said. "And then I'll tell you everything."

Reluctantly, they took up Erica's cell and each, in turn, listened to the message Marie had left for Erica what seemed a lifetime ago.

"Jason's here with me," she said when they were finished. "I noticed bruises on his neck and shoulder shortly after I picked him up from the school."

Garrett nodded. "I saw them, too."

"You did?" She glanced over at him.

"Right after you got off the ferry. That's the biggest reason I was suspicious when you first came here."

Now it made more sense.

"Jason told me his dad had hurt him." Erica leaned forward. "It wasn't Marie. It was Billy. She was finally going to leave him because he'd started hurting Jason. Please let him stay on the island with me."

The two cops said nothing.

"You don't have enough evidence yet to charge Billy Samson with anything," Garrett said. "Which means you don't have enough evidence to put the boy in protective custody."

"Please." Erica leaned forward. "If Billy finds out that Jason heard them fighting the morning Marie disappeared, Jason might disappear, too."

"How do we know the boy is safe?"

"They're staying with me for protection," Garrett said. "Since Billy showed up here the other night."

"One last question," one of the detectives said. "Who packed all your things?"

"I don't—"

"There was no sign of forced entry into your apartment."

How could Billy have gotten into her apartment? How? Suddenly she knew.

"About a year after Marie got married," Erica said, remembering. "I gave her a key to my apartment. I was worried about her. I told her any time day or night if she needed to get away to come stay with me. Billy must've found it."

The detectives looked at each other. "Do not leave this island," one of them said. "You disappear with Jason and we will come after you with everything we've got."

"I won't be leaving," she whispered. "And thank you." She stood and headed for the door.

"Erica?" One of the detectives stood and crossed the room. She turned.

"We're doing everything we can to find your sister." He patted her shoulder.

The other cop stood. "Billy Samson is just one cop. Most of us try to be pretty decent guys."

She nodded and glanced from one to the other. "I'm starting to understand that."

Garrett took her hand and led her from the room, but when he glanced back at the two detectives there was something in his expression that set Erica on edge. The moment they stepped outside, she touched his arm. "You know something you're not telling me."

He looked away.

"Garrett, please. I need to know everything."

"A couple months ago, they found traces of your sister's blood on the workbench in the garage at the Samson house. Billy claimed she cut herself on something." When he glanced up, she saw only resignation in his eyes. "But then last week, they were dredging a lake in some little town in Indiana for an unrelated drowning. They found Marie's car. There were traces of blood. Hers."

Reality sank in and the last ray of hope darkened inside her. "She's dead, isn't she?"

"I don't know."

"Garrett, don't lie to me."

"I don't know."

He held her so tightly she couldn't have pulled away even if she'd wanted to try, but she'd seen the truth in his eyes. He thought Marie was dead.

CHAPTER TWENTY-THREE

BILLY WOULD COME BACK to get Jason. Garrett had explained to Erica in no uncertain terms that although the man was now busy with the cops having turned their sights on him, Billy would be biding his time. When she least expected him, he'd be there.

Still, one day flowed quietly into the next. After the meeting with the Chicago detectives, her plan to leave Mirabelle at the end of the summer had necessarily fallen by the wayside. Before she fully realized it, a week had passed. The busy tourist season was winding down and Jason was talking about how excited he was about going back to school in the fall.

Erica came down the stairs in Garrett's house one morning, showered, dressed and ready to start the day and found Garrett putting away the clean dishes from the dishwasher and Jason at the counter, eating breakfast. They looked so comfortable together that any stranger looking from the outside in might've thought they were father and son and this their normal routine.

The sight was almost painful. They could be a family, the three of them. "Guess who has the entire day off?" she said, trying to lighten her own mood.

Garrett glanced up at her, and her heart nearly stopped. "You and me."

"And me," Jason said, with a big grin.

It was good to see him laughing. He'd even announced

to her several nights ago that he wanted to sleep by himself in the upstairs guest bedroom. Although it'd left her alone in Garrett's big bed, she was happy Jason was feeling more settled. She laughed. "Every day is a kid's day off!"

"Your point would be?" Garrett said, grinning.

"Oh, so now you're siding with him?"

"You don't need anyone to take care of you."

Erica moved by him and whispered, "Maybe I don't need it as much as I want it."

He narrowed his eyes and stepped back. "Let's go sailing."

"Yeah! Yeah!" Jason cried.

"Sailing? I thought there were supposed to be heavy storms coming."

"Storms are coming tomorrow. Today it's going to hit seventy with a light breeze. Sounds like perfect sailing weather to me."

In the end, Erica couldn't disappoint Jason, so after preparing a cooler filled with sandwiches, drinks and other munchies, they set off for Setterberg's rental shop. Garrett paid for an entire day on a small sailboat and came back outside with three life jackets. "Put these on." He handed one to Jason, held the other one out for Erica, and cocked his head at her. "You look like you don't want to do this."

"To be honest…boats kind of scare me."

"You're kidding, right?"

"No."

"City girls." He shook his head. "Right, Jason?"

"Yeah, city girls." Jason shook his head.

"Hey! That's not fair."

"You're living on an island. Get used to it." Garrett pushed her arms through the vest holes, tugged it on her, and zipped it up. "Besides, you're going to like this."

"Promise?"

"Yes. I promise."

They spent the morning sailing around Mirabelle. Erica was surprised by how large the island actually was and how much of it was undeveloped. A large part of the island was undeveloped state land, but there were two houses on the northwest end, an old log cabin with a red-trimmed porch and deck, and a pale yellow Victorian with white gingerbread. Other than the satellite receiver on the roof of the cabin, both looked deserted.

"Does anyone live there?" she asked, pointing to the structures barely visible amidst the thick trees.

"There was an old woman in the yellow house," Garrett said, leaning back in the boat. "But I heard she moved to a nursing home some time ago. Everyone in town swears the guy who owns the log cabin is crazy, but I've never met him."

Very soon, they lost sight of the houses and continued around the rest of the island. Garrett, who seemed to have mastered the art of sailing even though he'd been a city boy, taught Jason the concepts and safety rules. During the short time they'd been living at Garrett's, Jason had flourished. The timid, scared boy she'd picked up at school that cold April afternoon so long ago was nearly gone. In his place was a confident and happy camper, and much of the credit had to go to Garrett.

On finding a sandy stretch of beach on state parkland, they landed the boat to picnic and explore. They were sitting on a big blanket finishing lunch, when the absolute perfection of the moment hit her. Sunshine. Waves lapping gently on the sandy shore. Jason happy and content. Garrett, looking sexy as hell and ever so much like a…father.

"Are you all right?" Garrett reached for her hand.

"Just thinking," she said. "About how someday you're going to make a wonderful father."

He held her gaze. "You think?"

"I know."

As she looked into his eyes, she knew something had to change. The more time Jason spent with Garrett, the harder it would be for him to leave Garrett's home. Billy had made no move to come back to Mirabelle, so maybe it was time for her and Jason to start thinking about moving back into their own apartment. For Jason's sake.

And hers. Better she left Garrett before he left her.

GARRETT DREW A SOFT CLOTH down the surface of the natural cherry in one long stroke, feeling the finish, making sure it was ready. Smooth. Even. Perfect. He stood back and critically examined the end result.

A woodworker could disguise many mistakes with intricate carvings and complicated design, but on this bed with these graceful, understated lines even the slightest error, an uneven surface, a mistake of a few degrees, became glaringly obvious. King-sized with four tall pencil posts, a wide headboard and a footboard lined with old-fashioned rope pulls, the design he'd developed for this bed frame was simple and flowing, more Shaker than Mission, more contemporary than Shaker.

Reminiscent of the graceful curves of a woman lying on her side, these lines were faultless. This was, hands down, the most stunning piece of furniture Garrett had ever made. Not a single slab of that wood had been turned, cut, drilled, pounded, stained or varnished without thoughts of Erica filling his mind. He imagined her now, lying there, the curve of her neck to her shoulder, her narrow waist flaring into her hips, the gentle curves of her long legs.

"Garrett?"

Oh, God. Sometimes he wondered if he hadn't completely conjured the woman in his mind she seemed to have become so much a part of him.

"Do you mind if I come in for a minute?"

"Sure." He closed his eyes and swallowed, composing himself before turning around.

Something had been bothering her today and he hadn't been able to put his finger on the problem. Near as he could tell, they'd had a damned near perfect morning sailing together, but she'd been preoccupied. By the time they got back to Mirabelle, she was barely speaking to either him or Jason. Figuring she'd talk when she was ready, he'd given her some space and come out to his woodshop.

From the serious look in her eyes, she was ready. As if she were uncertain how to begin, her gaze moved past him and focused on the bed. "Did you make that?"

He nodded. "Designed it, too."

"Can I touch it?"

"Yeah. It's finished."

She ran her hand along one of the tall posts and then the headboard. "It's so smooth. The color of the wood is so warm. What is it?"

"Cherry. With a very light, natural stain. It'll darken over time to a rich umber color. The slight contrasts of light and dark you see now in the wood will intensify, creating something unique, something no man could ever plan."

Suddenly, he found himself hoping she'd be around in ten, fifteen, fifty years to see the wood age to perfection.

"I'll bet you'll be able to sell this for an arm and a leg." When he said nothing, she turned and looked at him. "You don't plan on selling this?"

Never. "No."

"So it's your bed?"

I made it for you. He nodded. *Share it with me?*

"Well, I…it's…beautiful." As if she guessed his thoughts, she quickly glanced away. "Why did you become a cop?"

"What?"

"You're so talented. Why a cop?"

He looked down at his hands. "Remember I told you my dad taught me woodworking?"

She nodded.

"He taught himself everything he knew while he was in prison."

She glanced up at him. "Prison?"

"Manslaughter. Killed a guy in a bar fight."

"How old were you when it happened?"

"About twelve."

"So he had a temper."

He laughed humorlessly. "That's putting it lightly."

"Did he ever hit you?"

"Yeah. He didn't drink often, but when he did, he was mean."

"Your mom?"

"Never touched her."

"What does that have to do with you becoming a cop?"

"I beat up a kid in high school. It scared me. Finding out what I was capable of doing. Of how much of my father was in me." He stared at the bed frame. "Getting sent to the workhouse, though, for a month was probably the best thing that ever happened to me."

Listening, she waited.

"There was a counselor there, who made me understand that it's not strength that matters. It's what a man does with his strength that counts. He made me believe that becoming a cop would put me on the straight and narrow. It worked for a long while."

"But?"

"I was turning into the criminals I put in jail."

"You keep in touch with your dad?"

"He passed a while back, but when he got out of prison, he moved back in with my mom. He was a changed man.

So calm, so controlled. Almost happy. He said it was the woodworking."

"So you picked it up."

"Yeah. Guess I have the best of both worlds up here." He paused, waiting to see if she was ready to talk. One minute flowed into the next. Whatever it was had her tongue-tied, and that was something. "Well," he finally said. "Will you help me carry this inside?"

"Up to your room?"

"*Your* room. You might as well sleep on it while you're here."

Several trips into the house later, they had all the pieces upstairs, the mattress and box spring off the old frame, and the space was ready for the new bed. Jason had joined them and had helped put all the pieces together. A short while later, they were finished.

"That's that." Garrett stood back.

"Looks nice," Jason said. "Can I go watch TV now."

"Sure," Erica said. "Thanks for your help."

The bed looked good in the big room, but there was something missing. "This room needs something."

"Color," Erica said. "Red."

She'd nailed it. "A big red down comforter." The color would set off the rich tone of the cherry. Not to mention her bare skin.

"Exactly." Her gaze connected with his. "I…need to talk to you about something. I think it's time for Jason and I to start thinking about moving back into our old apartment."

Leaving him. He should've seen this coming. Instead, he'd allowed himself to get used to them, enjoy their company. Now the thought of living in his house alone filled him with a deep and consuming emptiness. He looked away, feeling too raw to face her. She'd see. She'd know.

"Lynn's college kids will be gone in a few weeks," she

went on, "so the apartment will be open again. Billy's made no attempt to come back to Mirabelle—"

"No."

"I'm not asking your permission, Garrett."

"It's not safe." He stood and paced. She couldn't leave. What would he do without her? Without Jason? Without the sounds of their voices? Their laughter, their little arguments.

"I appreciate all you've done for me and Jason, but he's getting very attached to you and…it must be confusing for him. I plan on talking to Lynn tomorrow and then at the end of this month, we'll be moving out."

"You need to stay here."

"Why?"

Tell her. Tell her you want her to stay. Tell her you need her. "You know why," he whispered.

"Do I?"

"I can't protect you at your old apartment. I can't protect Jason."

"Well, it's time for me to protect…a couple of hearts." She walked toward the door.

"Erica?"

She stopped, but didn't turn. Her shoulders rose and fell quickly as if she was taking deep breaths, as if she were holding back. If he asked her to stay, would she? And if she stayed, what then? Next week, next month, next year, what would happen the first time he lost his temper? What would happen if he ever got angry with Jason?

Jason. Damn, he'd gotten unexpectedly attached to that kid. What had he been thinking? Starting something he couldn't finish? He clenched his jaw. "I…" He sighed. Even he could hear the resignation in the sound. "This is exactly what Billy is waiting for."

Without so much as a backward glance, she left the room. Anger built inside him until he felt as if he might burst from the pressure. *Break something. Go pound your hammer. Do something. Blow it off.* But in his heart he knew there was nothing that would make a difference, nothing that would take away the—not anger—but pain.

CHAPTER TWENTY-FOUR

THE STORMS forecasters had been warning the public about for the past few days hit Mirabelle early in the evening. The massive band of severe weather now stretched across the entire Midwest from Missouri all the way up to Canada and would be hitting Chicago about the same time as Mirabelle.

Wind battered the trees, blustery clouds formed overhead, and a biting cold cut through Erica's coat. She flipped the collar of her jacket up, hugged the grocery bag tighter and tucked her head down as she climbed the hill to Garrett's house.

"You really don't need to walk me home," she said to Arlo. "I'll be fine."

After Billy had shown up on the island, Arlo or one of the pub regulars had insisted on walking her up to Garrett's house every night after work. "No point in fussing about it," Arlo said. "We'll be there in a couple minutes."

"But it's such a terrible night out."

"All the more reason you can use the company."

After passing Arlo's stables, the golden glow of incandescent lights twinkled through the tree branches, and as she walked up his drive there was Garrett sitting at the kitchen table with Jason, talking and laughing. They looked to be playing a game.

"Thank you, Arlo." She reached up on tiptoes and lightly kissed his cheek. "You've done so much for me."

"You've got that all wrong, dear. You've done so much for Lynnie and me. See you tomorrow." Pulling his jacket tighter, he headed back down the hill.

Erica couldn't shake the feeling that Lynn and Arlo felt like the parents she'd never had.

She turned to go into the house. Her feet hit the porch steps, and Garrett spun around, his guard raised by the sound. Suddenly, she was overwhelmed with gratitude. First Arlo and now Garrett. He hadn't owed her and Jason anything and yet he'd opened his home and had promised to protect them. Making a special meal for him tonight seemed grossly inadequate for all he'd done for them, but it was all she could offer.

"You're home early," Garrett said after she'd shut the front door.

Home. If only.

As if he realized what he'd said, his smile disappeared.

"No one's out and about with the storm coming," she explained. "Lynn gave me the night off."

"Sweet!" Jason smiled. "Garrett's teaching me how to play chess."

"I can see that." She set the groceries on the counter. "Isn't that hard?"

"I almost beat him once," Jason said.

"If I'm not careful, he'll be crushing me the next time we play." *The next time.* Garrett's grin was laced with sadness.

"Have you two eaten?"

"Not yet."

"Good. I stopped at the grocery store, thinking I'd make a special meal."

"Special, huh?" His thoughts appeared to have drifted firmly away from the chess game.

She did her best to ignore him as she emptied the contents of the grocery bag. "A pasta dish. Something you two have never eaten before."

"Why not?"

"Yeah, why?" Jason said, following Garrett's lead in teasing her.

"Because, smart alecks." She smiled. "My order for special sausage from my favorite Chicago butcher only just arrived at Newman's."

"Ah."

"Your turn," Jason said.

Garrett moved a piece. "Check."

"Dang it!"

"In one move you can put me in checkmate. Do you see it?"

"Where?"

"You want me to show you?"

"No," Jason said quickly. "Not yet—there it is. Check-mate!"

"You did it." Garrett chuckled.

"Can we play again?"

"How 'bout some other time. Let's help Erica."

Jason hopped up on a stool at the island counter, but Garrett came to her side of the counter. "What can I do?" he asked, coming close. Very close. Too close.

She put the bottle of Chianti she'd purchased between them. "You can open this and pour two glasses."

For a breathtaking moment he looked as if he might take her by the arm and ask her to stay, but then he grabbed the bottle and took an opener out of a nearby drawer.

She brushed off a package of mushrooms. "Jason, can you slice these like I showed you before?"

"Yep."

She placed a cutting board and paring knife in front of him along with the package of white-capped mushrooms.

Garrett handed her a glass of wine. "I'm at your service."

She took a sip of wine and got Garrett going on slicing onions and various peppers. After getting the sausage browning on the stove, she set about cutting up the chicken breasts, sautéing the vegetables, and then simmering them in various spices and wine.

Garrett grated a chunk of Romano cheese. "Whatever this is, it smells amazing."

"I hope you like it."

"I love everything you make."

Erica set the food on the table as Garrett and Jason dove in, piling one thing after another onto their plates. The first meal she'd made for Garrett, she'd scoffed at the domesticity of it all. Maybe because it was something she'd never had, never knew she could have. Now, though, she was glad to be able to do something for this man.

"Come on," he said. "We're not eating until you sit down."

She joined them at the table. The family feel of Garrett's house was getting more and more comfortable with every passing day. While her apartment back in Chicago had fit the bill for many years, that place wasn't the picture that flashed in her mind when she thought of home. Home had somehow become this house, this kitchen. Family not only included Jason these days, but Garrett. These were things she didn't have a right to expect.

She hadn't even told Jason yet that they'd be leaving to go back to their own apartment, hadn't packed a single bag, and already her heart was breaking. Suddenly, she missed having a home. A family. A place where she belonged. How can a person miss something she's never had?

BLACK CLOUDS CHURNED overhead as a wall of driving rain made its way across Lake Superior. Erica stood by the window in Garrett's bedroom and watched the weather hit with amazing force, feeling an affinity with this natural phenomenon.

Rain slashed against the windowpane, wind whipped the nearby branches of a maple tree into a frenzy, and lightning lit sporadically over the water. She walked across the hall to check on Jason. He was sound asleep, oblivious to the storm. What a change from the boy who'd woken up crying in the middle of a rainstorm when they'd first come to Mirabelle.

Restless, she crossed the hall again. Lightning flashed, illuminating the lines of the headboard Garrett had made, curvy, sensual and bold. What she wouldn't have done in that moment to see his head on a pillow near that headboard, or any headboard, when it came right down to it.

A sense of desperation overwhelmed her. She'd be leaving soon. Out of Garrett's home. Very likely out of Garrett's life. This was it. Before she left, she wanted a taste of being with him. One taste. Who could blame her?

She crept back into the dark hallway. As she went down the stairs to the spare bedroom where Garrett was sleeping she worried she'd waited too long. What if he was asleep?

Quietly, she tiptoed toward his room. All of the shades were open to the storm outside. Lightning flashed, showing his bed empty, the blankets twisted and mussed as if he'd tossed and turned for some time. She stood in the doorway, now at a loss. Where was he?

Lightning flashed again. He was sitting in a chair by the window, watching the storm. But now his gaze was focused on her.

GARRETT WOULD'VE BEEN lying to himself to suggest that he was surprised to see her in his room. As he'd been getting ready for bed, he could practically feel her upstairs thinking about him. Knowing she was planning on leaving him, the tension culminating in the house was matched only by the storm gathering outside.

So when he heard her light step in the hall outside his room, it was all he could do to keep himself still. The hard-on, he could not stop. "You'd be doing everyone a favor by going back upstairs," he said, not moving a muscle, "and forgetting whatever it is you have in mind."

Without a word, she moved toward him.

"Erica, don't. This will only make you leaving all that much harder. For both of us."

She faltered, but then kept coming.

He didn't want to look at her, but when she knelt in front of him, he couldn't take his eyes off her face. He touched her cheek and pulled back. "My hands. They're too rough."

She snatched back both his hands and entangled her fingers in his. "I love your hands. Every single rough edge and callus. Every line."

"Don't do this," he whispered.

"You've known practically from the first moment we met that this was going to happen. You want it. I want it." She pushed his knees apart and inched toward him.

She kissed him and cupped his erection at the same moment and he expelled a breath into her mouth. "You don't waste any time, do you?" Breathing hard, he pushed her away. This woman was everything his body needed, but she'd rip his heart to shreds. "You may be what I want, but you're not what I need."

"No ties. No commitments. That's every man's dream."

"Not for this one." He flung her hands off him, pushed back his chair and stood. "Believe it or not, now I'm the one who wants the fairy tale. Having you and Jason here, with me, has made me see the possibilities. Now I want a wife and a houseful of kids. Happily ever after."

"Well, then, it's a good thing I'm not asking for forever."

"Erica, I lose myself when I'm with you. I—"

She silenced him with her mouth, and like a blazing hot ember her kiss burned away every one of his good intentions with its heat. Then her hands were pulling off his shirt, her fingers working the fly on his jeans. Once she'd touched him, stroked him, all caution left him. He couldn't get her naked enough fast enough. "You're crazy, you know that?"

He ripped her T-shirt in his haste to remove it. While she unhooked her own bra, he tugged off her jeans and thong in one sweep. Then she was naked and lying on his bed. If he hadn't been throbbing so badly with the need to be inside her, he might have taken a few minutes to drink in the sight of her, those flashes of pale beauty and dark desire.

He wasn't the only one in a hurry. She pulled him down, forcing him to land on top of her. "I'm too heavy. I'll crush you."

"I want to feel every inch of you over me. Every bone, every muscle. All of you."

Supporting part of his weight, he did cover her, completely. Her breasts pressed against his chest. Her smooth stomach to his abs. Her hips to—

"Now," she breathed. "It's been too long." She pulsed forward, took him inside and his full weight pressed upon her. "How can this be bad?" she whispered. "How can you not want this?"

Oh, he did want this. Her. More than anything. Over and over and over, and when he came inside her, again and again, thrusting into her, he took her with him. He could feel her body pulsing around him with every moan she breathed into his mouth. He collapsed against her, burying his face in her neck, her hair.

"Erica," he breathed.

He shouldn't have done it, but he pulled back and opened his eyes. Through that deep brown color, now glistening with emotion, he saw inside her for one instant.

He should've known. No commitments? No ties? For all her bravado, this woman's core was ripe with softness, raw with vulnerability, and all he wanted to do was fold her in his arms and, this time, make slow and sweet love to her.

They'd been hot and wild together, not crazy or scary, and he hadn't lost anything. Except for his heart. Sex wasn't the only thing he wanted from this woman.

He'd been fooling himself. This woman was everything he'd ever wanted—needed. She was strong, but loving. Tough, but kindhearted. He loved that she didn't back down, that she gave as good as she got with a passion that matched his. She'd taken everything he'd given and thrown it right back at him. Her intensity matched his stroke for stroke, and when she came to him, he burned bright and hot.

He didn't need sunshine and blue skies to soften his edges because the woman he loved had a few edges of her own. They were different in ways that made it exciting, and the same in every way that mattered. He'd fallen in love with her.

"Well, that was fun." She rolled onto her side, closing him off.

"Hey," he whispered, wanting to make love to her this time. Love. He kissed the back of her head, ran the back of his hand reverently along her side. He kissed her shoulder, slid his hand down her back, along her side, to come to rest at her waist. The bed he'd made wasn't perfect. She was. Perfect for him.

Erica closed her eyes. She'd wanted sex and sex is exactly what she'd gotten. A tear slipped onto the pillowcase. *Stupid, stupid, stupid.* How could she possibly have thought that having sex with Garrett would solve anything?

"Come here," he whispered.

When she didn't move, he came to her, pressing flush against her back, his arms enveloping her. Softly, he brushed her hair away from her neck and kissed the hollow below her ear.

"I wasn't through with you." His words flowed by her ear and her breath quickened.

His hand wrapped around her waist, moved on to her

stomach and pushed upward to her breast. The need she'd thought sated gathered all over again.

"I do want you. Over and over and over."

She shifted onto her back and reached for him.

"No." He grabbed her wrists and pinned her hands up by her head. "You set the pace last time. Now it's my turn." Then he lowered his mouth to hers, slowly, his eyes open and dark.

It was the sweetest, most gentle kiss Erica had ever felt. He made love to her mouth, then her neck, and then, sweet heaven, to her breasts. Her nipples hardened for him, and when he moved down her stomach, she squirmed and opened. He settled between her legs and patiently, quietly, expertly brought her to orgasm.

She hadn't expected this, hadn't dreamed it. After what seemed an eternity, she ran her hands through his hair and urged him upward. "Garrett," she cried. "Please."

"Please what?" he whispered against her.

"Make love to me."

"Isn't that what I've been doing?" His smile was tender, but heated.

"I want you up here, my arms around you."

The words had no sooner left her mouth than he was there, pressing against her, slipping inside, slowly making love to her. There was no fear. There were no worries. Tonight there was only the sweet sensation of Garrett inside her, the weight of him on her, his arms wrapped protectively around her. Only Garrett.

ERICA AWOKE BEFORE SUNRISE the next morning with Garrett's arm heavy over her side, his hand cupping the underside of her breast, and his face buried in her hair. His chest rose and fell in a soft, steady rhythm. He was so much bigger than she that the mattress dipped under him, keeping her flush against him, but there was no place else she wanted to be. Never in her life had she been quite this content.

It couldn't last. Even now, doubts threatened. Last night was last night. This morning, under the bright sunlight, Garrett would realize his mistake. He would see her for what she was, the exact type of woman he didn't want in his life, and he would turn away and leave. It's what men did. They left.

Better she prepare herself now. Better she protect what little was left of her heart.

GARRETT STIRRED IN HIS sleep. Something was wrong. Erica was gone. He snapped open his eyes and bolted upright. *Samson!* Then he saw light in the kitchen and heard the faint sounds of tinkering in the cabinets, water running in the sink, and he shut back down. Erica was fine. She'd just gotten out of bed.

Taking a big, calming breath, he pulled on a pair of boxers, dragged a shirt over his head, and walked quietly down the hall. Already dressed in jeans and a T-shirt, she was at the counter, making a pot of coffee. She fit there. In the kitchen. In the family room. And in his bed. Seeing her filled him with a deep sense of fulfillment. This woman, no other, belonged by his side, and as if these walls had been waiting for her all these months, this home suddenly seemed as much hers as his.

He moved behind her, drew her hair back and kissed her neck. "Take those clothes off and come back to my bed."

She moaned, bent her neck for a moment and then straightened. "I have to go into work early. I promised Lynn I'd make tiramisu for a dessert special."

"I'll help you," he whispered. "Later."

"Jason is probably confused enough as it is. I don't want him to wake up and find us."

"He won't be up for hours yet." He turned her within the circle of his arms. "That might be enough time for what I have in mind."

"Garrett." She pushed against his chest. "I have to go."

He dropped his hands to his sides and forced his feet to keep absolutely still. "What are you doing?"

"What do you mean?"

"This. Pulling back."

She looked away.

Tell her. Tell her you love her. Instead, he waited, silently.

"No commitments." She stepped backward, away from him. "Remember? No ties."

"That's bullshit."

"Let's be honest," she whispered. "Last night was… nice—"

"Nice?" Anger flashed. His guts churned with something akin to fear. He was going to lose her. *Tell her.*

"Shh! You'll wake up Jason."

"Maybe he should wake up. Maybe he should see what a coward his aunt is being."

She stalked toward the door. "I don't have to take this."

"Yes." He grabbed her arm. "You do."

She shook him off and faced him. "Between the two of us there isn't one single smooth edge. I'm not ready for the ups and the downs, the love and the hate."

"You sure seemed ready enough last night."

"Sex isn't enough, Garrett."

"Last night wasn't only about sex. You know it." *I love you.* If only he could say the words.

"I'm not what you want. Remember?"

She was so, so beautiful. "If you're going to cut me, you'd better make it deeper than that." As hard as it was, he made himself look straight into her eyes.

"All right." She pushed against his chest, and this time he let her go. "I don't love you, Garrett, and I never will. Turns out, *you're* not what *I* want."

"Dammit!" Furious, he turned around and swiped the counter clean with the back of his hand. A bowl smashed into pieces on hitting the ceramic floor. A stack of mail flew in the air. A couple of pots and pans clanked to the floor.

This sprite of a woman had snatched his heart right out of his chest, thrown it on the ground and stomped all over it. He threw back his head and nearly howled. The pain was gut-wrenching and devastating. With a sick feeling in the pit of his stomach, he knew it had only just begun.

"Go. Leave," he ground out. "In fact, why don't you pack up today? Instead of going back to that damned apartment, why don't you leave Mirabelle? You don't belong here, anyway. Not anymore than I do."

Without a backward glance, she left.

He clenched his fist, pent-up emotion coursing through him. Pacing now, he stepped on a shard of pottery and glanced at the floor. What was he doing smashing bowls and throwing pans? That wasn't going to change anything.

He went to the window and watched her stalk down the hill, holding her head so proudly. "I love you," he whispered into the silence, and telling her was the only chance in hell he had of taking away the pain.

CHAPTER TWENTY-FIVE

AT DUFFY'S THAT NIGHT, even the lighthearted jokes, conversation and laughter Doc, Bob and Dan brought to the bar wasn't enough to shift Erica out of the funk she'd been in all day. With the white noise of the TV and jukebox music in the background, they were chatting about a salmon fishing tournament that had taken place more than ten years back, but she barely heard their conversation.

Was Garrett right about her? If he'd asked her to stay, if he'd told her he loved her, what then?

"I'm telling you, that salmon was only twenty-seven pounds," Dan said, embellishing his statement with a good-natured pounding of his fist on the bar. "I remember it like it was yesterday."

"It was twenty-nine pounds if it was an ounce, dammit," Bob argued. "I caught it, I oughta remember."

"Humph."

"Doc?" Bob looked over at him. "Which one was it?"

Doc glanced at Erica and grinned. "I oughta be able to finagle a beer out of this one, don't you think?"

Erica chuckled. "You guys are nuts."

A body was pulled from Lake Michigan today...

The newscaster's words on the TV behind her pulled Erica out of the conversation. Slowly, she turned around. As if she'd suddenly sunk into a bubble, the noisy sounds of the bar fell silent. She slipped into slow motion, focusing her every sense on the TV screen as the world around her continued moving along. The waitresses kept taking and delivering orders. The bartender kept pouring drinks. Normal. Everything else went on while usual as her world fell apart.

The remains are believed to be those of Marie Samson. The mother of Jason Samson...

Her sister was dead.

"Oh, no," one of the men at the bar behind her said.

"Dammit."

"Erica, you okay there?"

The reporters fired questions at the detective being interviewed. *"Does this change the investigation in any way?"*

"Well, it's obviously a murder investigation now."

"Do you think Jason is still alive?"

"Yes. We're going under the assumption he's still alive."

"Erica?"

"Erica!"

A hand touched her shoulder. Lynn had come into the bar. She was out of breath and panting. "I came as soon as I saw the news."

Everything dulled around her, the light, the sounds, the smells. Then someone wrapped their arms around her and held on, kept her from falling. It was Lynn. She felt soft and warm, like a mother.

"My sister is dead," Erica whispered.

"I know." Lynn squeezed tighter.

She heard Billy Samson's name mentioned and quickly looked back up to listen to the TV newscaster.

A warrant has been issued for Billy Samson in connection with the murder of his wife, Marie Samson. Police have been unable to locate Samson....

"Good," Lynn said. "You don't have to worry about him any more."

"No," Erica said. "This is bad. Very, very bad."

"Why?"

"If they can't find him, that means he's coming here."

"What do you want us to do?" Dan asked.

"Just a minute." Lynn put up a hand quieting him. "How do you know he's coming here?"

"He wouldn't disappear without Jason." Erica ran for the door.

"Wait for Arlo."

"No time!"

"Where you going?"

"To get Jason!" she yelled. "He's having a sleepover with Brian."

Erica ran, flat out, to Sarah's apartment. Panting, she climbed the stairs. Except for a dim light shining through the kitchen shades, the apartment was dark. "Sarah!" she called, knocking on the door. "It's Erica. Open up!"

While Erica waited, a vision of Billy having already broken into Sarah's apartment flashed through her mind. *It's okay. It's late. They're probably asleep.* When no one came to the door, she knocked again, and then pounded. "Sarah!"

Finally, a light turned on inside, and Sarah, sleepy-eyed, drew back the curtain and opened the door. "What's going on?"

"Where's Jason?" Erica went inside and shut the door behind her.

"Asleep. More than an hour ago."

"I need to take him to Garrett's."

"Is everything all right?"

"No, but I don't have time to explain."

A look of concern passed over Sarah's features, but she didn't argue. "I'll get him."

Erica paced in the entryway. Only a moment later, Sarah returned with Jason trudging slowly behind her.

"Erica, why do I have to go home?"

"I'll explain on the way." She grabbed his hand.

"Is there anything I can do?" Sarah asked.

"Call Garrett. Please. Let him know I'm on my way."

"Will do."

Holding Jason's hand, Erica ran down the steps. When they got down to the bottom, she stopped, looked around, listened, making sure they were alone. "Hop up on my back, kiddo." She knelt down in front of Jason. "I'll give you a piggyback ride."

"What's wrong?"

She didn't want to frighten him. And she couldn't tell him, not now, not like this, that his mom was dead. "We have to hurry." As soon as she'd situated him on her back, Erica jogged as fast as she could through the back streets of town, keeping to the shadows as much as possible.

"Erica?"

"Shhh," she whispered. "I'll tell you when we get to Garrett's."

"I'm scared." His arms tightened almost painfully around her neck.

"I won't let anything happen to you."

When they reached the edge of the woods, the blackness of the night settled around them and she paused to listen. Other than one dim lamppost heralding the start of Garrett's drive, there were no lights.

Something told her not to move onto the pitch-black darkness of Garrett's driveway, but there was no other way to his house. To her right, she heard the sound of leaves rustling softly, too softly to be human. A small animal scurried on the forest floor.

Jason's breath sounded in her ear. She hiked him up a little higher and got ready to run.

"Jason." The voice was quiet and coming from the darkness. "Hey, buddy, how you doing?" Billy stepped into the circle of light.

"Dad?"

"Come here, son, and give me a hug."

Jason tensed on Erica's back, but then he slipped down to the ground and walked obediently toward Billy.

"You didn't think I'd forgotten about you, did you?" He lifted him up and hugged him, all the while keeping his gaze on Erica.

"No," Jason said.

"We're going to take a little trip, you and me. To some place fun." Billy pointed toward the marina. "Erica? Why don't you come and see us off."

"What about my stuff?" Jason asked.

"We don't have time. I've got a boat waiting for us."

"But my woodworking kit, my—"

"I said—" Billy glared at him "—we don't have time."

All at once, the past seemed to come back to Jason. The joy that had taken months to return into the little boy's life was wiped out within seconds. Fear filled his eyes and his arguments fell silent.

"You're not taking him anywhere." Erica held her ground between Billy and the shore.

"This boy is my son. And he's coming with me. Aren't you, buddy?"

"No," Erica said. "He's not."

"Jason?" Though Billy's voice was quiet, the underlying threat screamed out loud. "Move on by her."

Her nephew glanced at Erica, but then Billy touched his shoulder and steered him toward the marina. Jason put one foot in front of the other like a robot.

"No!" Erica screamed, and lunged at Billy.

Billy flung out his right arm and connected with Erica's cheek. She flew backward, stumbled and landed on the ground. "He's my son!" Billy softly bit out. "Stay out of this!"

"No!" Erica said, standing back up. "Not this time. Never again."

GARRETT CAME OUT OF his woodshop, where he'd been holed up from the moment late that afternoon when Sarah had come to get Jason for a playdate with Brian. He took a deep breath of crisp night air and turned his face to the black sky as crickets chirped slowly in the cooling air. He was tired. It'd been a long and awful day. He glanced at his watch and wondered what time Erica would be getting off. Would she come home or go to Sarah's?

Home. I'm sorry. Come home. He couldn't imagine the place without her. Without her voice, without the smell of her cooking, without her intensity bringing the place alive. He chastised himself again for the selfish, shortsighted, pain-induced, hurtful things he'd said to her that morning. He couldn't blame her if she never spoke to him again.

The faint sound of a voice filtered through the trees. At least he thought it was a voice. *Erica? What the—*

"No!" That was unmistakably her voice.

He raced down the dark drive and saw the outline of three people dimly lit in the light at the base of his drive. Erica, Jason and…Billy Samson. He knew it without even seeing the man's face. Keeping his distance, he pulled up short of the group. "Erica. Jason. You guys okay?"

"Garrett!" She glanced at him, but didn't move. "He's trying to make Jason leave with him."

"Jason," Garrett said. "Go on over to Erica."

"He's not going anywhere," Billy said, gripping Jason's arm and pulling him back. "Unless it's with me."

"Why don't you and I settle this alone? Keep Erica and Jason out of it."

"Oh, we'll settle it, all right." Billy reached inside his jacket, pulled out a handgun, and pointed it at Garrett. "Up at your house."

Garrett didn't move.

"Get your hands up and go. Now." He pointed the gun at Erica. "Or she's dead."

Without a choice, Garrett signaled for Erica to join him. The moment she reached his side, he headed with her up the hill.

"What are we going to do?" she whispered.

"Shut up and move," Billy said.

Garrett walked slowly. In a few minutes, they'd reach the house. Once inside, they wouldn't have a chance in hell of getting away. This guy was a cop, trained, and probably a damned good shot. The only option they had was to run into the woods in opposite directions and hope to jump Billy before he left with Jason. He had no way of communicating that to Erica.

"Billy, you don't need to do this," Garrett said. "I'm sure we can work something out."

"You think so, huh?"

He touched Erica's arm and signaled with his thumbs. She seemed to be following him. *You go right. I go left. One. Two. Thr—*

Behind him there was quick movement on the gravel road just before pain, blinding in intensity, shot through Garrett's head.

Erica screamed. "Garr—!"

CHAPTER TWENTY-SIX

INEFFECTIVELY, ERICA struggled against the twine tying her hands behind the chair. The thin string bit into her skin, and all she could do was mumble and groan around the scarf tied over her mouth as Billy dragged Garrett's unconscious body into the house, threw him onto a chair and tied him up.

The sight of poor Jason standing in the corner, frightened speechless, had her redoubling her efforts. If there was any humanly possible way for her to stop him, Billy was not getting off this island with her nephew.

Billy finished tying up Garrett. "Bye!" He mock saluted her and yanked Jason with him out the door.

Erica frantically glanced around for anything she might use to get free. If she could get her hands on the scissors by the phone, she might be able to cut through the twine cinching her wrists. She hopped the chair over to the desk and managed with her head to knock over the cup holding a menagerie of desk supplies. Pens and pencils scattered and the scissors slid to the edge. Turning her back to the desk, she grabbed the scissors in her hand, opened it and worked to cut through the twine.

This was going to take forever. Billy was going to be gone with Jason by the time she managed to get free. She felt herself panicking and almost dropped the scissors.

"Mmmm," Garrett groaned in pain, and blinked open his eyes.

"Garrett!" she mumbled around the scarf. "Wake up."

"What the hell?" He took in her tied-up state and struggled against his own bindings. "Dammit!" With great force, he hopped up and down on the chair, threw himself off center, managing to land lopsided on one leg and cracked the frame. Another few hops and the chair broke apart. He shook himself free of the wood pieces and then loosened the ropes.

He ran to Erica, grabbed the scissors and cut the rest of the way through the ropes binding her hands. While she worked off the gag, he cut through the binding on her feet.

"Let's go!" she yelled.

"Wait!" He ran upstairs. "I'm not going after him unarmed." He came back down a second later, carrying a gun.

"Billy killed my sister!" Erica said as they ran down the hill. "Her body washed up on the shore of Lake Michigan this morning."

"We'll get him, Erica. One way or another."

They reached town and raced to the marina. On hearing a commotion, Garrett slowed her down and then stopped her altogether. A few lampposts lit the area, making it clear a group of people had gathered. Arlo, Lynn and several pub regulars blocked Billy's access to the boats. Garrett and Erica met Herman as he came running into the marina, his gun ready.

"That way," Garrett whispered, pointing to his right. "Don't shoot unless you've got a clear shot at him."

"We're not moving," Arlo said. "Not until you let go of that boy."

"He's my son!" Billy yelled.

"Proves some people don't deserve to be parents," Lynn said.

These people, folks she'd known for such a short time, had all but adopted her and Jason. Why? How? It didn't make sense that they'd risk their lives like this.

"Get out of my way, old woman, or you'll be the first to die." Billy pointed the gun at Lynn.

"No!" Jason tugged away from Billy and ran to Lynn, throwing his arms around her waist.

"Get back here, Jason, or so help me—"

"No!" Jason yelled.

Good for you, Jason. Erica moved toward Billy.

Garrett grabbed her arm. "Stay back. This guy's got nothing to lose." He aimed the gun at Billy. "You're under arrest, Billy Samson. Put your weapon down!"

Billy spun around. And fired. Garrett was already moving. He jolted forward and tackled Billy. The gun flew from Billy's hand. Erica ran over, picked it up and yelled, "Stop!"

Billy had no intention of going down without a fight. He went after Garrett like a wild man. In no time, there was blood all over both of their shirts.

Garrett's blood, Erica realized with a sick heart. He'd been shot and was bleeding heavily. Garrett blocked several punches, threw a few of his own, and when Billy came at him again, managed to shift out of the way, tripping Billy and knocking him facedown onto the marina pavement. Garrett jumped onto Billy's back and wrestled his arms behind him.

Erica ran to Jason and threw her arms around him. "Are you okay?"

He nodded.

"You're done, Billy!" Garrett yelled.

Billy went deathly still as his gaze locked with Erica's. "You have to believe me. I didn't mean for it to happen. One day everything was fine and the next day Marie was asking for a divorce."

"So you killed her?"

"You think I wanted to?"

"Just because she was leaving—"

"It was an accident!" Billy thrashed back and forth. "I told her I'd do anything, but she'd already made up her mind. I tried to stop her, but she made it to the garage. I pulled her back, and she hit her head on the workbench. Wasn't that hard. Hell, she even made it into her car, but then she didn't move. I went to her, tried to wake her up. There was blood on her head." He went still. "Shoot me! Get it over with!"

"Oh, no." Garrett grabbed handcuffs from Herman and slapped them on Billy's wrists. "You're going to get exactly what you deserve. Prison for the rest of your life."

"WELL, THAT'S IT." Sitting in the conference room at the Mirabelle police station, the FBI agent closed his file. "I've got your phone number in case we need anything. You're free to go."

With the first pale light of sunrise illuminating the morning sky, Erica stared at the man. "What does that mean?"

The two Chicago cops who'd previously interrogated her were sitting at the other end of the table. One of them gave her a small smile filled with a lot of compassion. "It means, Erica, that you can stay here on Mirabelle. Or go back to Chicago."

"Whatever you want," said the other one, standing up. "Billy signed a full confession. You're free to go."

Free to leave Mirabelle. Free to get on with her life.

"Once you deal with custody over Jason," said the first Chicago cop, "you can move to France if you want."

Custody of Jason. She'd almost forgotten about that. She'd just assumed he'd be staying with her, but what if his paternal grandparents wanted to fight for custody?

All through the night, Mirabelle had been overrun by various forms of law enforcement and swarms of news reporters. Between the questioning from the cops and the interviews with reporters, she'd barely had a moment alone to think. In a day or two, they'd all be leaving. Life would get back to normal. Normal. She'd forgotten what that felt like.

She walked out of the conference room and found Garrett's office empty. She hadn't had a moment alone with him since this whole deal had come to a head. Out in the reception area, Jason was sound asleep in the chair next to Herman's desk. Sometime during the night, he'd overheard one of the reporters talking about Marie. Between that and what his dad had said down at the marina last night, the poor kid had put two and two together. He'd cried while she'd held him, but thankfully, exhausted after his ordeal, he'd fallen asleep. They'd have plenty of time to talk about what had happened, but now wasn't that time.

"You need some help getting home?" Herman whispered. "It's been a long night."

"We'll be all right, Herman." She smiled. "Thank you. For everything."

"No problem."

She touched Jason on the shoulder, hoping to gently rouse him. He stirred and quickly, as if frightened, opened his eyes. The moment he saw her, he flew into her arms.

"Hey. It's okay." She held him, rocking back and forth. The grip he had around her neck was so tight, she almost couldn't breathe. *Safe and sound, Marie. He's safe and sound.* "We're going to be all right, you and me."

"Promise?"

"Yeah, kiddo. I promise." Holding Jason in her arms, she stood up and headed for the door. She grabbed the handle and turned back. "Herman? Where's Garrett?"

"He left a couple minutes ago. Doc Welinsky insisted he get his arm stitched up."

Good. That was good. That meant she wouldn't have to say goodbye.

GARRETT SAT IN DOC WELINSKI'S office getting the gunshot wound to his arm stitched up. He'd wanted to wait until the feds were finished questioning Erica, but his damned arm was throbbing, and Doc had practically dragged him out of the police station.

"You were lucky," Doc said. "You lost a lot of blood, but that bullet was only a few inches away from an artery."

It hadn't hit anyone else, that's all that mattered as far as Garrett was concerned. Billy Samson was behind bars, and the FBI and several Chicago detectives, having been close on Samson's trail, were back at the police station, taking statements. Erica and Jason were safe. It was over.

"Well, I have to admit," Doc said. "All this excitement got my old ticker going, that's for sure."

There was a knock on the door, and a nurse poked her head inside the room. "Sally McGregor's on the phone for you."

"Tell her I'll call her back as soon as I'm done here," Doc said.

"Actually, Doc, she wants to talk to Garrett." The nurse held out the cordless phone.

Garrett glanced at the nurse. "Why?"

"She wouldn't say."

Doc grabbed the phone. "Sally, what is it? Garrett's a little busy getting stitches." Doc fell quiet, the phone to his ear, and Garrett turned woozy. He could hear a woman's voice coming over the line, but couldn't make out a single word. "All right. I'll tell him." Doc hung up the phone.

"What did she want?"

Doc quickly tied off the last stitch and snipped the thread. "It's Erica."

"Is she okay?" Garrett sat up. The room seemed to swim.

"Whoa!" Doc steadied him.

"Dammit, Doc. Tell me why Sally called."

"She saw Erica and Jason heading to Duffy's with two suitcases."

"What? Now?"

Doc nodded. "She said it looks like they're leaving the island."

Garrett hopped down from the table and nearly fell to his knees.

"Hold on there." Doc quickly slapped a large gauze pad over Garrett's wound and wrapped a strip of medical tape around his arm. "Okay. Go."

Garrett grabbed his shirt and pulled it over his head with his one good arm.

"Don't let that girl leave this island," Doc called as Garrett moved as fast as he could down the hallway. "Or that gunshot will be the least of your worries."

CHAPTER TWENTY-SEVEN

ERICA WAS EVEN WORSE at goodbyes than she was at hellos. It would be best for everyone if she and Jason left Mirabelle the same way they'd come. Quickly and quietly.

They'd gone as fast as they could up to Garrett's house and crammed as much as possible into the two suitcases she'd bought all those months ago. Then she'd taken all the clothes Lynn had given her at the beginning of the summer and placed them in a paper bag. Her hands started shaking as she prepared to leave Garrett's house, but she wouldn't let herself look around, wouldn't let this get any harder than it had to be. Together Erica and Jason headed back down the hill toward the town center.

They hadn't gotten very far when Jason asked, "Erica, where are we going?"

"I need to drop a few things off for Lynn, and then we're going back to Chicago."

At that he stopped.

"Are you leaving me in Chicago?" he asked, his voice tight and small.

"What? No." She struggled to find the right words, knowing she wouldn't be able to talk about Billy without the hostility she felt toward him tainting every word. She wasn't sure that was what Jason needed to hear. "We have to talk about who you're going to live with and where."

He looked down at the ground. "I know."

She wasn't sure what kind of a relationship he had with his paternal grandparents, but they could be the kind who bought ponies and spoiled kids. "Your grandparents might ask if you could live with them. What do you think?"

She was scared, scared that he'd choose his grandparents over her. "You can be honest with me," she said. *Even though it might break my heart.* "You can tell me exactly what you're thinking. No matter what you say, I will always love you." When he didn't say anything, she knelt in front of him. "Jason, do you want to live with your grandparents?"

He looked into her eyes. "Don't you want me?"

"Of course I want you."

"Really?"

"Really. I don't know what I ever did without you in my life."

"Then I want to live with you."

She pulled him into her arms and hugged him as tightly as she thought his little frame could stand. "Okay, then. That's the way it's going to be. You and me."

"What about Garrett?"

Erica hated the idea of uprooting him from Garrett's house, from this island, but it was time to move on. *She* had to move on. "Garrett has his own life. Here on Mirabelle. He was helping to protect us while we needed it, and now everything's okay. We don't need to live with him any longer."

"We could still stay here. On the island."

"Our lives, yours and mine, are back in Chicago. I think it's best if we go home."

Jason nodded, but didn't say a word.

They continued on toward Duffy's. This early in the morning no one would be about. They could easily sneak through the back door to return the clothes Lynn had lent to her at the beginning of summer along with the notebook detailing all of Erica's recipes and the set of keys Lynn had given her to the restaurant.

After leaving their suitcases in the alley, she unlocked the back door and, holding Jason's hand, walked quietly to Lynn's office. She set the bag of clothing on the floor and the recipe notebook and keys on top of Lynn's desk. A note seemed appropriate, but she wouldn't have known what to say.

"Let's go." She reached for Jason's hand, stepped out into the bar and took one last look around, emotions clogging her throat.

"I'm going to miss this place," Jason whispered.

"Me, too."

The back door opened and footsteps sounded down the hallway. Erica clenched her jaw and closed her eyes for a moment. *You're doing the right thing. For everyone.* She turned.

Lynn came into the bar. "So after everything we've been through together—" she stalked toward Erica and stopped ten feet away, as if she didn't trust herself to come any closer "—I don't even get two weeks notice?"

"I thought it would be better this way."

"Better for who?"

"Everyone."

"Well, I got news for you, dearie. *Everyone* is going to miss you and Jason." She bent down and Jason ran into her arms. Holding him in her arms, she stood. "Even Sally McGregor. From her post office window she saw you coming down the hill with suitcases and figured I'd want to know."

"I'm sorry, Lynn. I didn't want to make this harder than it had to be." Erica swallowed back the tears. "The police said I could leave. So I thought this would be for the best."

"You don't have to leave."

"Yes, I do." This place was too painful. She felt open and raw and exposed. "There's nothing here for me. For us."

"You're about as wrong about that as anyone could be." Lynn set Jason back down, but held his hand. "You've got a job and a place to live. Jason could start back at school. What's the hurry?"

"We came here, running away from something, Lynn. This isn't our home."

"It could be. If you want."

She wanted a sweet, quiet, safe place to call home, but no matter what had happened to change her over the last several months, she was still Erica Corelli. An Italian cook—not a chef—from Chicago.

She thought of her apartment back home, her old job, her old friends. She wasn't sure she fit anywhere any longer. "Everyone on this island has been so good to me and Jason. You and Arlo, especially. I have no way to thank you for what you've done."

"A hug would be nice."

For a moment, they looked into each other's eyes and the ebb and flow of their relationship these past months came together in this moment. They were more than friends, and they both knew it. Lynn opened her arms wide.

Erica fell into her like a child. "Goodbye, Lynn."

Lynn's eyes turned red. "You've become like a daughter to me. And, you." She looked down at Jason. "Like a grandson." She lifted him high in her arms. "You are the best little boy in the whole world, and I love you with all of my heart."

As he squeezed his arms around her neck with tears streaming down his cheeks, Arlo came in from the alleyway. This is exactly what Erica had wanted to avoid. "Oh, hell." They had to get out of here before someone called Garrett.

"Life is messy, isn't it?" Lynn said.

They finished saying goodbye to Arlo only to find Bob and Dan waiting their turn. Even the Setterbergs had come to wish them farewell. By the time Hannah, Missy, Sarah and Brian joined the group, Erica was a mess and Jason's eyes were swollen and red.

"You should stay," Hannah said.

"Yeah," Sarah and Brian echoed.

Missy tilted her head. "You leaving isn't in the cards."

From the windows near the lake came the sound of the ferry's horn announcing its imminent arrival at the pier.

"We have to go." With one last look at everyone, she took Jason's hand and headed out the back door into the alley. Every step felt weighted with all the memories loaded into what now felt like such a short time.

"Don't forget us," someone called out.

"Call," Lynn said. "Or e-mail. Or both."

"Better yet," Arlo added, "come back and visit."

They stepped outside, into the now bright morning sun and the ferry tooted again. In a few minutes it would dock. As they headed toward Main, Jason hung his head, looking at least as forlorn as he had back at Charlie's restaurant in Chicago, all those months ago.

"Look at the bright side," she said. "You'll get to go back to your old school in Chicago and play with your friends. We'll figure out a place to live that's close to your old neighborhood."

The moment they reached the sidewalk and the new windows in front of Duffy's, he pulled his hand from hers. "I don't want to go back to Chicago. I like it better here."

"Jason, we're going home."

"No!" He crossed his arms over his chest. "I'm not going."

"Wha—" Erica stared at him. Her first reaction was to argue with him, but then she realized what it had taken for him to stand up for himself after everything he'd been through. Once the dust settled, Jason was going to be okay.

The ferry horn tooted its arrival at the pier. "We have to go," she said, calmly, patiently. "This isn't our home."

"You can't make me." He was pouting now, but she couldn't find it in herself to be mad at him. Searching for the right words, she glanced up.

Garrett was coming slowly toward them, his face, pale and drawn, looked as if it had been made from Lake Superior stone. He was furious. He stopped a few feet in front of her. "Just like that, huh?" he said. "You don't even have the decency to discuss this with me. As if I don't have a say. As if I—" He stopped, looked away.

"I'm trying to do you a favor." She turned. "Don't you get that?"

"No." He grabbed her arm. "I don't want you to go. I don't want Jason to go, either."

"That's not what you said yesterday. Yesterday—"

"I'm an idiot. Nothing I said before matters! Nothing." He knelt in front of Jason. "I need to talk to Erica for a few minutes alone. Is that okay?"

Jason nodded, walked over to Duffy's front entrance and peered through the windows. Lynn unlocked the front door and let him inside.

"The ferry's leaving," Erica said. "We don't have time."

"You've got five minutes," Lynn whispered, and left them alone on the street.

Garrett turned back to her. "I don't blame you for being angry at me. I was an ass. Give me another chance."

"To break my heart? Another chance to make me feel—"

"I was wrong. Everything I said was wrong." He stepped toward her, but she backed away. "Erica—"

"No." She shook her head. Tears glistened in her eyes. "Don't."

"I lo—"

"Don't!" She shoved him away.

"I love you! Erica, look at me!" He grabbed her arms. "Look at me, dammit!"

She glanced into his eyes.

"It's too late," he whispered. "I love you. There's nothing you can do or say to change that."

"What about peace and quiet? What about that calm, fairy-tale life you want so badly?" She was trying to make him mad. It would make her leaving so much easier.

"I don't want quiet. I need messy and passionate and crazy. I want you. In my life."

"You're saying that to get me to stay."

"No." He took her hand and wrapped his fingers through hers.

"It's because of what happened with Billy—"

"No. I knew it before." He reached out and ran his fingertips along her cheek. "You and I…we're the same. It's good between us. We're good. Sometimes so good it scares the hell out of me." His arms went around her neck and pulled her close. "Stay," he whispered. "Please."

"My life. Jason's life. We left everything back in Chicago."

"You're telling yourself you need to go back because you're scared. Even more than me. Erica, you belong here. You fit. You were meant to be here. With me. With these people who've become—whether you want to admit it or not—your friends. Everything that matters—now—in your life is here on Mirabelle." He tilted her face toward his. "Give us a chance. Maybe we can make our very own fairy tale come true."

The ferry horn sounded a warning. It would be leaving within minutes.

Jason stuck his head out Duffy's front door. "Are we staying?" he asked, his eyes bright. "Can I go play with Brian?"

Erica glanced up and saw the entire Mirabelle farewell committee with the addition of Doc standing inside the bar, waiting expectantly. She'd left Illinois without a backward glance and hadn't missed it much. Her old boss had no doubt hired someone to replace her at the restaurant. Her apartment? Except for her kitchen supplies, she'd barely thought of it. And Marie was gone.

Mirabelle, on the other hand, she knew with certainty she would miss. This place had changed her, deep inside, and she didn't want to go back.

"Are you sure?" she asked Garrett. "You really want me to stay?"

"You leave," he said, resignation filling his voice, "and I'll be right behind you. Moving back. I'm in your life to stay. Whether you want me there or not."

Her throat closed. He looked so fierce, so strong, so beautiful. All she wanted to do was let go, wrap her arms around him and love him for the rest of her life. Love him. This strong, compassionate, giving and protective man. She loved Garrett.

She'd slipped quietly, but completely down a path from which there was no return. The truth settled in her heart like a warm blanket over cold legs, a feeling so right, so perfect, so real and so consuming that she couldn't remember ever not having felt this way. There was no more running from it. She no longer wanted to run from it.

"Jason and me, we're a package deal."

"I wouldn't have it any other way," Garrett whispered. "He's as much a part of me as you are."

"I love you." She rested her hand on his chest.

"I know," he whispered, his eyes darkening with emotion and so much more. "I'm sure you'll find some way to prove it to me later."

"Erica?" Jason said.

"Yes, Jason!" She laughed. "You can go play with Brian." She wrapped her arm around Garrett's waist, rested her cheek against his chest, and whispered, "I get to play with Garrett."

He tilted her chin up and kissed her.

"Does that mean we're staying?" Jason asked.

"Yeah, kiddo." She jumped into Garrett's arms, the strongest, yet safest and most loving arms she'd ever felt. This tattered princess had finally found her knight, a bit tarnished and worn, but all hers. Apparently fairy tales did come true every once in a while.

"We're home!" she said to the sound of hoots and hollers and claps from the islanders, her friends, standing inside Duffy's Pub. "To stay."

* * * * *

*Be sure to pick up Helen Brenna's next
Mirabelle Island book,
THEN COMES BABY, in December 2009!
Discover the secrets of the mysterious islander
who lives in the cabin on the wild, north shore....*

*Celebrate 60 years of pure reading pleasure
with Harlequin®!*

To commemorate the event, Silhouette Special Edition
invites you to Ashley O'Ballivan's bed-and-breakfast
in the small town of Stone Creek. The beautiful inn-
keeper will have her hands full caring for her old flame
Jack McCall. He's on the run and recovering from a
mysterious illness, but that won't stop him from trying
to win Ashley back.

*Enjoy an exclusive glimpse of Linda Lael Miller's
AT HOME IN STONE CREEK
Available in November 2009 from
Silhouette Special Edition®.*

The helicopter swung abruptly sideways in a dizzying arch, setting Jack McCall's fever-ravaged brain spinning.

His friend's voice sounded tinny, coming through the earphones. "You belong in a hospital," he said. "Not some backwater bed-and-breakfast."

All Jack really knew about the virus raging through his system was that it wasn't contagious, and there was no known treatment for it besides a lot of rest and quiet. "I don't like hospitals," he responded, hoping he sounded like his normal self. "They're full of sick people."

Vince Griffin chuckled but it was a dry sound, rough at the edges. "What's in Stone Creek, Arizona?" he asked. "Besides a whole lot of nothin'?"

Ashley O'Ballivan was in Stone Creek, and she was a whole lot of somethin', but Jack had neither the strength nor the inclination to explain. After the way he'd ducked out six months before, he didn't expect a welcome, knew he didn't deserve one. But Ashley, being Ashley, would take him in whatever her misgivings.

He had to get to Ashley; he'd be all right.

He closed his eyes, letting the fever swallow him.

There was no telling how much time had passed when he became aware of the chopper blades slowing overhead. Dimly, he saw the private ambulance waiting on the airfield outside of Stone Creek; it seemed that twilight had descended.

Jack sighed with relief. His clothes felt clammy against his flesh. His teeth began to chatter as two figures unloaded a gurney from the back of the ambulance and waited for the blades to stop.

"Great," Vince remarked, unsnapping his seat belt. "Those two look like volunteers, not real EMTs."

The chopper bounced sickeningly on its runners, and Vince, with a shake of his head, pushed open his door and jumped to the ground, head down.

Jack waited, wondering if he'd be able to stand on his own. After fumbling unsuccessfully with the buckle on his seat belt, he decided not.

When it was safe the EMTs approached, following Vince, who opened Jack's door.

His old friend Tanner Quinn stepped around Vince, his grin not quite reaching his eyes.

"You look like hell warmed over," he told Jack cheerfully.

"Since when are you an EMT?" Jack retorted.

Tanner reached in, wedged a shoulder under Jack's right arm and hauled him out of the chopper. His knees immediately buckled, and Vince stepped up, supporting him on the other side.

"In a place like Stone Creek," Tanner replied, "everybody helps out."

They reached the wheeled gurney, and Jack found himself on his back.

Tanner and the second man strapped him down, a process that brought back a few bad memories.

"Is there even a hospital in this place?" Vince asked irritably from somewhere in the night.

"There's a pretty good clinic over in Indian Rock," Tanner answered easily, "and it isn't far to Flagstaff." He paused to help his buddy hoist Jack and the gurney into the back of the ambulance. "You're in good hands, Jack. My wife is the best veterinarian in the state."

Jack laughed raggedly at that.

Vince muttered a curse.

Tanner climbed into the back beside him, perched on some kind of fold-down seat. The other man shut the doors.

"You in any pain?" Tanner said as his partner climbed into the driver's seat and started the engine.

"No." Jack looked up at his oldest and closest friend and wished he'd listened to Vince. Ever since he'd come down with the virus—a week after snatching a five-year-old girl back from her noncustodial parent, a small-time Colombian drug dealer—he hadn't been able to think about anyone or anything but Ashley. When he *could* think, anyway.

Now, in one of the first clearheaded moments he'd experienced since checking himself out of Bethesda the day before, he realized he might be making a major mistake. Not by facing Ashley—he owed her that much and a lot more. No, he could be putting her in danger, putting Tanner and his daughter and his pregnant wife in danger, too.

"I shouldn't have come here," he said, keeping his voice low.

Tanner shook his head, his jaw clamped down hard as though he was irritated by Jack's statement.

"This is where you belong," Tanner insisted. "If you'd had sense enough to know that six months ago, old buddy, when you bailed on Ashley without so much as a fare-thee-well, you wouldn't be in this mess."

Ashley. The name had run through his mind a million times in those six months, but hearing somebody say it out loud was like having a fist close around his insides and squeeze hard.

Jack couldn't speak.

Tanner didn't press for further conversation.

The ambulance bumped over country roads, finally hitting smooth blacktop.

"Here we are," Tanner said. "Ashley's place."

* * * * *

Will Jack be able to patch things up with Ashley,
or will his past put the woman he loves in harm's way?
Find out in
AT HOME IN STONE CREEK
by Linda Lael Miller
Available November 2009 from
Silhouette Special Edition®.

This November,
Silhouette Special Edition®
brings you

NEW YORK TIMES
BESTSELLING AUTHOR

LINDA LAEL
MILLER

At Home in
Stone Creek

*Available in November
wherever books are sold.*

Blackout At Christmas

Beth Cornelison,
Sharron McClellan,
Jennifer Morey

What happens when a major blackout shuts down the entire Western seaboard on Christmas Eve? Follow stories of danger, intrigue and romance as three women learn to trust their instincts to survive and open their hearts to the love that unexpectedly comes their way.

**Available November
wherever books are sold.**

REQUEST YOUR FREE BOOKS!

2 FREE NOVELS PLUS 2 FREE GIFTS!

HARLEQUIN®

Super Romance®

Exciting, emotional, unexpected!

YES! Please send me 2 FREE Harlequin® Superromance® novels and my 2 FREE gifts (gifts are worth about $10). After receiving them, if I don't wish to receive any more books, I can return the shipping statement marked "cancel." If I don't cancel, I will receive 6 brand-new novels every month and be billed just $4.69 per book in the U.S. or $5.24 per book in Canada. That's a savings of close to 15% off the cover price! It's quite a bargain! Shipping and handling is just 50¢ per book*. I understand that accepting the 2 free books and gifts places me under no obligation to buy anything. I can always return a shipment and cancel at any time. Even if I never buy another book from Harlequin, the two free books and gifts are mine to keep forever.

135 HDN EYLG   336 HDN EYLS

Name	(PLEASE PRINT)	
Address		Apt. #
City	State/Prov.	Zip/Postal Code

Signature (if under 18, a parent or guardian must sign)

Mail to the **Harlequin Reader Service:**
IN U.S.A.: P.O. Box 1867, Buffalo, NY 14240-1867
IN CANADA: P.O. Box 609, Fort Erie, Ontario L2A 5X3

Not valid to current subscribers of Harlequin Superromance books.

**Are you a current subscriber of Harlequin Superromance books
and want to receive the larger-print edition?
Call 1-800-873-8635 today!**

* Terms and prices subject to change without notice. Prices do not include applicable taxes. Sales tax applicable in N.Y. Canadian residents will be charged applicable provincial taxes and GST. Offer not valid in Quebec. This offer is limited to one order per household. All orders subject to approval. Credit or debit balances in a customer's account(s) may be offset by any other outstanding balance owed by or to the customer. Please allow 4 to 6 weeks for delivery. Offer available while quantities last.

Your Privacy: Harlequin is committed to protecting your privacy. Our Privacy Policy is available online at www.eHarlequin.com or upon request from the Reader Service. From time to time we make our lists of customers available to reputable third parties who may have a product or service of interest to you. If you would prefer we not share your name and address, please check here. ☐

HSR09R

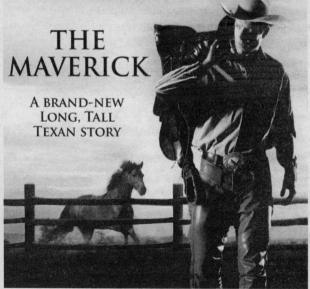

HARLEQUIN® *Super Romance*®

COMING NEXT MONTH

Available November 10, 2009

#1596 LIKE FATHER, LIKE SON • Karina Bliss
The Diamond Legacy
What's worse? Discovering his heritage is a lie or following in his grandfather's footsteps? All Joe Fraser *does* know is that Philippa Browne is pregnant and he's got to do right by her. Too bad she has her own ideas about motherhood…and marriag

#1597 HER SECRET RIVAL • Abby Gaines
Those Merritt Girls
Taking over her father's law firm isn't just the professional opportunity of a lifetime—it's a chance for Megan Merritt to finally get close to him. Winning a lucrative divorce case is her way to prove she's the one for the job. Except the opposing lawyer in the divorce is Travis Jamieson, who is also after her dad's job!

#1598 A CONFLICT OF INTEREST • Anna Adams
Welcome to Honesty
Jake Sloane knows right from wrong—as a judge, it's his responsibility. Until he meet Maria Keaton, he's never blurred that line. Now his attraction to her is tearing him between what his head knows he should do and what his heart wants.

#1599 HOME FOR THE HOLIDAYS • Sarah Mayberry
Single Father
Raising his kids on his own is a huge learning curve for Joe Lawson. So does he really have time to fall for the unconventional woman next door, Hannah Napier? Time or no that's what's happening.…

#1600 A MAN WORTH LOVING • Kimberly Van Meter
Home in Emmett's Mill
Aubrey Rose can't stand Sammy Halvorsen when they first meet. She agrees to be a nanny to his infant son only because she's a sucker for babies. As she gets to know Sammy, however, she starts to fall for him. But how to make him realize he's a man worth loving?

#1601 UNEXPECTED GIFTS • Holly Jacobs
9 Months Later
Elinore Cartright has her hands full overseeing the teen parenting program, especially when she discovers *she's* unexpectedly expecting. Not how she envisioned her forties, but life's unpredictable. So is her friend Zac Keller, who suddenly wants to date her *and* be a daddy, too!